PRAISE FOR DHARMA KELLEHER

"Shea Stevens is just about the most interesting and sympathetic criminal you'll meet."

— Paula Berinstein, author of the Amanda Lester detective series

"A thrilling ride that will have you turning pages into the wee hours of the morning!"

— Renee James, author of SEVEN SUSPECTS

"Dharma Kelleher breaks new ground and breaths new life into a great genre. The best thing to happen to crime fiction since V. I. Warshawski."

— Greg Barth, author of SELENA

BLOOD SISTERS

BLOOD SISTERS

A SHEA STEVENS THRILLER

DHARMA KELLEHER

SNITCH: A SHEA STEVENS THRILLER

Copyright © 2020 by Dharma Kelleher.

Published by Dark Pariah Press, Phoenix, Arizona.

Cover design: Damonza

All rights reserved. No part of this story may be used or reproduced in any manner whatsoever without written permission from the author except in the case of brief quotations embodied in critical articles or reviews.

This is a work of fiction. Names, characters, places, and incidents are products of the author's imagination and are not to be construed as real. Any resemblance to actual events, locales, organizations, or persons, living or dead, is entirely coincidental.

Ebook ISBN: 978-1-952128-03-5

Print ISBN: 978-1-952128-04-2

ACKNOWLEDGMENTS

I am so grateful for the support and input from multiple sources who have made this book possible.

First and foremost, the passionate and dedicated subscribers of the Dharma Kelleher Readers Club. You inspire me to keep writing!

Also I am grateful for the expertise provided by Detective Adam Richardson of the Writers Detective Agency podcast and the many others who provide input via the podcast's Facebook group. You help me get more of the details right.

I want to thank the many members of the intersex community for sharing their experiences, especially River Shannon Aloia and Nicky Phillips. It's time to end Intersex Genital Mutilation. Long past time.

And last but not least, I want thank you, dear reader, for purchasing this book. Your support helps me to continue to write stories about marginalized people and their ongoing fight for justice. Let's make a better, safer world for everyone.

*Thanks as always to my wife, Eileen.
You are my light in this world of darkness.*

1

Shea Stevens's blood ran cold. A skull painted against a Confederate flag background glared at her from the gas tank of one of the countless bikes in the dusty Cortes County Fairgrounds parking lot. It wasn't just some rando's attempt to add racist flair to their Harley Fat Boy. It was the Johnny Reb, emblem of the Confederate Thunder Motorcycle Club. It meant trouble.

"It can't be." Tendrils of fear snaked down her spine while she stared at the motorcycle. She nervously ran a hand through her butch pixie haircut, ignoring the harsh summer sun turning her tanned skin red.

"Aunt Shea, come on!" Annie Wittmann, her twelve-year-old niece, pulled at her arm.

The two other women with them stopped and turned.

"Something wrong, Havoc?" asked Rah-Rah, a golden-haired woman with the girl-next-door looks.

Indigo followed Shea's gaze. Her black-and-cobalt-blue braids fell still as the whisper of a breeze died. "Shit."

The three women wore leather cuts identifying them as members of the Athena Sisterhood Motorcycle Club. Annie wore a cutoff denim vest with the words Little Sister stitched on the back.

"Gotta belong to one of their hangarounds or someone's old lady," Rah-Rah said.

"Or a member from an out-of-state chapter," Indigo suggested.

Shea checked the back of the bike. "Arizona plates. They're local."

"Can't be a patched member then," Rah-Rah insisted. "They're all in prison. Won't even be eligible for parole for another four years."

"Let's hope so." Shea exchanged a look with Indigo that communicated volumes about their brutal history of dealing with the Thunder. If they were out of prison and knew the Sisterhood was responsible for putting them there...Shea didn't even want to think about what could happen. To her. The other members of the Sisterhood. But worst of all, to Annie.

"Aunt Shea, can we go in already? I'm melting out here in the parking lot."

"Yeah," Shea said. "Let's go in. Uncle Terrance is probably wondering where we are."

At the entrance to the fairgrounds, a heavyset man in a Harley Davidson T-shirt said, "Welcome to the High Desert Biker Festival. Tickets are ten dollars each."

Shea held up her vendor's badge. "Iron Goddess Custom Cycles." She handed him a ten-dollar bill. "This is for my niece."

After Indigo and Rah-Rah paid, the four of them wandered through the maze of booths that sold everything from clothing and riding gear to aftermarket parts and motorcycle insurance. Shea scanned the leather-clad crowds for anyone wearing a Confederate Thunder cut.

Fortunately, they reached the Iron Goddess booth without seeing another Johnny Reb.

Under the white ten-by-twenty canopy tent, Terrance Douglas, Shea's business partner, sat in front of a banner that read Iron Goddess, Custom Cycles for Women. He was a muscular black man with a trim afro, a full beard, and an approachable smile. A sport bike with a tank painted like a checkered racing flag sat in the middle of the tent, flanked by racks of helmets, jackets, gloves, and Iron Goddess–branded clothing.

"Ladies," Terrance said with a nod.

"Morning, T," Shea said.

"'Bout time y'all showed up." He stood. "I was beginning to worry."

"My fault," Rah-Rah said, pulling off a pair of shades she'd bought at one of the booths on their way in. "I couldn't decide between this pair and some retro Ray-Bans."

"Hi, Uncle Terrance," Annie said, giving him a hug.

"Hey, sweetie. You excited about starting soccer camp tomorrow?"

Annie shrugged. "A little nervous."

"Nervous? Girl, I've seen you play. You got moves like Megan Rapinoe. What've you got to be nervous about?"

"I don't know."

"You just go out there, show 'em who's boss. It'll be all right."

"Thanks, Uncle T."

"You two ready to check out the rest of the festival?" Rah-Rah asked Indigo and Annie. "I saw a jewelry vendor a few aisles over selling cute earrings."

"Can I?" Annie looked to Shea.

"Yeah, but do what Rah-Rah and Indigo tell you." Shea

handed her a couple of twenties. "And try not to spend it all in one place."

"Geez, you act like I'm five."

"She'll be all right," Indigo said. "We'll also keep an eye out for you-know-what. We'll meet back up at the awards ceremony if we don't see you sooner."

"See you 'round." Shea gave each of them a hug and a clap on the back then turned to Terrance. "Getting any customers?"

"Some. Sold three jackets, a few pairs of gloves, and several T-shirts. A couple women asked about custom bikes and took business cards."

A woman and man strolled into the booth and walked around the sport bike. She was skinny with long blond hair secured with a studded leather hair wrap. He sported an unkempt beard and wraparound shades. His leather cut identified him as a patched member of the Desert Devils, a one-percenter motorcycle club with close ties to the Confederate Thunder. Maybe it was his bike they saw in the parking lot, though usually they decorated theirs with red devils, not the Johnny Reb.

"Let us know if you have questions," Terrance said, but the couple ignored him.

"Why you want a bike of your own, honey?" asked the guy.

"Cause the bitch seat is hard and uncomfortable is why." The woman threw a leg over the sport bike. She wore a cutoff denim jacket with the words "Property of Dugger" stitched on the back. "I can picture me riding something like this."

"A pissant crotch rocket?" Dugger chuckled. "Girl, you'd kill yourself, fer sure."

"It's got twice the horsepower of a Harley with the same displacement," Shea said, meeting the woman's eyes. "And much better clearance, so you can take corners faster. You could leave your boyfriend here in the dust."

The woman's face split with a mischievous smile. "Sounds like my kinda ride."

Dugger stepped between Shea and his girlfriend on the bike. "Lady, I suggest you mind your own business."

Shea stepped into his space. "This here is my business. I built this bike. You're not afraid your old lady will leave you behind, are ya?"

He glanced down at her vest. "I recognize them colors. You one of them Barbie bikers."

"Athena Sisterhood. I see you're one of the Thunder's lap dogs. They haven't patched you over yet?"

"Shea," Terrance warned. "Don't."

Shea's eyes locked with Dugger's. She didn't want to be the first to look away. At the same time, she didn't need club rivalries spilling over into the business she shared with Terrance.

She turned to the girlfriend. "When you're ready to buy, call us. My man Terrance here'll give you a good deal."

"Thanks." The girlfriend picked up a business card, and the two of them walked on to the next tent.

"What the hell was that?" Terrance asked.

"What can I say? I'm not good with people. Especially assholes. You should have Lakota, Kyle, or Monica helping you run the booth. Even Vince would be better than me."

"Vince, Kyle, and Monica were all here yesterday. Lakota will be here this afternoon. You owe it to your team to put in your time."

Shea took in a deep breath and let it out. "You're not wrong." She sat on the bike in the tent. "After the festival, give me the keys to the truck. I'll trailer the show bike back to the shop. You can drive this bike home." She patted the bike's fairing.

"Deal. Now I gotta take a piss. Do us both a favor and try not to kill any future customers while I'm gone."

Shea laughed darkly. "That's a big ask."

Terrance walked out of the tent then turned. "The award ceremony's at seven. Encourage people who stop by the booth to vote for our Flying Tree bike."

"Will do."

2

A DUST DEVIL blew a flurry of sand, dust, and litter through the crowd gathered around the fairgrounds' main stage.

"Shit." Shea rubbed the grit from her eyes and brushed the dust from her cut. The glare of the setting sun cast the fairgrounds in golden hues and long shadows.

Most attendees of the biker festival had already left, having spent their limit on leather, chrome, and bling. But Shea, Terrance, and Lakota White River, the shop's mechanical engineer, stood among a few dozen hardcore bikers waiting for the winners of the custom motorcycle contest to be announced.

Shea and Lakota had spent four months crafting a motorcycle with a polished wood fairing that curved around a state-of-the-art cylindrical power cell. The result looked like an exhibit from a modern art museum, but with the speed and agility of a high-end crotch rocket.

A heavyset man onstage blew into the microphone. "Sorry 'bout that dust devil, folks. I call that a desert baptism."

"Get on with it," shouted Terrance.

"Not nervous, are ya, T?" Shea nudged him with her elbow.

"Sales are down twenty percent from last year," he replied. "We need a win to boost sales, or we could close our doors in the next year."

Annie gave them a worried look. "Iron Goddess is in trouble?"

"Nah," Shea replied. "Uncle Terrance is just being his usual paranoid self."

"We hope," Lakota whispered. She stood three inches taller than Shea. Her salt-and-pepper hair stretched halfway down her back in twin braids.

"Now, where was I?" The man on the stage squinted at the paper in his hand. From a nearby table, he picked up a small trophy with a golden plastic motorcycle on top. "Ah, yes, the winner for Best Design in the Cruiser Category is Steve Jansen from Jansen Customs in Mesa, Arizona."

A smattering of applause greeted Steve Jansen, a wiry blond in a Sturgis T-shirt. He climbed the stairs to the stage, flashed a gap-toothed smile, and accepted the trophy.

"Best Design in the Sport Bike Category goes to…"

A swarm of deranged butterflies fluttered in Shea's stomach. Yeah, Terrance was always worried about sales, but even she had noticed a dip in traffic in the shop.

The announcer adjusted his glasses. "I swear, the older I get, the smaller the text gets. And I'm the fool who wrote this."

"Announce it already," Shea shouted.

"Okay, okay, Best Sport Bike goes to Michael Vasquez, Eloy Motorsports in Eloy, Arizona."

"Fuck," Shea muttered under her breath when the winner took the stage to accept his trophy.

"Language," Annie said in a taunting singsong voice.

Lakota put a hand on her shoulder. "There's still a couple more categories we could win."

"Best Design in the Electric Category goes to Gavin Redmond and Amy Marana of Red Rock Customs, Moab, Utah."

Shea clapped despite her disappointment. Amy Marana, or "Switch" as she was known to friends, had worked for Iron Goddess until she took the job in Moab a year earlier.

"Good to see Switch getting recognition," Lakota said. "I hear she's thriving there at Red Rock Customs."

Switch and a man Shea assumed was the owner of Red Rock Customs mounted the stage. Switch looked like a deer in the headlights while her partner accepted their trophy. Shea felt for her. Neither of them cared much for the limelight.

"Way to go, Switch!" Shea shouted when her former employee walked past.

Switch turned, and her face lit up. "Shea. Thank you." She pounced at Shea and wrapped her in a tight, unexpected hug.

When Switch let go, she vanished into the crowd without another word. Typical Switch, Shea thought.

When the applause died down, the crowd grew quiet for the top prize.

"Last, but certainly not least..." The announcer hefted up a large trophy of wood and brass. "The winner for Best in Show is..."

Shea tried to tell herself it didn't matter. Odds were she wouldn't win, and life would go on. But a part of her clung to the smallest shred of hope.

"Shea Stevens and Olivia White River, Iron Goddess Custom Cycles, Sycamore Springs, Arizona."

Shea wasn't sure she heard correctly. Maybe it was her

mind playing tricks on her. Time slowed. And yet the people around her were jumping and clapping and slapping her on the back. Shea realized she was walking through the crowd, being pulled along by Lakota. She climbed the stage, feeling her heart thudding against her rib cage.

"Care to say a few words?" asked the man.

Shea was about to speak when she spotted two familiar faces in the crowd. One was Dugger, the biker she had butted heads with several hours earlier. Next to him stood One-Shot, the president of the Cortes chapter of the Confederate Thunder. He should have been in prison. How was he here?

"I...uh...yeah, thanks." Shea turned to Lakota, who stepped up to the mic.

"I'm Olivia 'Lakota' White River, Iron Goddess's mechanical engineer. Our goal was to create a motorcycle that's as badass as it is planet friendly. All of us at Iron Goddess Custom Cycles are grateful for your support. Thank you."

Another roar of applause washed over Shea while she and Lakota stepped down from the stage.

"You okay?" Lakota elbowed Shea. "Looked like you got a little stage fright, girl."

"I'm all right." Shea searched the crowd for One-Shot and Dugger, but all of the faces were silhouetted against the setting sun.

"You call that contraption a motorcycle, chica?"

The familiar voice drew Shea's attention from the crowd to a Latinx woman. The patches on her cut identified her as the president of the Athena Sisterhood. "Looks more like a coffee table attacking a droid from *Star Wars*."

"Fuego!" Shea laughed nervously and gave her a one-armed hug. The weight of the trophy almost threw her off balance. "Call it what you like, but it'll leave your Kawasaki Vulcan in the dust."

Indigo stood nearby with her wife, Savage, a stocky white woman with short-cropped, bleach-blond hair. She wore a Cortes County EMS polo shirt.

"Congrats on the win, Havoc," Savage said, using Shea's street name. "Chalk one up for the biker shop for misfit toys."

"Thanks. Glad you could make it."

"Got off shift a few hours ago. Didn't want to miss the festivities. What'll you do with the motorcycle?"

"Terrance'll put it up for sale on the website. I just build 'em. He's in charge of selling them."

"Thank goodness for that," Terrance said as he joined the group. "If it were up to Shea, she'd just add it to the stable of motorcycles filling up her garage."

"Some women collect shoes. I collect motorcycles." Shea handed the cumbersome trophy to Terrance. "Show it off to whoever you like."

"There's a magnificent spot in the front window. Monica and I can build a display around it."

"Ms. Stevens?" called an unfamiliar voice.

Shea turned to see a petite white woman with rimless glasses and a floral-print shirt. "Yes?"

"Elia Quinn. I'm a journalist for the *Cortes Chronicle*. Congratulations on winning Best in Show."

They shook hands. "Thanks."

"I understand Iron Goddess hires a lot of second-chancers—ex-cons, recovering addicts, and the like. That's what your friend meant by the shop for misfit toys. Am I right?"

Shea was always leery of revealing her employees' pasts. "Yeah."

"I'd love to do a cover story about you and your shop."

Shea was about to say no, but Terrance stepped between them and shook Elia's hand.

"Hi, Elia. I'm Terrance Douglas, Iron Goddess's business manager. We'd love for you to do a story on the shop. Besides our award-winning bike, which we've nicknamed The Flying Tree, we have some very innovative custom motorcycles in the works, all specifically designed for women, which is our specialty. When would you like to come by?"

"Would tomorrow be too soon?" Elia asked.

"Not at all." Terrance beamed.

"Great. See you all in the morning. Say ten o'clock?"

"We look forward to it."

Shea sidled up next to Terrance after Elia walked away. "What innovative customs do we have in the works?"

"The touring bike for Ms. Hughes. It's a custom."

"Custom, yes. But hardly innovative and not much more than a frame at this point."

"Sorry, guess I got a little carried away, but we need all the press we can get. I want to capitalize on this win as much as possible."

"I just don't like reporters asking a lot of questions, especially about our crew."

"Fair enough. No intrusive questions about our employees. I'll steer the interview toward the bikes we build."

"I'll pull out some of the designs I've had on the back shelf for a while. Give Ms. Puff Piece something to write about."

"Good."

"Aunt Shea, can we go now?" asked Annie. "I'm hot, and I got soccer camp in the morning."

Shea looked at her watch. It was nearly eight o'clock. "Yeah, we can go. We still have to load the show bike into the trailer and drop it off at the shop."

That earned a major eye roll from Annie. "That's gonna take forever," she said with exaggerated drama.

"Sorry, Doodlebug."

"Please stop calling me that. It's embarrassing."

"Embarrassing? You used to love me calling you Doodlebug."

"Yeah, when I was a kid. I'm almost a teenager."

"Sor-ry! I'll try not to do it anymore. Let's get moving so we can get you home."

3

THE HAIR on the back of Detective Toni Rios's neck stood up when she entered the Blue Bar, a watering hole popular with the deputies in the Cortes County Sheriff's Office. Something was wrong.

Even on a Sunday night, the bar in downtown Ironwood should have been bustling with her fellow officers taking a drink after a shift. But the room was empty, dark, and quiet as a mausoleum.

There'd been no mention of the bar on the radio she carried on her belt. Just the usual chatter; a callout for a wrong-way driver on I-17, a frat party getting out of hand on the other side of Ironwood, and a report of gunfire up in Bradshaw City.

Toni drew her sidearm and flashlight, scanning the main room. Next to the dark jukebox, she spotted a figure lying on the ground. Her pulse sped up when she recognized her partner, Detective Ebony Johnson.

Ebony had asked Toni to meet her at the Blue Bar to discuss a case they were working.

"Ebony! Ebony! Are you okay? What happened?" Toni knelt down, checking her partner for injuries. Her hand came away wet and sticky when she touched her fellow detective's torso. The flashlight revealed a mess of red. "Mierda."

"Toni," Ebony whispered in a hoarse voice. She mumbled something else that Toni couldn't make out.

"What? What'd you say?" Toni leaned closer, putting her ear next to Ebony's mouth.

Ebony leaned up and kissed Toni on the cheek. "Will you marry me?" Her voice was filled with mirth.

The lights of the bar flashed on, blinding Toni for a moment. From somewhere in the glare, multiple voices shouted, "Happy twenty-fifth anniversary!"

Her gun arm instinctively rose toward the sound before she realized what was happening. A banner reading "Congrats on 25 Years of Service" hung above the bar. She reholstered her weapon, heart hammering in her chest, grateful she didn't pull the trigger.

She stood and offered a hand up to her partner. "Hijo de puta, I could have shot one of you."

"Glad you didn't." A red wet stain stretched across Ebony's shirt and arm. From the smell of it, Toni realized it was ketchup.

Lieutenant Goodman emerged from the crowd, carrying a plaque. "Congrats, Detective."

Toni took the plaque from him and shook his outstretched hand. "Thanks, LT."

"First drink's on me."

Toni approached the bar while her fellow officers patted her on the back and congratulated her. The bartender, a retired officer named O'Neill, popped open bottles of beer and set them in front of Goodman, Johnson, and herself.

"I should kick your ass, compañera," Rios said to Johnson. "Nearly gave me a heart attack."

"You're right. Not nice of me to scare an old lady. I promise to do better, ma'am." Johnson winked at her.

"Old? Puta, I'm only thirty-eight, and I can still kick your ass. And what was that 'Will you marry me' crap? Last thing I need is for rumors to circulate that you and I are dating."

"Relax, Toni. It was a joke."

Toni bristled. Despite her attempts to keep her personal life on the DL, rumors about her sexual orientation had been drifting through the Violent Crimes Division for years. Eventually, she came out to her lieutenant when she agreed to be the Lambda Resource Center's police liaison.

She took a long pull on her beer. "This mean you don't want to marry me, chica?"

Johnson gave her a sideways glance. "Sorry, partner. I prefer someone more masculine. And younger."

"Gee, thanks a lot."

"Seriously, you'd be a total catch for the right woman."

"She'd have to be pretty desperate." A memory of a crush she had years ago flitted through her mind. But the woman was an ex-con and a CI to boot. Starting a relationship with her would have broken all kinds of regs.

"Tell me, Detective. Now that you got your twenty-five in, you planning on pulling the pin?" Goodman asked.

"And leave this county in the hands of you people? Not a chance. Besides, what would I do with my time? Take up knitting? Grow heirloom tomatoes? Sheriff Keeler's almost seventy. If he can stick it out, so can I."

"Glad to hear it," replied Goodman. "I'd hate to lose someone with your experience. Any updates on the Wolf Ridge Arms hijacking?"

"Two guards and a driver were killed. Initial reports

point to at least two shooters. Still waiting on ballistics and the report from the M.E.'s office. According to our contact at Wolf Ridge Arms, over four hundred weapons were taken, half of which were semi-automatic rifles. The rest were pistols of various calibers."

"How did the hijackers know where the truck would be? I'd think the company would keep that information confidential."

"They do. We're looking at an inside man. Or woman. Johnson and I have been interviewing employees and running backgrounds. So far, no leads."

"Find those guns, Detective. Last thing we need is some mass shooting in our county at the height of the tourist season."

"Yes, sir. We'll get them."

"Detective Rios," an all-too-familiar gravelly voice drawled behind her. She nearly choked on her beer.

She turned and found herself facing Sheriff Buzz Keeler. The buttons on his uniform strained to contain his belly, which hung over his belt like a sack of potatoes. His nose was dark with gin blossoms. His eyelids drooped. He'd already had a few before Toni arrived.

She saluted him out of instinct rather than respect. "Sheriff Keeler."

The room quieted, leaving an awkward energy sizzling in the air.

"Never woulda thought you had it in ya. Twenty-five years. And only killed—what was it?—One, no, two of your fellow officers."

Toni stiffened while a thousand justifiable retorts played through her mind, all of which could get her written up for insubordination. "Yes, sir."

"All due respect, sir," chimed in Goodman, "the situation with Sergeant Foster and Detective Edelman was unfortunate, but they were running a heroin trafficking ring and had kidnapped a young girl. I doubt any officer could have handled it any better than Rios here. Her closure rate is the best in the Violent Crimes Division. She's good police and a genuine asset to the department."

Keeler eyed Goodman and harrumphed. "Not bad for a beaner dyke with a badge." He turned back to the bar and slammed his tumbler on the polished mahogany. "Gimme another."

When the bartender refilled the glass, Keeler shuffled off into the crowd.

"Thanks for that," Toni whispered to Goodman.

"Keeler's a bigoted ass. But as long as the citizens of Cortes County keep reelecting him, we can't do anything about it."

It was a reality Toni had dealt with for years. Other officers had filed harassment complaints, but they went nowhere. Those who spoke up eventually resigned.

A friend of Toni's on the interagency organized crime task force had urged her to apply to the FBI. But despite Keeler and others like him, she refused to let the bigots drive her away from her mission to protect the citizens of the county.

After two beers and an equal number of glasses of club soda and lime, she sidled up to Johnson. "I'm packing it in for the night."

"Already? It's only nine o'clock."

"I want to get an early start in the morning. Goodman's wanting us to close the Wolf Ridge Arms hijacking yesterday."

Johnson looked at her with a skeptical gaze. "You okay to drive?"

"¡Sí, abuela! I'm all right. See you mañana."

"Watch your back, girl. It's a full moon. Lotta crazies out there up to no good."

Toni waved to her comrades while she made her way out of the bar. The moon loomed large over the downtown buildings. Heat from the day still radiated from the pavement, causing sweat to pool under her breasts. She couldn't wait to get home and pull off the bulletproof vest underneath her blouse.

While she walked along the sidewalk to the public lot where she'd parked, her mind reviewed what she knew so far in the weapons hijacking case. The truck routes and schedules weren't published anywhere. And yet the hijackers dispatched the driver and guards with surgical precision. Someone at Wolf Ridge Arms was involved.

"Hey, Rios!" shouted a male voice just after she unlocked the door with a key fob.

Toni turned and glimpsed two men in the shadows on the other side of the lot. Two gunshots shook the air, and pain exploded in her chest. She fell back against the car next to hers. Pushing against the pain, she drew her sidearm and fired four shots toward her assailants.

After ducking down behind her car, she scanned the lot. No one in sight, but she could hear cries of pain. She'd hit someone.

Another muzzle flash lit up the night, and her driver's door window shattered. Rios fired three more rounds and dropped down between the cars. Every breath she took felt like daggers in her chest.

She pulled her radio off her belt. Through gritted teeth, she said, "4-Lima-35. Request backup and RA unit. Shots fired. I'm hit. One suspect is down. Public lot, 4500 block of North Monterosa, Ironwood."

"Roger that, 4-Lima-35. Backup and medical are en route."

Adrenaline surged through her, making the pain in her chest barely an afterthought. Another gunshot echoed through the parking lot, and shattered glass rained down on her from the rear window. She dropped the radio and fired three more rounds. Shadows scurried across the lot.

"Stop where you are. Drop your gu—unh!" Searing pain erupted on the side of her head. She fell back against the other car, choking on blood. A motorcycle engine roared to life somewhere in the lot and faded away.

Keep breathing, she told herself. But every gurgled breath brought a fresh wave of pain.

Faces appeared in the darkness. Voices familiar but distorted. "Hold on, Detective. Medical's on the way."

Her pulse boomed like a kettledrum in her ears. A bright light flashed in her eye, and then more pain when someone lifted her onto a gurney.

"Just hang in there. We're gonna get you patched up."

Something over her face. More faces stared down at her, and then everything faded. Light. Pain. Everything.

4

SHEA DROVE through their neighborhood in the cycle shop's pickup truck. Annie slept slumped against the door beside her.

Shea braked suddenly to avoid hitting an adult bobcat with three kits crossing the dark road in front of them.

Annie jolted awake. "What—what happened?"

"Sorry. Bobbie Jean and her babies ran across the road."

"Where?" Annie had named them a few weeks earlier when she spotted them lounging in their backyard.

Shea pointed between two of their neighbors' houses. "Disappeared over there."

"Damn, I wished I'd seen them."

"We're almost home."

"Good." Annie sat up and rubbed her eyes. "What time is it?"

"Almost eleven."

Shea pulled the shop truck into their driveway and stopped at the pullout beside the house. She pressed the garage door opener.

The door creaked and groaned like a portcullis in a

medieval castle. Shea had kept meaning to oil it up, but other things kept taking priority.

She stepped out of the truck and felt the cool steel of a gun barrel press against the back of her head.

"I wanna hear you say it, bitch." The pinched, nasally voice was familiar, though Shea was surprised to hear it. "I want you to admit you set us up with that drug deal."

"Mackey." She turned and glared into the outlaw biker's beady eyes, ignoring the snub-nosed revolver he held in her face.

"Aunt Shea?" The passenger door of the truck opened.

"Stay in the truck, Annie." To Mackey, Shea said, "Thought you and the boys were in prison."

"Got out yesterday. We all did."

Mackey's beak nose and weak, scruffy chin made him look more like a weasel than ever in the stark light coming from the garage. His leather cut, dusty and dry from three years in storage, bore the worn patches of the Confederate Thunder Motorcycle Club. Reddish-brown splotches stained his wrinkled white shirt. Barbeque sauce? Ketchup? Or blood?

"Appeals judges threw out the case. Called it entrapment."

Shit, thought Shea. "Well, goody for you. Why the hell you stinking up my driveway?"

"The DEA refused to name who snitched on us. But I know you's the one who set us up."

"You forget. I grew up around the Thunder. I don't snitch. No one in the Sisterhood knew about the roadblock. If you're looking for a rat, best check your own ranks. Wouldn't be the first time the feds got a man inside the Thunder."

"Don't lie to me, cunt. I spent three years in federal lockup cuzza you." The revolver trembled in Mackey's hands. His nostrils flared. "Shoulda known something was up when you dykes-on-bikes gave us Bonefish's stash without wanting nothing in return. Sure as hell wasn't outta the goodness of your little rug-munching hearts."

"We gave y'all the dope to stop the violence between the clubs, dumbass. The Athena Sisterhood's a law-abiding club. We got no use for that shit."

Uncertainty mixed with fury in Mackey's shifting eyes. His breathing was staccato and sharp. "I shoulda shot you the day we met."

Shea stepped toward him, pressing her forehead against the gun barrel. "You wanna kill me, ya little shit? Go ahead. Just do me a favor and smile at the security camera mounted on the wall behind me."

A muscle twitched under Mackey's left eye. His finger curled around the gun's trigger. Shea refused to look away.

Mackey screwed up his face and raised his arm as if to shoot the camera. In a flash, Shea snatched the gun away before he pulled the trigger and smacked him across the face with it. He collapsed onto the concrete, blood dripping from his nose.

"You really are stupid. The video feed's stored in the cloud. Shooting the camera won't do shit." She caught a whiff of burned gunpowder coming off the revolver. Her pulse quickened. "This gun's been fired recently. Who'd you shoot?"

Mackey grinned, blood smeared across his teeth. "Ain't telling you shit, bitch."

She clocked him on the side of the head. "Listen up, dipshit. Nobody wants another war between our clubs. Too many folks on both sides died last time. So, do everyone a favor and stay the fuck away from me and the Sisterhood. Now get the hell outta here before I pop a cap in your ass with your own gun."

Mackey picked himself off the ground, wiping blood from his face onto his arm. "You're a lying rat. I'm gonna prove it to One-Shot, and we gonna bury you."

"We both know your prez has more sense than to start that shit up again."

"You think so, huh?" He flipped her off with both hands and backed down the driveway.

Shea watched him stumble down the street and throw a leg over a Harley parked a few houses down. The bike chortled to life and disappeared into the night.

Shea turned to Annie. "You okay, Doodl—I mean, Annie?"

"I-I'm okay." Annie stared down the road. "You think Gramma Julia's outta prison, too?"

"Dunno." Shea steered Annie between the motorcycles parked in the garage and opened the door into the kitchen. "Why? You wanna go see her?"

"I miss her."

Shea put an arm around Annie's shoulder and kissed the side of her head. To Shea's surprise, Annie didn't resist. "I'll look into it in the morning, okay, kid?"

"All right."

"Now go to bed and get some rest."

Annie shuffled into her bedroom and shut the door.

Shea locked Mackey's revolver in a small gun safe she kept in her bedroom closet then pulled out her phone.

"Bueno," said an accented voice on the other end of the line.

"Fuego? It's Havoc," said Shea.

"Hola, Veep. What's up?"

"The Thundermen are out of prison. Mackey showed up at my place with a gun, accusing me of dropping the dime on their club."

"I thought the DEA was supposed to keep your identity confidential."

"They were. He's grasping at straws. We've had a mutual dislike for some time now."

"So I recall. You and Annie okay?"

"We're fine. I took the gun away from him and sent him on his way. Getting to be a tradition with us. But if *he* suspects me or the Sisterhood, chances are some other Thundermen do too. We gotta get a handle on this before it escalates."

"I heard on the news a cop got shot in Ironwood earlier. You think it's related?"

"Possible. Mackey's gun smelled like it'd been recently fired. And he had blood on his shirt." Shea replayed her conversation with Mackey, and concern gripped her heart. "They mention which cop was shot?"

"Not so far. Reporter said one person dead, but didn't specify who. Watch your back, hermana."

"You too, Prez."

Shea turned on the TV, hoping to catch a news story talking about the cop getting shot. The local news programs were over. CNN and MSNBC were too busy mocking Trump's latest narcissistic tweets to be bothered with local stories.

Shea surfed the news stories on her phone, opening an article that had been updated only minutes earlier. Detective Antonia Rios of the Cortes County Sheriff's Office had been shot during a confrontation with an unnamed assailant outside a bar popular with local law enforcement. The assailant was killed in the exchange.

Shea felt nauseated. She and Rios had history. One of Rios's earlier partners, Detective Edelman, had tried to kill Shea a few years earlier after she threatened to expose his heroin-trafficking organization. Rios had killed Edelman to save Shea.

Months later, Rios had forced Shea to be a confidential informant to infiltrate the Athena Sisterhood, who were suspected at the time of dealing drugs laced with strychnine.

After Shea revealed the source of the drugs was a dealer named Bonefish, Shea had remained with the Sisterhood and eventually become the club's VP.

Shea held a begrudging respect for the detective. Rios wasn't a bully with a badge like so many others who worked for Sheriff Buzzkill. She seemed to care for the county's citizens, including those who didn't normally garner much respect.

Shea called Rios's cell number, but it went to voicemail. "Hey, Detective, it's Shea Stevens. I heard about what happened. I...I don't know what to say, but I'm sorry. You're really nice. Call me." Shea's face grew hot with embarrassment when she hung up. Her message sounded as cheesy and insincere as a middle-school valentine.

She replayed her confrontation with Mackey in her mind. Serious shit was about to go down. She could feel it like a monsoon storm on the horizon.

5

"Annie! Come on! Your breakfast is getting cold, and you're gonna miss your ride to soccer camp." Shea sat at the breakfast bar, sipping coffee and reading the news on her phone.

Detective Rios was reported in stable condition. The assailant she'd killed in the shooting turned out to be a two-time loser named Kevin "Nuggets" Chaikin, a member of the Confederate Thunder. Shea'd never met him but knew the nickname from her previous interactions with the Thunder.

"One less scumbag," Shea said to herself.

The news story reported that another unidentified person was being sought in connection to the shootout. Mackey, no doubt.

"I ain't got no clean socks!" Annie cried from her bedroom.

"Crap," Shea muttered. She had meant to run a load of laundry before the bike festival. "Just use the ones from yesterday!"

"Ew, gross!"

"I'm sorry. I forgot to run the wash." Shea walked into Annie's bedroom.

Annie sat on her bed, her chin resting on her hands. She was dressed in a red Windcrest Soccer Camp T-shirt with black shorts. "What am I s'posed to wear?"

"I can give you a pair of mine."

"No." Annie rolled her eyes and shuffled to the wicker basket that served as her laundry hamper. She dug through the clothes until she pulled out two matching socks and gave them a sniff test. "I'll just wear these. But if other kids make fun of me, it's your fault."

"I'll take the hit. Just get your socks and cleats on and eat your breakfast before Fatima Ali's mom gets here to pick you up."

As Shea returned to the kitchen, her phone rang. The number on the caller ID wasn't familiar. "Shea Stevens."

"Good morning, Shealene. It's Julia Mueller."

After Mackey's visit the night before, Shea knew it was only a matter of time before she heard Julia's cigarette-scorched voice. "Heard y'all got released the other day."

"We did."

"Good for you," Shea said without enthusiasm.

"Some folks thinking you and the Athena Sisterhood mighta had something to do with us gettin' locked up."

"You think I'd snitch? Last thing the Sisterhood wanted was to make things worse between our clubs." It was a lie. They had set the Thunder up, but Shea would never admit it. "Besides, you're family, more or less."

"First I've heard you say it."

"Is that Gramma Julia?" Annie rushed into the kitchen with her eyes lit up like a Christmas tree.

"Eat your breakfast," Shea replied. "You can talk to Gramma Julia later."

Annie pouted but hopped onto a stool at the breakfast

bar and began eating, her attention clearly on Shea's phone conversation.

Shea sighed. "Raising Annie the past few years taught me how much you musta done for Wendy after Mom died."

"Your mother was my best friend, Shea-Shea. I was honored to raise your sister and would've happily taken you in too, had you stuck around."

Shea couldn't help thinking that both her mother and her sister Wendy would still be alive if they'd not been involved with the club. "I suppose you wanna spend some time with Annie."

"Like a junkie jonesing for a hit."

"Maybe this coming Saturday."

"Thunder's having a welcome-home barbecue at the Church tomorrow night. Gonna be tons of food, a live band, and a bouncy house for the kids. You and Annie can come hang out, just like old times."

The Church was the nickname for the Confederate Thunder's clubhouse, an old renovated church building west of Bradshaw City, twenty-five miles north of Sycamore Springs.

Shea bristled and walked to the other side of the room where Annie couldn't hear her talk. "The Thunder thinks I set them up to get busted, and you think it's a good idea for me and Annie to show up? How stupid do you think I am? I'd probably get shot dead before I took two steps inside that fence."

"Aw, bullshit. I wouldn't invite ya if I didn't think it were safe."

"Yeah, right. Besides, I don't want Annie hanging around the Thunder. I've spent the last three years deprogramming her."

"Deprogramming her?" Julia coughed a laugh. "Girl, you make the MC sound like a cult."

"Maybe not a cult, but definitely a racist, sexist criminal organization, or are the one-percenter patches the boys wear just for show?"

"Aw, come on. We're not that bad."

"Says the woman who just spent three years in prison for drug trafficking."

"I won't even dignify that with an answer. Fact is, we're out. And as I said, rumor is the Athena Sisterhood set us up. If you showed up, we could keep the two clubs from turning the county into a slaughterhouse again."

"What does One-Shot say to all this? He's the Thunder's prez."

"I ain't spoken to One-Shot directly, but I talked to Hooch. He thinks you oughta show up, maybe with a few officers from your club. We'll clear the air once and for all."

"Who the hell's Hooch?"

"Thunder's VP."

Shea had attended countless parties at the Church back when her father was the Confederate Thunder's president. Lots of drinking and drugs and the occasional fistfight, usually over someone's old lady or a football game or who's bike was faster or over nothing at all.

At the time, she'd thought it was hilarious to watch the patched members and their old ladies get wasted and act stupid. Now, as Annie's legal guardian and the VP for the Athena Sisterhood, Shea had a different perspective.

"You can tell Hooch and One-Shot that we'll meet them on neutral ground. Not at the Church."

"They figured you'd say that. The party's already scheduled. This is you and the Sisterhood's chance to stop the bloodshed before anyone starts something that can't be stopped."

"Mackey already started something. Showed up last night threatening me with a revolver."

"That boy, I swear. I'll talk to One-Shot and Hooch. They'll see he stays away from you. But only till tomorrow night. After that, I can't promise anything."

Shea wanted to tell her to go to hell. But there were too many lives at stake. "I'll talk to my prez and let you know."

"You need to be there, Shea-Shea. We got other things to discuss."

"Such as?"

"Stuff we ain't oughta discuss on the phone."

That didn't sound good. "Yeah, all right." The more Shea thought about it, the more this invitation sounded like walking into a lion's den wearing a bathing suit made from flank steak. "By the way, I heard about Nuggets getting killed."

"Fucking cop gunned him down in cold blood."

"Cold blood? I heard he shot first."

"Heard from who? The cops? What do you expect them to say?"

"Heard it on the news. And they say he wasn't alone. I'm guessing it was Mackey. That's why he had blood on him when he showed up at my place. It was Nuggets's blood."

"Shealene, I can't discuss club business. Why do you care so much about some cop, anyway?"

"It ain't about the cop. It's about keeping Annie away from the Thunder's violent shit." A car horn honked outside. "I gotta go. We'll see you tomorrow night."

Shea hung up. Annie was cramming scrambled eggs into her mouth as fast as she could.

"You got your bag?" Shea asked.

Annie nodded while she chewed and lifted her bag.

"All right. Get outta here, Doodlebug, er, sorry, Annie." Shea hugged her. "Have fun at soccer camp."

"Love you, Aunt Shea!" Annie said through a mouthful of egg while she raced out the door.

When the car drove off, Shea sat staring out the front windows.

In terms of sheer numbers, the two clubs were evenly matched—a couple dozen patch members in each. But the Thundermen had a ruthlessness the Sisterhood couldn't match. A majority of them had served time in prison. The women, for the most part, had not. They were decent, law-abiding citizens. And that made them vulnerable.

Her phone pinged. Fuego had sent a message that the Sisterhood officers were meeting at eight.

In her bedroom closet, Shea opened the gun safe and stared at the revolver she'd taken off Mackey. She thought about him and Nuggets ambushing Rios. *Stupid little shit.*

She grabbed her Glock .40-caliber, tucked it in a pancake holster at the small of her back, and relocked the safe. Until a new truce was in place, she didn't intend to be caught unarmed.

She slipped on her Athena Sisterhood cut over a mesh motorcycle jacket, tossed her helmet into the cab of the Iron Goddess pickup truck, and drove north out of her neighborhood.

The road twisted in switchbacks fifteen hundred feet up the side of Sycamore Mountain. The warm morning air was sweet with the scent of yucca that studded the mountainside. White blossoms towered on ten-foot-long stalks above the spiky plants.

At the top of the hill, she entered Olde Towne Sycamore Springs, a stretch of quaint, tourist-oriented shops that included Iron Goddess Custom Cycles. She pulled the truck into the shop's back lot and locked it up.

Her own motorcycle, a black Iron Goddess 750cc custom called Sweet Betsy, was still parked in the lot. Annie had been too tired to ride two-up on Sweet Betsy, so they'd taken the truck back home. Shea threw a leg over her seat and took off to meet with the Sisterhood officers.

Once past Olde Towne, Shea pinned the throttle on Sycamore Highway toward the college town of Ironwood. The road meandered through grass-covered hills dotted with juniper and rocky outcroppings. The wind roared in her ears, giving her the sensation of flying while she raced through the gentle curves. This was wind therapy.

While the landscape blew past, the tangled knot of concerns in her mind unraveled. Would she and the Sisterhood be able to reestablish a truce with the Thundermen? Could they keep Cortes County from turning once again into a blood-soaked battlefield?

What if the meeting at the Church was an ambush after all? Would they be able to fight their way out? It seemed unlikely. And then what would the rest of the Sisterhood do in response? Would the Thundermen then take them all out one by one?

What would happen to Annie? Even if they managed to prevent a gang war between the clubs, Shea didn't want Annie to have anything to do with Julia so long as she was involved in the Thunder. But keeping Annie away from her wouldn't be easy.

6

THE ROLLING HILLS of rural Cortes County gave way to the business-lined city streets of Ironwood. With Central Arizona University's spring semester over, a smattering of tourists from Phoenix and Tucson escaping the summer heat had replaced the throng of students who usually clogged the Downtown district.

Shea drove to Downtown Square and cut into an alley that ran behind the buildings on Prospector Avenue. A few doors in, she parked next to a familiar black Kawasaki Vulcan in the lot reserved for ASMC Enterprises, the Athena Sisterhood Motorcycle Club's clubhouse.

The instant she stepped inside, Shea recalled the moment she and the Sisterhood first discovered the storefront was a drug lab run by a woman named Bonefish. The place reeked of what smelled like a mix of burned plastic and cotton candy.

After the DEA seized the property, the Sisterhood purchased it on the cheap at auction and had it decontaminated. But the chemical stench lingered, if only in Shea's mind.

A hallway led to the club's chapel, where the MC's officers met to discuss business. Several chairs surrounded a wooden table. On the far wall, a fierce owl with outstretched wings and clutching talons was painted above the words Athena Sisterhood MC.

"Morning, Prez."

Fuego sat with a wooden gavel next to a cup of coffee from a nearby café. She looked up when Shea plopped down beside her.

"Hola, Havoc," she said. "You get Annie off to *fútbol* camp?"

"Barely. How's business at Gertie's?"

"Slower now that school's out. Those college lesbians love to drink."

"Hang in there. Fall is coming."

Savage, Indigo, and two other women soon walked in, each wearing their cuts identifying them as Sisterhood officers.

One of them, a woman with short-cropped black hair and an amiable smile, gave Shea a high five after she took her seat. "Heard congrats are in order. Best in show, huh? Well done."

"Thanks, Raven. Credit goes to my team, especially Lakota."

"You're too damn modest, Havoc. No one designs custom bikes like yours. Especially for women," said Dragon, an Asian American woman with a piercing gaze. Her biker cut looked incongruous over her white silk blouse. Although not a club officer, her experience as a criminal defense attorney helped the Sisterhood maintain its law-abiding status. At least most of the time.

Fuego rapped the gavel on the table. "*Hermanas*, in case you haven't heard, those *pinche putos* in the Confederate Thunder are out of prison."

The announcement prompted a stream of profanity from the women around the table.

"Why the hell'd they get released so early?" Savage, the club's sergeant-at-arms, asked.

"Their convictions were overturned," Dragon replied. "The appellate judges ruled there was no probable cause for the stop. They excluded the seized drugs as fruit of the poisonous tree. No evidence, no conviction."

"Are you serious?" asked Shea. "I was their CI. I called them with a legitimate tip."

"Unfortunately, the appeals court ruled differently. That's the nature of the justice system, I'm afraid."

"Justice system," Indigo scoffed. "Betcha them charges would've stuck if they'd been black."

A blanket of awkwardness settled on the group. A year earlier, Scottsdale cops had arrested Indigo on trumped-up murder charges and put her in the men's jail because she was transgender. She'd been brutally assaulted.

"However they got the convictions tossed," said Raven, "we gotta keep relations with them from turning violent again."

"They already have," Shea said. "One of their patches showed up at my place last night. A prick named Mackey pulled a gun and accused me of ratting them out. I denied everything and took the fucker's gun. But they're looking for payback."

"It's not just us they're after," Indigo added. "Last night, two Thundermen shot the detective in charge of the task force that busted the Thunder. I've worked with her as the Lambda Resource Center's liaison to the sheriff's office. She's an honest cop. Not like some of them bastards."

"She's alive, at least," Savage replied. "And killed a Thunderman named Nuggets during last night's shoot-out."

"Nuggets may not've been alone," said Shea. "Mackey's gun had been recently fired when he jumped me."

"Are we looking at another war between the clubs?" Raven looked from one woman to another. "Some of us barely survived the last one. Not to mention what those fucking animals did to Goth and Pixie."

"Julia Mueller called me this morning," Shea replied. "Her late husband was a Thunderman named Monster. They raised my sister after our mom was killed. Helped raise Annie too."

All eyes were on her.

"She told me the Thunder's having a welcome-home celebration at their clubhouse tomorrow night. They want a few of us there for a sit-down to hash things out and keep things from going back to the way things were."

Savage shook her head. "Sounds like an ambush."

"Total ambush," Raven added.

"It could be," Shea admitted. "But Julia still considers me kin. I doubt she'd invite me up there if she thought they were planning to kill me. She all but confirmed to me that Mackey was with Nuggets last night. I think it speaks to her sense of loyalty to me."

"Unless she's trying to get custody of Annie," Dragon pointed out.

"Yeah," replied Indigo. "Besides, even if your godmother cares about you, she sure as hell wouldn't shed no tears if them white boys shot my black ass."

"Get them to meet us on neutral ground," Fuego said. "But going up to their clubhouse is loco."

Shea knew they were right. But the threat of another gang war chilled her. "They won't agree to neutral ground. And if we refuse, they're going to come after us. I know it's a risk. Hell, it may even be a suicide mission. I'm willing to go alone. I don't want to put anyone else in danger."

"Not a chance. Someone's gotta watch your six," Savage said. "I'll go with you."

Indigo put her hand on Savage's. "Well, fuck. You ain't going without me. I'm in if there's no other option."

"I'll join you," said Fuego. "Those racist pendejos don't scare me none. And since I'm the chapter president, I should be there for any negotiations. Dragon?"

Dragon looked grim. "I think this is a remarkably bad idea. But I'm in."

"Good," Fuego said. "All in favor of meeting with the Thunder, say 'aye.'"

All the women announced their approval.

"Nays?"

No one spoke.

Fuego clacked the gavel. "It's decided. Any other business we need to discuss?"

After an awkward silence, Dragon asked, "Havoc, where's the gun you took off Mackey?"

"In my gun safe."

"You think Mackey shot Detective Rios?"

"Wouldn't surprise me."

"I suggest you turn the gun over to the sheriff's office."

"Reporting Mackey to the cops could jeopardize our sit-down with the Thunder," said Fuego. "They already suspect we were in on the drug bust."

"If Mackey's gun was used to shoot a sheriff's deputy, we have to turn it over. If it comes out later we withheld evidence, we could all be charged with conspiracy after the fact."

"I'll take care of it," Shea promised, though she wasn't sure how. She didn't trust anyone in the sheriff's office other than Rios.

"Any other matters before we break?" Fuego asked.

No one else spoke.

"There's a Shell station on Pinellas Parkway, just west of Bradshaw City. We'll meet there tomorrow night at six and ride to the Thunder's clubhouse together." Fuego banged the gavel and closed the meeting.

7

THE SQUEAK of a door opening roused Toni Rios from the misty depths of unconsciousness. Ebony Johnson and Johnny Bello, another detective in the Violent Crimes Division, appeared in her field of view.

Disorganized blips from the night before flashed through her mind. The party at the Blue Bar. Walking to the parking lot. A voice calling her. Then gunshots and pain. It took her a moment to realize she was in the hospital.

"Shit," Bello said, stroking his goatee that made him look like a slightly younger Al Pacino. The top button of his shirt was undone, and his tie was loosened.

Ebony elbowed him. "Hey, Toni. How ya feeling, girl?"

"Hurts to talk." Toni's voice crackled like glass in a food disposal. The left side of her face burned with pain, and the inside of her mouth felt stuffed with cotton.

"Not surprising." Ebony's eyes glistened. "Doc says a bullet tore through your left cheek, just missing your teeth. Another penetrated the outer cartilage of your left ear. A couple inches to the right, we wouldn't be having this conversation."

Bello gave her a forced smile. "You won't be winning no beauty contest anytime soon, but hey, you're alive. Got lucky if you ask me."

Yeah, lucky me, Toni thought.

"And if it's any consolation," Ebony added, "you put that dirtbag in the morgue. Some Thunderman named Chaikin. Buddies call him Nuggets. Detective Morris is meeting with the M.E. right now, or she'd be here as well."

Rios reached out with her hand and made a gesture as if she was writing.

"Of course." Ebony pulled out a notepad and pen and handed them both to Toni. "Here, girl."

"Were 2," Toni wrote. The pulse oximeter on her index finger bounced with each stroke.

"Were two?" Ebony asked. "I don't understand."

"2 perps."

"What do you remember from last night?" Bello asked.

"Walking to car. Dark." Toni flipped to a fresh page and tried to sort out the memories. "Perp called my name. Then shot me in vest."

The vitals monitor beside the bed began beeping. Part of the screen flashed red. She ignored it and continued writing while a montage of images cluttered her mind.

"Returned fire. 3." She scratched out the number. "4 shots."

"Could you ID the shooters?"

"Too dark. In shadows. NE corner of lot. 50–60 ft away." She took a breath, pushing back against a wave of panic. "Called 4 backup. Don't remember more."

A nurse entered. "Miss Antonia, your heart rate is getting way too high." She glanced at Bello and Ebony. "You two best wrap this up. Your friend's endured a lot. She needs her rest."

"Almost done," Bello assured her.

She didn't look convinced. "How's your pain level, sweetie?"

"Hurts."

"I'll request another dose of pain medication." The nurse strode back out of the room.

"Any idea who Chaikin's buddy was?" asked Ebony.

Toni shook her head. The movement sent waves of pain burning through her face.

"Why would they go after you?" Bello pressed. "Is the Thunder connected to a case you two are working?"

"No se," she wrote.

"Nose?" Bello asked. "I don't understand."

"*No sé*. She doesn't know," Ebony clarified. "Last I heard, the Thundermen were in prison after you busted their punk asses. Musta got released."

Bello nodded. "Whoever he is, we'll find the other muthafucker who shot you and nail his ass to the wall. Hopefully, Ballistics can get a match with the rounds CSU recovered."

Ebony's expression hardened. "Just a head's up, Officer Blythe from SIU's been lurking around wanting to take your statement." Special Investigations Unit was the department assigned to all officer-involved shootings.

"Fucking SIU vulture," Bello said. "I'll put a call in to CLEA and get a union rep here pronto before they talk to you. Well, I better blaze, see if I can't track down this other shooter." He patted Toni's shoulder and headed toward the door.

"Gracias, Bello," Toni said despite the pain.

"Take care of yourself, Rios."

After he left, Toni wrote, "Gun hijacking?"

"I've pulled in Detective Tolliver while you're recovering. ATF Special Agent Rudy Powell has his people canvassing Wolf Ridge Arms employees and compiling a list of potential suspects."

Toni's frustration from being left out of the investigation was so visceral, it was worse than the pain she was feeling from her injuries. "Where's my stuff?"

"Your clothes are in evidence. They were soaked with blood. You would've tossed them, anyway. I can stop by your place and pick you up something comfortable to wear so you don't have your ass hanging out of a hospital johnny."

She opened a nearby drawer and held up a clear plastic bag. "Your purse is here. Phone, wallet, credit cards, cash, everything looked accounted for. When you're ready, go through it. You find anything missing, let me know."

"Phone please?" Toni wrote and held up the notebook.

"Sure." Ebony reached into the purse and handed Toni her phone.

Toni took it, pulling against the IV in the crook of her left elbow.

"You need anything from home besides clothes? Toothbrush, something to read, a laptop?"

"Laptop." Toni held up her phone and pointed to the charging port.

"Charging cord? You got it, partner. You on any dietary restrictions?"

"Clear liquids," she wrote.

"Shit. Yeah, kinda hard to eat with your injured cheek, huh?"

Toni gave her a frustrated look.

"When they let you eat solid food again, you tell me. I'll bring you whatever you desire. The medical care here's top notch, but the food not so much. When I was in here after that tweaker knifed me last March, I ordered chicken and dumplings. You know what they brought me? Campbell's chicken noodle poured over a hamburger bun, sesame seeds and all. So, you just say the word, I'll bring you some actual food."

"Gracias, compañera," Toni murmured.

"De nada." Ebony put a hand on Toni's arm. "I'll be back in a while with your clothes and stuff. Keep the notebook to talk with the nurses. I've got plenty of spares."

As the door closed behind Ebony, Toni opened her phone. Only ten percent battery remained. Lots of texts from her fellow officers, mostly the detectives in the Violent Crimes Division, wishing her a speedy recovery. She'd express her thanks later when she was feeling better.

She flipped through her voicemail messages. One caller ID caught her attention. She played it and almost dropped her phone. She hadn't spoken with Shea Stevens in over a year, not since Toni had released the ex-con from her confidential informant agreement.

A warmth flooded her body. Shea Stevens was no beauty. Scarred face and a wiry physique. And she was an ex-con who still played fast and loose with the law.

But something about her got Toni's senses buzzing. Not that she'd ever act on it. Sheriff's deputies weren't allowed to date felons.

Rios's thumb hovered over the button to return the call. She sighed and set the phone down on the bedside table. The thunder of gunshots echoed in her mind. Muzzle flashes lighting up the night like a strobe. The shock of taking two in the vest. Then the agony from when she was hit in the face.

The nurse reappeared and emptied a syringe in her IV port. Eventually she drifted off into a troubled sleep.

8

Shea headed south from Ironwood, picking up Highway 89 off the Ironwood Bypass. She pushed Sweet Betsy well above the posted limit, only slowing when she approached the hill past Meeker Ranch Road.

As she crested the rise, she spotted the ever-present CCSO patrol car parked on the shoulder waiting to catch speeding tourists. Locals knew to slow down.

Twenty minutes after ten o'clock, she cruised into Olde Towne Sycamore Springs. Just past the Kokopelli Café, she turned up a side street and parked in the Iron Goddess back lot.

She entered the service bay, where a half dozen bikes stood on lifts in various stages of repair. The familiar bouquet of rubber, engine grease, and a hint of ozone filled the air. It was to Shea what lavender or vanilla were to normal people—familiar and calming.

"You're late, dude," Kyle Flores taunted in a singsong voice. The four-foot-tall mechanic worked to fit a new tire onto the front wheel of a Suzuki Boulevard that stood on a nearby lift.

"Whatever. I'm also the boss."

"Oh yeah," replied Kyle. "Almost forgot that for a microsecond."

"That reporter here?"

Lakota paused from tack-welding a custom fuel tank and raised her mask. "In the office with her photographer talking to Terrance."

"They're wanting to take pictures of us," Kyle added, this time with more concern than snark in his voice. "There are people from my past I'd rather not know where I am, if you get my drift. People who aren't above causing serious harm to little bodies."

"I'll tell the reporter to keep your photo and name out of the story. Anyone else prefer to remain anonymous?"

Vince Roberts, a woman with a purple fauxhawk hairdo and built like a bulldozer, was elbow-deep converting the drive belt on a Harley Softail to a chain drive. She raised a grime-smeared hand.

"My ex is a fucking headcase. Don't need her finding out where I landed after rehab. She's still in LA last I heard, but I don't want my deets showing up on the interwebs. Can't deal with her level of crazy no more."

"Fine," Shea said. "I'll tell them no names or photos unless you give permission."

She opened the door that led to the office, leaving behind the sounds and smells of the shop. Terrance sat behind his desk, with the reporter, whatever her name was, in the chair opposite him. A skinny guy in his twenties with wild, bleach-white hair stood nearby. He reminded Shea of a human-sized Q-tip.

"There she is," Terrance was smiling, but the look in his eyes said, "Where the hell you been?"

"Sorry I'm late. Had some personal business that took longer than expected."

"You remember Elia Quinn from the *Chronicle*," Terrance continued.

Shea shook her offered hand.

"And this is my photographer, David Walsh."

"Nice to see you. Did Terrance give you the tour?"

"Yes, it's quite a business you've built for yourselves."

"Well, the original owner believed in giving people a second chance. Hired mostly ex-cons, including the two of us. When he died ten years ago, he left the shop to Terrance and me. We've been business partners ever since."

"And you've continued the tradition of hiring ex-cons?"

"Ex-cons, recovering addicts, other people rebuilding their lives for one reason or another. Everyone except our salesperson Monica out front. She's the only normal one among us."

"Thus, the motorcycle shop for misfit toys." Elia grinned. "Have you had any problems with employees stealing or getting violent?"

Shea thought about the break-in five years earlier but said nothing. It was a can of worms she'd rather not reopen.

Terrance spoke up. "The culture we've developed encourages recent hires to take advantage of this opportunity to leave past lives behind and become responsible, upstanding citizens. All in all, it has worked."

"I'd love to talk with some of your employees," Elia said. "Their success stories would be so inspirational."

"No," Shea said sharply. All eyes turned to her. "Our employees are busy meeting tight deadlines."

Elia flashed her a reassuring smile. "Oh, we won't take up much of their time."

"They also prefer to avoid any publicity."

"We can keep them anonymous. No names, I promise."

"What Shea is trying to say is that we encourage our people to focus on the present rather than the past."

"I see," Elia said. "How about you, Shea? What's your story?"

Shea rolled her eyes. *Here we go*, she thought.

"I was a runaway, got into trouble, spent a little time in the can, then got out and started working here. Not much of a story."

"Really? Aren't you the daughter of Ralph Stevens, the former head of the Confederate Thunder biker gang? At least until he murdered your mother. What a trauma you endured. To go from that to become an award-winning motorcycle builder. That is a story that must be told. How about I buy you a coffee next door and you tell me about it? Meanwhile, David can take some photos of the shop, starting with the bikes in the showroom."

Shea wanted to tell her to go to hell, that she had no interest in digging up old shit. But Terrance was giving her a look that said, "Don't blow this. We need the publicity."

"Fine. Just no pictures of my employees. Got it?"

"Agreed."

Shea led Elia out into the showroom. A few customers were wandering the aisle, shopping for gear or parts. At the front counter, Monica was ringing up a customer. With her bleach-blond locks and centerfold figure, she resembled the models draped across motorcycles in the biker magazine ads, if a decade older.

"I'll be back soon. That photographer's gonna take some pics."

Monica flashed her a gleaming-white smile. "Okay, boss."

The Kokopelli Café next door was an all-wood building that dated back at least fifty years. It was popular with tourists, especially bikers stopping in for a quick breakfast before going on a ride in the high country. The tables were mostly occupied, filling the room with chatter, laughter, and the clink of dishes.

The hostess seated them in the corner at a two-top with wobbly chairs. She dropped off a carafe of coffee with two mugs and promised the server would be with them shortly.

"What d'you wanna know?" Shea asked.

"I'm sorry, Ms. Stevens. I brought you here under false pretenses." An embarrassed expression colored Elia's face.

"False pretenses?"

"I have a friend who needs your help." Elia's eyes held Shea's.

"With a motorcycle?"

"No, nothing like that. She...she's in trouble."

Shea felt a prickle along her spine. "What kind of trouble?"

Elia picked apart a napkin. "She had an affair with a powerful politician she worked for several years back. A married man. Long story short, she got pregnant. She wanted to have the baby, but he hounded her until she had an abortion. Now he's running for reelection and has been intimidating her to keep quiet about the affair and the abortion."

"Who's the politician?"

"State Senator Joseph Connelly."

"Connelly? The head of the Arizona Senate? Mr. 'Pray the Gay Away'? The one who refused to resign even after his fake charity got shut down by the feds? That asshole?" Shea's blood boiled at the thought of all the anti-LGBTQ bills he'd tried to ram through the Arizona legislature over the past few years. "Isn't he sponsoring an anti-abortion bill in the senate right now?"

"He is. No doubt an attempt to rally supporters in his bid for the open U.S. Senate seat against Graciela Perez in

November. Which is why he's pressuring my friend to stay quiet."

"If you've got the dirt on him, why haven't you published it already? Why get me involved?"

"My friend is reluctant to send me the proof I need to convince my editor to run the story. We risk being sued for libel if we go to print without it. All I have is her word. I haven't been able to verify the facts from any other sources."

"Why won't she give you the proof?"

"Fear of retaliation. She claims he already slashed her tires, busted up her kitchen, and left her threatening messages warning her to keep quiet."

"Has your friend talked to the police?"

"Connelly is close with both Sheriff Keeler and County Attorney Kavanagh. Any attempt to prosecute him could backfire. You're the vice president of the Athena Sisterhood. I know you help women in tough situations. I'm hoping you could convince him to leave her alone."

Shea considered what Elia was asking. They had protected women from abusive boyfriends, taken down drug dealers hurting women, and rallied around one of their own who was wrongly accused of murder. But going up against a well-connected guy like Connelly was unfamiliar territory.

"Getting a guy like Connelly to back off won't be easy. He's used to getting what he wants, whatever he wants. As you pointed out, he's got a lot of friends in high places. If she wants to bring him down, she should go public about the affair and abortion."

"She's terrified of what he'll do if she does. Not only is he well connected, he's vindictive too. A graphic designer sued him for nonpayment and won a judgment against him. A month later, the graphic designer's wife died in a hit-and-run. His dog died from ingesting a toxin. And a ransom virus hit the company's computer system, forcing them into bankruptcy. None of it could be traced back to Connelly. But I've done enough digging to know that dreadful things happen to people who cross him. That's why we need you and your biker gang to protect her and convince him to leave her alone."

"So he can come after us too? How is the Sisterhood supposed to protect your friend from a psycho like that? Hit-and-runs, murdering pets, and ransom viruses? This isn't a favor you're asking. It's a suicide mission."

Elia leaned back against her seat, arms folded, with a look of disappointment on her face. "Huh, never thought I'd hear a member of the Athena Sisterhood cower to the patriarchy. Much less their VP. That'd be a helluva story in itself."

"I prefer to see it as choosing one's battles. We're already dealing with a serious matter of our own."

"The Confederate Thunder, I'm guessing."

This caught Shea's attention. "What do you know about it?"

"I heard the charges against them were dropped on appeal. The drug evidence thrown out on some technicality."

"Fucking legal system."

"That's why I need your help, Shea. The legal system won't help my friend. She's in genuine danger."

"Who's your friend?"

"You're willing to help her out?"

"I'm willing to talk to her and see what we can work out."

"Her name's Deirdre West. I'll give you her number. I appreciate any help you and the Sisterhood can provide."

9

"You ready, David?" Elia asked the walking Q-tip when they returned to Iron Goddess. He and Terrance were standing next to a bobber with wrapped pipes and an electric blue tank.

"I think so. FYI, Linda called. Murder-suicide up in Bradshaw City. She told us to get on it."

"Right." Elia turned to Shea and Terrance. "Thank you both for talking with us. This will be a marvelous story, sure to bring new business."

"Thanks for doing this," Terrance replied, shaking their hands. "We appreciate the publicity."

"Our pleasure." Elia and her photographer grabbed their gear and trundled out the door.

"I think this story could be a real sales boost, especially after winning the design award. I've already received some interest from potential buyers of the Flying Tree bike."

"That's great, T." Shea stared across the room, too preoccupied with what Elia Quinn dropped in her lap to pay attention to what Terrance was saying.

"What's wrong? Miss Elia ask too many personal questions?"

"What?" Shea met his gaze. "Oh, nothing like that. Friend of hers needs help with something."

"What kind of help?"

"Athena Sisterhood kinda help."

A cloud of dread passed over Terrance's face. "Girl, what kinda trouble you getting yourself into now?"

"Me? You're the one all gung ho about Miss Elia Quinn doing a write-up on Iron Goddess. Turns out she wanted the Sisterhood to help her friend."

"Just keep whatever this is away from the shop. We don't need any more shoot-outs, break-ins, or other trouble that drives away customers."

"Don't worry. I'll handle it." Shea patted Terrance's shoulder.

Terrance looked no more convinced than Shea felt. "That's what I'm afraid of."

He wandered back into the office while she pulled out her phone and saw she had a text message from Rios.

Glad you called, Shea. I'm alive, but have trouble speaking. Text me when you can.

SHEA'S PULSE QUICKENED.

I don't think Nuggets was the only shooter.

Who else?

Thunderman named Mackey threatened me with a gun last night. Used to be their VP. Had blood on him. Gun smelled like it'd been fired. May have been with Nuggets.

Shea sighed, feeling the familiar nausea from when she

was a confidential informant. Snitching went against everything her father taught her when she was a child.

> R U okay?

Rios's concern caught Shea off guard.

> I'm fine. Shook up my niece.

> You call 9-1-1?

> Come on, Rios. You know me better than that.

> I'll have Det. Bello call you. He's lead on case.

"Shit," Shea said aloud. She didn't want to deal with anyone but Rios. But it made sense she wouldn't be investigating her own shooting.

> You gonna tell him I was your CI?

> No.

> Thanks. Feel better soon.

Shea felt awkward, unsure what else to say. Rios replied with a red heart emoji. Shea waited for more, but there was no other response. The conversation was over.

"Excuse me?"

Shea looked up to see a woman in an orange-and-black leather Harley jacket. "Yeah?"

"Any idea where they keep the chain lube?"

"Aisle three."

"Thanks."

Shea looked back at her phone and realized the detective had called her by her first name. In the past, Rios had almost always addressed her as Ms. Stevens. She tried not to ascribe any meaning to it. But that and the red heart emoji left her wondering.

She shook her head to clear out the silly thoughts and dialed the number for Deirdre West that Elia had given her. It went straight to voicemail.

"Hey, this is Shea Stevens, VP for the Athena Sisterhood. Elia Quinn said you needed help with a situation. Call me. I'll see what we can do."

Shea put away her phone and stopped by the office on her way to the service bay. Terrance was on the phone, no doubt reaching out to all of his media contacts about the award.

"If anyone needs me, I'll be working on the Hughes bike."

He nodded.

The sizzle of welding and the buzz-whine of a pneumatic wrench helped settle her nerves. She found Lakota examining the fuel tank she had tack-welded earlier.

"How'd it go with the reporter?" Lakota asked.

"It went. How're we coming on the Hughes bike?"

"Got the frame, handlebars, and the front forks finished up. Wheels ordered. The fenders are cut out but need to be shaped. I'm about to do the final weld on the tank. Still have to fabricate the seat frame and the oil pan. Then sand everything down before sending it off to paint and chrome."

"Sounds good. I'll start shaping the fenders."

"Right on."

Shea strolled over to the table where two oblong pieces of sheet metal lay on the set of plans that she and Lakota had put together for the bike.

Before hiring Lakota several years ago, Shea had fabricated custom bikes by gut instinct. Some turned out better than others. Lakota brought her mechanical engineering skills to the mix, and since then, the bikes they created had been more solid. Fewer complaints, even when they raised the prices.

Rather than limit her creativity, this gave Shea the courage to further push limits, knowing that if they met with Lakota's expert approval, they would be solid creations.

Shea reviewed the plans for the Hughes bike, picked up one of the fender pieces Lakota had cut from aluminum sheet, and slid it into the English wheel. Back and forth she drew it, adjusting the pressure to create the perfect curved shape.

It was a tedious process but one Shea enjoyed because it got her mind off of other things. Shaping the metal was like meditation to her. She felt at one with both metal and machine, guiding the aluminum molecules where she needed them to go. Gradually, the flat piece of metal took shape into a fender.

She pulled it out, examining the lines, checking for flat spots that needed further work. When she was satisfied, she went to work on the rear fender.

By the time two o'clock rolled around, the bike was finally looking like something. Lakota had finished the tank and the oil pan.

Her phone rang. The caller ID showed the same number she had called earlier. Deirdre West.

"This is Shea."

"You're with the Athena Sisterhood?"

Shea looked around. "Hold on a minute. Let me get somewhere I can talk." She stepped out the back door to the parking lot. Vince was leaning up against the wall, smoking a cigarette. Shea continued to the far side of the lot for privacy. "What's the deal between you and Connelly?"

"Not over the phone. Can we meet somewhere this evening?"

"Where d'you have in mind?"

"There's a bar south of the university on Peppermill Avenue called Millie's. Know where it is?"

"No, but if it's listed on the web, I can find it. What time?"

"Six o'clock?"

Annie would be home from soccer camp around five. Shea wasn't comfortable leaving her at home after Mackey's visit the night before. She'd have to find someone to look after her until this meeting was over.

"All right. How will I recognize you?"

"I'll be wearing a navy business suit and a white blouse. How about you?"

"Leather biker vest, Athena Sisterhood patches on the back."

"Great. I'll see you at six. And thanks for helping me out."

"Yeah."

Shea considered calling Fuego but figured it could wait until she heard the full story from Deirdre. Instead, she returned to the office. Terrance was off the phone, finally.

"Hey, T, you mind watching Annie this evening for a while?"

"This have to do with that Athena Sisterhood business you mentioned earlier?"

"I'm meeting with that friend of Elia Quinn's and would rather not leave Annie home alone. A Thunderman named Mackey paid me a visit last night. Things got a little heated."

"As much as we'd love to have her over, Jake and I have a date tonight since I was at the festival all weekend. Sorry."

"Not a problem. I'll check with some of the Sisters."

Shea called Rah-Rah, but after four rings, it went to voicemail. Shea hung up without leaving a message and called Indigo, filling her in on the situation.

"We'd love to have her over. Savage is off duty, so we're making pizza. Annie'll make it a party."

"Thanks, Indigo. We should be there a little before six."

10

Shortly after five, Shea arrived home to find Annie lying on her bed, still in her soccer clothes.

"How was your first day of soccer camp?"

Annie sighed. "Felt more like boot camp. Never ran so much in my life. At least tomorrow we're focusing on kicking."

"Well, change into street clothes. I'm taking you over to Indigo and Savage's for pizza."

"Do we have to? I'm not that hungry. My belly hurts."

Shea sat down on Annie's bed next to her. "You drink enough water?"

"I thought so. Water. Gatorade. Juice."

"You feeling constipated?"

"Ew. Gross."

"I'm just trying to figure out what's going on. When was the last time you pooped?"

"This morning."

"You know what it could be?"

"What?" Annie had a worried expression on her face.

"Your first period. You are twelve. You've said some of your friends have already had theirs."

"Why does it have to start during soccer camp?"

"Happens that way sometimes. Welcome to womanhood, kiddo. I've got to meet someone at six o'clock. So, whether or not you eat, I gotta drop you off at Indigo and Savage's for a couple hours."

"Can't I just stay here? I'm almost a teenager. I can look after myself."

"Normally, I'd say yes. But after what happened last night, I'd feel better if you weren't here alone. Besides, Auntie Savage is an EMT. Maybe she has a secret remedy to make you feel better. Now go take a shower and put on clean clothes. I'll get the laundry started so you have clean clothes for tomorrow."

"Oh, thank God. I thought you'd forget again."

"You're old enough to do your own laundry now."

Annie groaned dramatically. "Whatever." She pulled herself into a sitting position.

"I'll give you a couple Pamprin for the cramps and some panty liners, in case Aunt Flo officially arrives."

"Aunt Flo? Seriously, sometimes I wonder what century you're living in."

An hour later, they were riding two-up on Sweet Betsy. The sun ducked between hills, lighting the canvas of clouds in scarlet, tangerine, and lilac. Dusk settled into the valleys. Shea would've loved to open up the throttle, but with the haziness of twilight came deer, elk, coyotes, bobcats, and other critters oblivious to the dangers posed by her six-hundred-pound motorcycle. With her niece on the passenger seat, she didn't want to take a chance.

It was ten minutes to six when she pulled into the driveway. Annie slid off the back first, followed by Shea, who opened up the top case on the back to take out Annie's daypack.

They were halfway to the front porch when Indigo opened the front door. "Hey, Stretch!" she said to the gangly girl. "How's my favorite soccer player?"

Annie shrugged. "Okay, I guess."

"Uh oh. Something wrong?" Indigo hugged Annie and led the two of them inside.

"We think she's about to get her first period," said Shea.

"Hello? Private information! Gah!"

"Sorry. My bad." They walked into the kitchen, where Savage was rolling out pizza dough.

"If it's any consolation, I'm still waiting for my first one," Indigo said with a sardonic grin.

Annie got a confused look on her face. "Do trans girls get periods?"

"No, they don't, sweet cheeks," Savage said. "Indigo was making a joke."

"Hey, you never know," Indigo added. "Miracles happen."

The timer above the stove beeped. A cloud of steam rose when Savage opened the oven and slid the pizza onto a large wooden cutting board. The air filled with the tangy aromas of tomato sauce, cheese, spices, and pepperoni. Shea's stomach rumbled. She wished she was staying for dinner.

"Hope you're hungry." Indigo used a large knife to slice the pie into six pieces.

"I appreciate you looking after Annie while I meet with this woman." Shea debated snagging a piece before she left, despite the time.

"After what happened last night, you shouldn't go alone." Indigo turned with a concerned expression. "Give me a sec to pull on my motorcycle boots and jacket."

Shea considered saying no. She preferred handling things herself.

"Sure." Shea turned to Annie. "Indigo's coming with me. You behave for Aunt Savage."

With Indigo following on her own motorcycle, Shea motored south through northern Ironwood's suburban streets into the University District. School was out for the summer, so traffic was light. Only the stalwart year-round residents and the students taking summer classes remained.

Once past the college buildings, Shea found Peppermill Avenue with its many restaurants, bars, laundromats, and payday loan stores. A red neon sign flashed the word "Millie's" above a red-brick building. Shea pulled into the lot.

"Never been here," Indigo said while they walked from the parking lot.

"Me neither." Shea checked her watch. They were twenty minutes late. "Hope she's still here."

The interior lighting was subdued but not dark. Dark wood paneling and polished brass dominated the decor. The clientele had a professorial look about them. Mostly older white guys not quite dressed well enough to be business executives.

A woman in a dark-blue suit with pale skin and shoulder-length copper-colored hair sat in a booth reading from a tablet. Next to her, a pale-pink pig the size of a cocker spaniel sat making little grunts, snuffling the air and eyeing Shea and Indigo. A brightly colored cocktail rested on a damp napkin in front of her.

"Deirdre West?" asked Shea.

11

THE WOMAN LOOKED UP. She was somewhere in her thirties or forties. Her eyes had a tired hollowness to them. "Are you Shea Stevens? I was beginning to worry you weren't coming."

"Sorry." Shea sat in the booth across from her. Indigo slid in next to her. "This is my friend, Indigo. She's the Sisterhood's secretary."

"Nice to meet you both. This is Sophie Bacon. She's my emotional support animal."

Indigo shot Shea a glance that said, "What've you got me into?"

A server approached and asked for their drink order.

"What's your poison?" asked Deirdre. "My treat."

"Sam Adams," Shea replied to the server.

"Got anything non-alcoholic?" Indigo asked.

"St. Pauli's NA, ginger beer, cola, club soda, cranberry juice, OJ."

"Gimme a ginger beer," Indigo said.

"Great. I'll have those to you shortly."

"I love the smell of beer, especially dark ales," Deirdre

replied. "But turns out I'm severely allergic to hops and barley. No beer for me. I prefer cosmos anyway. Too many episodes of *Sex and the City*, I suppose."

"What's the deal between you and Connelly?" Shea asked, not interested in small talk.

"Seven years ago, I was working on Joe's communications team, helping him shape his message as a state representative."

"You shaped his message?" Shea asked. "The man is a sexist, homophobic dirtbag. Great message."

"You forgot racist and transphobic," Indigo added.

"Joe was more moderate then. Some pundits speculated he might jump to the Democratic party."

Indigo smirked. "Clearly, *that* didn't happen."

"Who initiated the affair?" Shea asked.

"Joe did. It started with compliments about my work. Then little gifts. When he started coming on to me, I was flattered. Here he was, this handsome, influential man, and he was giving me all of this attention. I guess I ignored the fact he was married."

"How long did this affair with Mr. Wonderful last?" Indigo asked.

"About a year. Then after he won the 2014 election, I discovered I was pregnant."

"It was his?"

"I wasn't sleeping with anyone else. At first, I wasn't sure what to do. I knew he wouldn't leave his wife. And I never imagined myself as a single parent. But I was thirty-three. The longer I waited to start a family, the harder and riskier it would be. So, I decided to keep it."

"How did he react when you told him?"

"At first, he denied it was his. He'd just been elected to the Arizona Senate and had a lot of people calling in favors for their support. I guess he thought I'd wreck everything."

Shea rolled her eyes. "Because it's all about him."

Indigo nodded.

"When I threatened a paternity suit, he backed down and insisted I get an abortion. I refused. I'm pro-choice, but I wanted this baby. Our baby. But he kept badgering me and badgering me. He'd show up at my apartment at all hours of the night, banging on the door until I let him in. He'd call and leave me voicemail messages, saying I'd be branded a home-wrecker and a whore, that our child would be called a bastard and worse."

"Did he ever hit you?" Shea asked.

Deirdre stared into her glass. "He shoved me around a few times, smashed a dish or two, but never punched me. He wasn't abusive."

"What happened?"

"I gave in. What else could I do? Wasn't worth dealing with him anymore. He paid for the abortion and gave me an additional ten thousand dollars to keep quiet about the entire thing."

"That was years ago. Why do you need the Athena Sisterhood now?"

"After the abortion, I ended things with Joe and got a job with Thunderbird Image Consultants, a PR firm here in Ironwood. Two weeks ago, I was talking to my coworker, Regina. She was telling me about when she had an abortion years ago. I mentioned what I went through with Joe. My supervisor walked in and told Regina to get back to work. He said I best keep that story to myself. An hour later, security appeared outside my door and told me I was terminated. No notice, no severance. I pushed my way into my boss's office."

"What'd he say about firing you?"

Emotion colored Deirdre's face. "He said, 'Joe sends his regards.' Turns out Joe and my supervisor are fraternity brothers. Security practically frog-marched me out of the building."

"I'm sorry to hear that."

"I have some savings and a little side hustle going, but not enough to pay all my expenses. My mom's in assisted living, which is expensive. I've applied for several positions, both here and down in the Valley. But so far, nothing." She took a deep breath and let it out slowly. "I called Joe and told him I'd go to the press unless he paid me fifty thousand dollars. He's running for the U.S. Senate now. He's neck and neck with Graciela Perez, so the stakes are high. He's bringing in the high-dollar donations from his wealthy corporate supporters."

"You're blackmailing him?" Shea looked at her incredulously.

Indigo raised her glass in salute. "Good for you, girl. Stick it to that bastard."

"I'm not proud of it, but I'm desperate. I have to protect my mom. She doesn't have but a few months to live, but she likes where she's been staying. Fifty grand would give me a little breathing room to find a new job. And after what happened between us, he's a hypocrite for using this anti-abortion bill and his so-called family values rhetoric to get elected."

"Your boy gonna pay up?" Indigo asked.

"He refused. He said if I talked to the press, he would sue me for libel. I told him I had proof. All the records from the clinic, transcripts of our text messages, recordings of phone calls and voicemail messages."

Shea chuckled darkly. "That must have made his day."

"He got angry. Told me he knows I'm looking for work, and he'd make sure nobody hires me unless I turned over the evidence to him. Still, I told him to go fuck himself. Give me the money or I'd go public."

Sophie Bacon started grunting fervently. Deirdre pulled a Ziploc bag of peeled carrots out of her purse, and the grunts turned into fervent squeals until Deirdre set some carrots on the table. Sophie quieted and munched away on the snack.

"Next morning, I found my tires slashed. All four. Day after that, someone broke into my townhouse, smashed all my dishes, and left a printed note that read 'Keep Quiet.'"

"You go to the cops?" Indigo asked.

"I can't prove it was Joe. None of my neighbors saw who slashed my tires or broke in. Besides, he has a lot of influential friends, including Sheriff Keeler. Even if I filed a complaint, it wouldn't go anywhere."

"So, you contacted Elia."

"She was my media contact with the *Chronicle* when I was at Thunderbird Image Consulting. We became good friends over the years and used to get together for drinks once a week. Last Friday, I told her what happened. I wasn't sure whether I wanted her to publish the story. Not after my tires were slashed and my condo broken into. She said she'd talk to someone who could help. I guess that's you two."

"What're you asking us to do?"

"Ideally, I'd like you to get him to pay me fifty grand and then leave me alone."

Shea chuckled. At one time, she would've said yes and relished putting the screws to someone like Connelly. But now she was a parent and a business owner. The Sisterhood was a law-abiding club, at least on paper. Going full outlaw biker on Connelly could come with a steep price.

"Much as I'd love to see him pay for being a prick, we can't help you blackmail him. We can tell him to back off and inform him the Sisterhood has your back. It won't get you any money, but maybe he'll leave you alone long enough to get Elia Quinn to print your story and expose him. Whether it hurts his reelection, who knows?"

"And what if he comes after me or my mother? Ever since the break-in, I don't feel safe at home."

"Getting you a safe place to stay temporarily shouldn't be a problem," Shea said. "The Sisterhood works with a network of women's shelters."

Deirdre shook her head. "I looked into that. I called Megan's Place and several other shelters. They won't let me bring Sophie. I have friends in Camp Verde, but they're up in Vancouver this week."

"I'd offer you my couch, but I don't think my cat Ninja would take kindly to your pig." Shea exchanged a glance with Indigo.

"Well, my wife and I got a spare bedroom not too far from here. You and, uh, Sophie are welcome to stay until you feel safe to return home. What about your mama?"

"That's my biggest concern. When I talked to her the other day, she said a strange man showed up asking if she knew what a slut I was."

"Connelly?" Shea asked.

"Not sure. Her mind isn't what it was. She could have just imagined it, for all I know. I asked the nurses, but they hadn't seen Joe or anyone else in her room. They won't let me look at the security footage. Only the police can do that, and even then, only with a warrant. Would it be possible for someone to watch over her? At least during visiting hours, in case Joe shows up."

Indigo smiled. "Sure, I can talk to Savage."

"Savage?" Deirdre looked alarmed. "I don't want anyone to frighten my mother."

"Don't worry. Savage is one of the sweetest people I know," Shea said. "She's Indigo's wife."

"She's off tomorrow and Wednesday, but then she goes on another twenty-four-hour shift," Indigo added.

"I can see if our other members could volunteer as a bodyguard for a while." Shea pulled out her phone and sent out a group text to the patched members and their prospects. Within minutes, Raven and two prospects, Bama and Moon Cat, volunteered to take shifts as needed.

"We can keep her protected. Anything else?" Shea asked.

"No." A tear ran down Deirdre's cheek. "Once I'm sure she's safe, I can talk to Elia about running the story."

Shea took a long pull on her beer, the spicy brew burning all the way down her throat. She hated men like Connelly. She hated that they got away with everything. It was a risk to get involved. Things could get very complicated. Even bloody.

"Let's go to your place so you can pack a suitcase."

12

SHEA AND INDIGO followed Deirdre's lemon-yellow Kia Soul east from Millie's until they came to Whispering Oaks Estates, a townhouse complex bordered by imposing hardwood trees. A golden moon on the horizon filtered through the leaves. Victorian-style street lamps in the complex's parking lot revealed brick townhouses with black faux shutters.

Shea and Indigo shared a parking space marked for guests. With Sophie the pig on a leash, Deirdre led them to a red door, unlocked it, and let them into the townhouse. The living room was spacious, with an overstuffed couch and matching chairs. A breakfast bar separated the airy kitchen, where a rack of polished copper pots hung over an island. A stack of large cardboard boxes lay next to the kitchen table. Along the left wall, a carpeted staircase rose to the second floor.

"Nice apartment." Shea said.

"It's a condo. But thanks. I love the space, though the neighbors can be a bit snobbish. A lot of rich white kids from back east. And the HOA's not real fond of Sophie and her tendency to root around in the landscaping."

"What's with the boxes?" Indigo asked. "You planning on moving?"

"No, I sell organic health and beauty products from Gaia's Essentials on the side. Ever use them?"

"Can't say I have." Shea took the measure of the place.

"They are amazing. Especially their CBD oil. It's my best seller. Great for chronic pain, anxiety, and many other conditions. Fully organic."

Shea and Indigo followed Deirdre upstairs. Warm pastel colors decorated the master bedroom. Like the rest of the house, it was clean and tidy. A floral comforter covered the queen-size bed. The left wall featured a framed photo of a cabin set in the woods. Next to that was a large print Shea recognized as the wind-carved walls of Antelope Canyon.

Deirdre pulled two suitcases out of her closet and began filling them with clothing, accessories, and personal care products. Shea helped her pack while Indigo called Savage to update her on the situation.

The doorbell rang. A mix of fear and frustration crossed Dierdre's face.

"That's probably Betty, one of my Gaia's Essentials clients. She comes by on Monday nights to pick up her orders. I meant to call her." She headed toward the staircase, but Shea intercepted her.

"Hold up. Let me see who it is first."

Fear flashed in Deirdre's eyes. "Oh, crap. You could be right."

"Wait up here." Shea drew her Glock and crept down the stairs. Indigo followed with her own pistol in hand. Through the peephole, Shea recognized the man standing on the porch and opened the door.

Connelly was a white man in his late forties. He was slim, with charismatic looks and a conservative haircut. His hands were manicured and his suit expensive.

Next to him stood a bookish guy in a gray chambray shirt under a black sport coat. He sported a stubbly but manicured beard and glasses with circular lenses, giving him the look of an older Harry Potter.

A dark Mercedes SUV sat parked illegally at the red-painted curb in front of the townhouse, its taillights glowing in the night.

"Sir, I really don't think..." the man beside Connelly said before turning to face Shea and Indigo.

"Harriman, I got this. Just wait in the car," Connelly replied with a dismissive tone.

Harriman glared briefly at Shea and Indigo then turned on his heel and climbed into the SUV.

"Well, well," Indigo said, holstering her gun. "If it ain't Senator Con Job. How's the fake charity business, Con Job?"

"I'm here to speak with Ms. West."

Shea glared at the man. "Fuck off, asshole. Deirdre don't wanna see you."

"Who are you?" Connelly quipped.

"We ain't the welcome wagon, if that's what you're wondering." Indigo snorted a laugh. "So, get the hell outta here before we call your wife and tell her you here making a booty call."

Rather than getting angry as Shea expected, the senator smiled warmly. "I'm sorry. There appears to have been a terrible misunderstanding. De's a friend of mine. I heard she lost her job and wanted to see how I can help. If I can just speak with her—alone." His tone was warm, reassuring, and polished. Almost seemed genuine.

"Like I said," Shea repeated, "she don't wanna—"

"Joe?" Deirdre appeared next to Shea. "What are you doing here?"

"I told you to wait upstairs," Shea replied.

"It's all right." Deirdre stepped between Shea and the senator. "You here to give me what I asked for?"

Shea and Indigo backed up, while Deirdre and Connelly faced each other in the doorway.

"De, honey. I realize you're in a tough spot. I want to help. Come sit with me in my car a moment. Without Joan Jett and Janet Jackson here." The look he shot Shea and Indigo was venomous.

"Whatever you have to say, you can say in front of my friends."

Connelly's gaze went back and forth from Deirdre to Shea. "I know you talked to a reporter. You need to kill the story before things turn ugly. Don't embarrass yourself like this. Believe me, you don't want all the publicity, the press hounding you, calling at all hours. Take it from me, it's a nightmare."

"The voters deserve to know who they're voting for and what you've done."

"I know we sinned. But it's best for all of us to leave the past behind us and let bygones be bygones."

"Write me a check for fifty grand, and I'll forget all about it."

He put his hands on her arms. "Oh, sweetie, nothing would please me more. But right now, all my funds are tied up with this darned election. You know how it is."

"You forced me to have an abortion, and now you're sponsoring an anti-abortion bill to help get elected. And you expect me to stay silent."

"I didn't sponsor the bill to get elected. I'm trying to save the lives of countless unborn children. You're a smart girl. You can appreciate that."

"Didn't care so much for our unborn child when you forced me to have an abortion, did you? 'Do as I say, not as I do.' Is that it?"

"Now, sweetheart, I never forced you to do anything, I merely encouraged you. But yes, I believe what we did was wrong. The affair, the abortion, all of it. I'm trying to do the right thing now, the righteous thing. You should want that too."

"Bullshit." Shea stepped forward.

"Excuse me?" Connelly glared at her. "This isn't your concern."

"As a woman fighting for the rights of women, it's very much my concern." A fire ignited in Shea's gut. Her old self. The one who played by her own rules.

"Damn straight," Indigo leaned an arm on Shea's shoulder.

"I could have all three of you arrested for extortion."

"Try it," Shea replied. "Turn your affair and your abortion into a major media sensation. Good luck getting elected to the U.S. Senate then."

"Deirdre," he said in a saccharin, pleading voice, "please. I don't want things to be ugly between us. Kill the story. Give me the documentation of our indiscretion. Let's move on with our lives."

"And if I refuse?"

His face turned ugly hard, his voice icy. "You don't want to refuse. That wouldn't be smart."

"What the fuck's that mean?" Shea stepped between them.

"It means things could get worse than losing your job. Think of your mother, Deirdre. So fragile. So vulnerable. Awful things happen in care facilities all the time. Did you know I'm on the board for Silver Hills Assisted Living? Chairman, in fact."

Shea grabbed him by the lapel. "You threatening to hurt her mother, you piece of shit?"

"Shea, don't hurt him," Deirdre said.

"Stay away from her, asswipe," Shea growled and shoved him away.

"Or what? You'll beat up Arizona's next U.S. senator? I'll have you locked up for assault faster than you can blink. You ever been to prison, Miss Shea? By the look of you, I reckon you have. But I can make sure you don't see daylight for a long time. There's doing time, and there's doing hard time. You get my drift?"

"Fuck you, Con Job. I hope Perez kicks your ass in November."

Indigo pulled Shea back. "Ease up, girl. Don't wrinkle the prick's pretty threads."

"Deirdre, keep your mouth shut," Connelly said over Shea's shoulder. "For both our sakes. And maybe get yourself a better class of friends than this diesel dyke biker trash."

He turned on his heel, climbed into the Mercedes SUV, and drove away.

"Charming guy," Indigo said with a sarcastic chuckle.

"He was nice when I was working for him."

"Uh-huh. When he used his position as your boss to coerce you into sleeping with him?"

Deirdre closed the front door and sighed then led them back upstairs. "He was persistent. Though I confess, I have a thing for married men."

"Why?" Shea asked.

Deirdre shrugged. "Just something about them. They're like caged tigers yearning to be free. I feel sorry for them."

Shea shook her head. "Wow! That's the most fucked-up thing I've heard all day."

13

When Deirdre finished packing, Shea and Indigo helped her carry her suitcases to her Kia. Sophie Bacon trotted behind on a leash. Connelly's SUV was gone, but Shea didn't get the impression he was done intimidating Deirdre into silence.

"Indigo, you wouldn't mind if a few of my clients dropped by your house to pick up their orders, would you?" Deirdre put the suitcases in the back seat of her Kia.

Indigo exchanged a glance with Shea. "Uh, I guess not. Long as it's not too late."

Deirdre smiled for the first time since Shea met her. "I appreciate that. I'll be right back." She disappeared into the house, leaving Shea holding Sophie's leash.

The pig made little grunting noises while her brush-like tail wagged back and forth.

"I think she likes you," Indigo said with a wry smile.

"Lucky me."

Shea didn't understand having a pig for an emotional support animal. Pigs were livestock, not pets. Not that she cared either way.

Deirdre re-emerged with two boxes of her Gaia's Essentials products and put them in her trunk.

"You ready?" Shea offered her the pig's leash.

"I think so." Deirdre opened the passenger door. Sophie hopped into the seat. "I guess I'll follow you two, since I have no idea where we're going."

"You follow Indigo." Shea turned to Indigo. "I'll ride sweep. Make sure we're not followed."

Her sister biker gave her a thumbs-up. "See ya there, Havoc."

Shea watched Indigo and Deirdre cruise out of the complex and followed.

Periodically, she checked her side mirrors to make sure no one was following. At Mission Street, a light turned red just as Deirdre went through it.

Shea should have stopped, but she didn't want to be left behind and allow Connelly to follow them to Indigo's. Instead, she ran the red light and nearly got creamed by a FedEx delivery truck.

Twenty minutes later, Shea pulled into Indigo and Savage's driveway, stopping next to Deirdre's car. Indigo stood on her porch, light pouring out of the open front door.

"Is it okay if I park here?" Deirdre had parked behind Indigo's Jeep Grand Cherokee.

"It's fine for now. If we need you to move it, we'll let you know."

Shea grabbed a suitcase and followed Indigo, Deirdre, and the pig inside.

Motorcycle magazines covered a rustic wooden coffee table in the center of the living room. A black leather sectional faced a glass entertainment center on which sat a television with tall speakers on either side. Savage and Annie were playing an auto racing video game. Savage stood and approached her guests. Annie barely looked up, too engrossed in the video game.

"Hi, I'm Savage. Welcome to our home."

"Thanks. I'm Deirdre West. And this is Sophie." The pig grunted several times while she took in her surroundings. Annie looked up wide-eyed at the sound.

"Wow, is that a pig?" Annie tossed aside the controller and petted Sophie's head. Sophie snuffled and grunted contentedly. "Never known anyone with a pet pig."

"Sophie's my emotional support animal." Deirdre picked up the pig, and it squealed to be put back down.

"This is my niece, Annie. She loves animals."

"Don't worry," Deirdre said when she caught Savage's concerned look. "She's trained to go potty outside. Just like a dog."

Savage exchanged glances with Indigo and Shea. "I suppose it'll be all right. We're not allergic and don't have any other animals. So long as she's housebroken and doesn't pee or poop on the carpet, I don't see a problem."

"Thanks. Where should I put my stuff?"

"I'll show you." Savage led them down the hall and turned into the first room on the left. A bedside lamp was lit next to the double bed covered in a purple-and-green floral comforter. Shea set the suitcase on the bed.

"How long do you think you'll need to stay?" asked Savage.

"Not sure." Deirdre opened a suitcase and hung up dresses and business suits in the wall closet. "Until I'm sure Joe won't hurt me or my mother. You think I should get a restraining order against him?"

"You could try," said Indigo. "I've known a lotta battered women who got restraining orders against their abusers. Sometimes it helps. Sometimes it makes the situation worse."

"Worse? How could it be worse?" Deirdre froze, staring at Indigo like a deer in the headlight.

No one said anything for a moment.

"Oh," Deirdre said at last.

"Connelly doesn't strike me as a person easily intimidated," Shea said. "In his mind, rules are for other people, not him. I doubt a piece of paper would keep him away from you."

"Well, fudge." Deirdre looked dejected.

"Focus on finding a new job. We'll deal with Connelly. Just gotta convince him that retaliating against you is a terrible idea."

Shea pulled out her phone. "Hey, Dragon. Think you can arrange a meeting with Senator Joe Connelly?"

"Connelly? Why would you want to meet with him?"

"He's harassing a woman he had an affair with several years ago. Forced her to have an abortion. Now he's threatening her if she doesn't remain quiet about it."

"Oh?" Dragon chuckled on the other end of the line.

"She's staying at Indigo and Savage's for the time being, but we need to convince this guy to back off."

"I'll make some calls. See if I can schedule a meeting with him."

"Thanks."

Shea hung up. "Our friend Dragon's a lawyer. She'll get us a sit-down with Connelly. Maybe we can coerce him to leave you alone." Though she wasn't too hopeful.

Deirdre nodded. "I appreciate that."

"You okay here?"

"Me and Sophie should be all right for now. Thanks, all of you, for your help."

Savage smiled. "We'll keep her safe."

"Thanks." Shea followed Indigo and Savage back to the

living room, where Annie was fawning over a very contented Sophie Bacon.

"Time to go," said Shea.

"Aw, come on," Annie pleaded. "I never played with a pig before."

"We have a load of laundry to do unless you want to go to soccer camp again with dirty socks."

Major eye roll. "Oh, all right."

They said their goodbyes. Shea and Annie climbed onto her bike and drove off into the night.

14

WHILE SHEA DROVE HOME, she considered how she could convince Connelly to leave Deirdre alone. But no obvious solutions came to her.

He was the son of Timothy Connelly, an international finance tycoon. Senator Connelly's family legacy gave him access to Arizona's power brokers, including other business moguls, religious leaders, the media, and law enforcement.

Relatively young for a career politician, Joe Connelly's Kennedy-esque charm had, at first, earned him a reputation as a bridge builder between Arizona's dominant conservative right and the rising progressive left.

But with the recent rise of conservative extremism, Connelly's views had slid further to the right. He demonized moderate Republicans as liberal sellouts and embraced hard-right positions he'd eschewed earlier. He championed anti-LGBTQ conversion therapy, shut down clinics that provided reproductive health, and pushed for a more draconian anti-immigrant "papers please" law.

Even if the *Chronicle* published the story about his affair and the abortion, Shea wondered if his rabid followers would care. They weren't known for holding powerful white men accountable for the wrongs they committed, so long as those men thumped the Bible and waved the flag of white nationalism. Connelly had already been caught running a money-laundering operation disguised as a fake charity. But even after the bogus nonprofit was shut down, the prosecutions went nowhere, and his popularity increased.

Could Shea and the Sisterhood do anything to keep him from retaliating against Deirdre? She'd always believed everyone had a weakness. But what was Connelly's?

When Shea pulled into their neighborhood at the bottom of Sycamore Mountain, she kept an eye out for Mackey's motorcycle or any other vehicles that didn't belong. She saw nothing out of the ordinary.

They walked in the house without incident, and Annie collapsed on the love seat in the living room. Ninja, their fifteen-year-old black cat, hopped onto her lap.

"Get off!" Annie whimpered and pushed her away. The cat meowed in protest and hopped down.

"Still got stomach cramps?"

"A little. Comes and goes. I think the Pamprin helps."

"Any sign of your period starting?"

"No."

The doorbell rang, followed by a series of hard raps. Shea stiffened and turned toward the door. *Is Mackey back to finish what he started? Or did Connelly recognize me and track me down to get to Deirdre?*

"Annie, go to your room. Lock the door."

She raised her head. "Ugh, why?"

"Just do what I say. Now."

Annie groaned while she stomped into her bedroom and slammed the door.

Shea drew her Glock and peered out the peephole. A

white man with a goatee stood on her front porch. She didn't recognize him.

"Who the hell are you?"

"Detective John Bello, Cortes County Sheriff's Office." He held up his shield and ID so Shea could see it through the peephole.

"What d'you want? I ain't broken no laws." At least not recently.

"I'm investigating the attempted murder of Detective Rios. I understand you've contacted her recently."

She remembered her text exchange with Rios, reholstered the pistol, and opened the door. "I'd rather talk to Rios herself."

"She's in the hospital, recovering from her injuries. I'm investigating the shooting. Mind if I come in? I have a few quick questions."

Shea let him inside, but his presence in her living room felt invasive. She wasn't used to having cops in her home. She didn't sit down or offer him a seat. Didn't want to give him the impression he was welcome.

Bello glanced around, studying the room. "You alone in the house?"

"My niece is in her bedroom."

"Anyone else?"

"No."

He appeared to relax just a fraction and pulled out a notepad and pen. "How do you know Detective Rios?"

"Let's just say we have history."

He studied her face for a moment. "Weren't you the one who killed Sergeant Willie Foster?"

Shea glared at him. "I defended myself from a corrupt cop who was working with members of the Jaguars drug gang."

"Right. I remember. That was an unfortunate situation."

"Unfortunate? The motherfucker kidnapped my niece and murdered my sister. My niece had to have her ear surgically reattached. It wasn't unfortunate. It was a fucking nightmare."

"Yes." He paused for a moment before continuing. "In your texts to Detective Rios, you said you knew something about her getting shot. What can you tell me?"

She held his gaze for a moment, looking for signs if she could trust him. "Nuggets wasn't alone when he ambushed Rios."

"How do you know that?"

Shea filled him in on Mackey's visit the night before, leaving out the part about disarming him.

"Why did Mackey show up here?"

"The Thundermen just got outta the can. Mackey thinks I helped put them there."

"Did you?"

"No comment."

"Oh, you're Rios's CI." There was a hint of surprise in his voice. "Is Mackey his first name or last name?"

Shea shrugged. "Hell if I know."

"After Mackey threatened to shoot you, what happened?"

She tensed. If Bello arrested Mackey, it could turn the Sisterhood's meeting with the Thunder into a bloodbath. "I disarmed him."

"You took the gun away from him?"

"Yeah."

"Where's the gun now?"

"Got rid of it." Drifting further from the truth made her more uncomfortable. Too easy to get caught in a lie.

"Where?"

"Tossed it off the side of a mountain in the Cortes National Forest, south of Ironwood."

"Any place in particular? A favorite scenic pull-off, perhaps?"

"No pull-off. Just tossed it while I was driving."

"Why'd you get rid of the gun if you thought it was used to shoot a sheriff's detective?"

"I didn't know Rios had been shot until I saw it on the news later that night. By then, I'd tossed the gun."

"What time did Mackey show up here?"

"Late. Maybe eleven o'clock."

"And after he left, you took a late-night drive into the national forest. Where was your niece when you were getting rid of the gun?"

"Here."

"How old is she?"

"Twelve."

"Her name?"

"Annie Wittmann."

"Wittmann. Wasn't there a Thunderman named Wittmann?"

"Annie's father. He's dead." Shea's memory of putting a bullet in Hunter Wittmann's skull remained vivid in her mind.

"Ms. Stevens, your getting rid of evidence tied to an officer-involved shooting is a problem."

"Like I said, I didn't know Mackey'd shot Rios until after."

"But you suspected he'd shot someone."

"I suspected he'd fired the gun. For all I knew, he shot it up in the air to celebrate getting out of prison."

"But you said he had blood on him."

"I'm done answering questions for tonight. Or do I need to call my attorney?" Shea reopened the front door and waited expectantly.

"Do everyone a favor, Ms. Stevens. Find the gun and call

me." Bello handed her a business card. "It might help us put Mackey back in prison. I know you and your lady biker gang aren't exactly fans of the Confederate Thunder."

"I'll see what I can do. Can I see Rios? I'd like to talk to her."

He stepped out onto the front porch. "Right now, only law enforcement and medical personnel may see her. Have a good night."

Shea locked the door behind him. "You can come out now, Annie."

Annie opened her bedroom door. "You think Mackey shot that cop?"

"You were listening."

"The walls ain't all that thick."

"Gramma Julia seems to think he was involved."

"Why'd you lie to the cop about the gun?"

"What d'you mean?"

"It's still in the gun safe."

"How the hell d'you know that?" Shea stared at the kid as if she had two heads.

"I guessed the combination. My mom's birthday."

"Shit. You stay out of the safe. Ya hear?"

"What's the big deal? You let me shoot at the gun range."

"Only with adult supervision. Guns ain't toys."

"Don't you think I know that? I'm not a baby."

"No, and you're not an adult either."

"I'm about to have my first period. That makes me a woman."

"You're twelve. Not even a teenager."

They stared at each other.

"Look, my gun safe, my rules. Those rules are for your safety, even if you don't understand why. Got it?"

"Whatever," Annie said with a sigh.

"Good. Now help me put the laundry in the dryer so you don't have to wear dirty socks again tomorrow."

"Can't you do it? I don't feel good."

"Want me to treat you like a grown-up? Grown-ups do their own laundry, even when they don't feel like it."

"So, if I do my own laundry, I can go into the gun safe?"

"Hell no. Laundry is only step one."

"How many steps are there?"

"A gazillion."

"Whatever."

15

THE NEXT MORNING, Shea was drinking her coffee when Annie shuffled in dressed in a soccer camp T-shirt, shorts, long white socks, and black cleats. "How are you feeling this morning?"

Annie hopped onto a barstool at the breakfast bar and rested her head on her arm. "'Bout the same. And before you ask, nothing's happening down there."

"Give it time." Shea fried a couple of eggs. When they were done, she put a banana on a plate next to the eggs and slid it over to Annie.

"This should help. I put panty liners and a travel-size bottle of Pamprin in your gear bag. Don't drink too much Gatorade today. The salt could make you feel bloated. Stick with water."

"Thanks." Annie looked up at her, a piece of egg on her fork. "You know, you're getting good at this."

"At what? Cooking eggs?"

"Being a parent. I mean, I know I give you shi—crap. And you still do things that embarrass me. And I wish Mom and Dad were here. But..."

"Stop! Now you're embarrassing me."

"I just wanted to say, I'm glad I got you."

Shea's throat tightened with emotion. She would not let herself cry in front of the kid. "Thanks. I'm glad I got you too." Shea sat down beside her and sighed. "And I wish your mom was here as well."

Shea's mind flashed with the last memory she had of her sister Wendy, lying in the street, her head half blown off from a gunshot. She remembered dragging a much-younger Annie away from her mother's body. Annie's anguished screams and the endless gunfire continued to echo in her mind.

Shea and her sister had only just reunited after being estranged for two decades. And in the blink of an eye, Wendy was dead. Guilt tightened around her heart like a boa constrictor.

"Tonight, we're going to a welcome-home party for the Thunder at the Church."

Annie's expression brightened. "Really? Will I get to see Gramma Julia?"

"Yes, you will. We're meeting the other Sisterhood officers at a gas station outside Bradshaw City, and we'll ride in together."

"Wow, I never thought you'd let me go to anything at the Church again."

"Well, the Thunder and the Sisterhood have things to work out to make sure everything stays civil between the clubs. And Gramma Julia wanted to see you."

"Oh my God, I can't wait."

Shea's phone rang. "Hey, Dragon. What's the news?"

"I made some calls. Connelly refuses to meet with us. I could send him a letter warning him to stay away from Ms. West and her mother. Perhaps the threat of a harassment lawsuit will get through to him."

"Worth a try, I guess."

"I'll see you at six then."

No sooner had Shea hung up when a car horn beeped outside. "There's Ms. Ali. Grab your bag."

Annie wiped her face, grabbed her gear bag, and started walking toward the door.

"How about a hug?"

"Aunt Shea, they're waiting."

"Come on." Remembering her sister had triggered maternal feelings.

Annie leaned in for a hug. "So embarrassing."

"Go kick some balls."

"Hilarious. Not." Annie rushed out the front door.

After Annie left, Shea considered Dragon's offer to send Connelly a letter. Threatening him with a lawsuit seemed as effective as shooting spitballs at him. The only way to get through to powerful people like him was to show them how powerful they weren't.

She pulled out her phone again and made a call. Part of her hoped it would go to voicemail. But she needed answers.

"Ballou Fugitive Recovery. Jinx Ballou speaking."

"Hey, Jinx. It's Shea."

Silence filled the connection for what felt like hours. "Shea. I, uh, I'm surprised to hear from you."

"I'm sorry how we left things. It was a difficult situation, and you did what you thought best."

"Shea, I really don't want to rehash our relationship now."

"I'm not calling about that. This is a business call. I need information. You might be the best person to get it for me. And I'm in a bit of a time crunch."

"What kind of information?"

"About Senator Joe Connelly. Specifically, his home

address and any dirt you can dig up on him. Hoping your skip tracer Becca could hook me up."

AN HOUR LATER, Shea was sitting at Connelly's kitchen table, having coffee with his wife, Evangeline. A box of donuts that Shea had brought lay open between them.

"How long have you worked for my husband, Ms. Bullion?" Evangeline selected a second French cruller from the box.

Shea smiled as genteelly as she could. Instead of her usual T-shirt and jeans, she had dug into her closet and pulled out an outfit that most resembled business attire, a blue silk blouse and dark slacks. Some makeup left behind by her ex-girlfriend, Jessica, helped hide her facial scars and feminized her appearance. Shea almost didn't recognize herself in the mirror.

"Not long. I'm based out of Phoenix, handling a lot of the oppo research," Shea lied. "And please, call me Laura. Ms. Bullion sounds so formal."

"If you'll call me Evie." She turned to the sound of someone approaching the kitchen. "Here he is now. The next U.S. Senator from the great state of Arizona."

"I understand that, Harriman, but they need to keep their guys in line. This gangster nonsense puts us all at risk. If they want this deal with the Border Patriots to go through, they need to cool their jets, or so help me God, I will bring it all down on their heads."

Connelly's eyes locked on Shea. "I'm gonna have to call you back." He tucked his phone into his inside jacket pocket. "Who the hell is she?"

"Joe, please. Language. Besides, Laura drove all the way up from Phoenix to drop off the latest opposition research."

Shea picked up a large white envelope. She'd printed Connelly's campaign logo in the upper-left-hand corner and filled it with printouts containing the dirt on the senator that Jinx Ballou's skip tracer had found. That and the box of donuts was all it took to get inside the house.

"Relax, Joey. Why don't you and me have a private conversation on what I found?"

"My heavens, you're ... you're that woman from last night."

"Joe, what's going on?" Concern edged Evie's voice.

"Don't worry, Evie," Shea said, keeping her gaze on Connelly. "He didn't mean to make it sound like he's having an affair. At least not with me."

"It's nothing, honey. I'll be out in a minute." Connelly looked ready to put his fist through a wall. He pointed down the hall, glaring at Shea. "In my office."

Shea followed him down the hall to a large office with a floor-to-ceiling dark wood bookshelf and a desk to match. The Arizona state flag stood on one side and an American flag with golden military fringe on the other. Odd considering Connelly never served in the military.

Connelly slammed the door shut and locked it. "How dare you break into my home. I should call the police."

"Go ahead. I didn't break in. I was invited in. Besides, I brought donuts. And this."

"What the hell's this?" He snatched the envelope from her hand and ripped it open.

"Just some financial statements that show money being transferred from your shell companies to some shady organizations, along with payoffs to judges, a little money laundering, and tax evasion. I'll admit, a lot of it was over my head. The money trails are convoluted. But I'm sure an FBI forensic accountant could have a field day with it."

"Where'd you get this?"

"Seems a friend of a friend of mine's been keeping tabs on you ever since you wriggled out from under that fake charity scam. They were more than happy to share what they've found."

"You trying to extort me?"

"Nah, Joey. Nothing like that." Shea said, taunting him with the nickname. "All I'm asking is that you make some calls and get Deirdre West a new job. Hardly rises to the level of extortion. After all, you got her fired from her old job."

"I never got that bitch fired. She was terminated for spreading lies about me."

"Lies, huh?" Shea wanted to smack that brilliant white smile off his face. Instead, she scooped up the envelope and turned to leave. "Well, I guess we'll let the FBI and their accountants sort out the lies from truth."

Just as Shea's hand hit the office's doorknob, Connelly barked the word, "Wait."

Shea turned back. His eyes smoldered with anger.

"Yes? You'd rather I keep your dirty financial deeds our little secret?"

"If I agree to this, Deirdre keeps her mouth shut. No talking to the press about our...previous interactions."

"Previous interactions? You mean your extramarital affair and the abortion? Not part of the deal. She talks to whoever she damn well pleases. This is America. Free speech. Freedom of the press. I woulda thought you'd have learned that Constitution stuff, being a state senator."

"If she does, I'll sue her for libel."

"Look, I'll admit I never finished high school, but based on what I heard, it's only libel if what she tells the press isn't true."

"And she can go broke paying a lawyer to prove it." His grin was serpentine.

Shea glared back at him, unblinking. "Meanwhile, all that money you been getting from the Arizona Liberty Council and other right-wing organizations dries up, your political career tanks, and your marriage to sweet, innocent Evangeline goes bye-bye."

Connelly's smirk faded.

"Do yourself a favor, asshole. Get Deirdre a job, then leave her the fuck alone. Don't call, don't text, don't visit. Maybe she'll be more inclined to keep your dirty little secrets. I won't share this with the feds, and everyone lives happily ever after."

He glowered at her. "I'll see what I can do."

"Good boy. And remember, our conversation stays private. Or I release my findings to the feds, and you go to prison. I've been there. Not a lot of fun."

"Bitch."

"I'm so glad we could reach an agreement, Joey." Shea opened the office door. "I'll let myself out. Oh, and thank Evie for the coffee. You really don't deserve her."

16

After meeting with Connelly, she had washed off all the makeup, hoping it would also wash away how disgusted he made her feel. It hadn't. She spent hours at Iron Goddess working on the Hughes custom cruiser, but all she could think about was how best to come at Connelly.

Shortly after five, she picked up Annie from the house and headed north to Bradshaw City to meet up with the other Sisterhood officers. Her leather cut fluttered over her armored jacket while she drove with Annie in her denim Little Sister vest on the passenger seat.

At quarter to six, they arrived at the Shell station outside Bradshaw City. Shea navigated past the gas pumps to where Savage, Fuego, Raven, and Indigo were waiting.

"We ready?" she asked Fuego.

"Just waiting for Dragon." Fuego nodded at Annie. "¡Hola, mi'ja! You coming with us?"

"I wanna see my Gramma Julia. I missed her while she was in prison."

"You think it's safe having her along?" Indigo asked. "What if…"

"It's all right. Julia ain't no Mother Teresa, but she'd take a bullet before she let anything happen to her grandbaby." At least, Shea hoped it was true.

Dragon arrived a few minutes later. "Sorry I'm late. Judge Martin called us into chambers after we recessed. She can be a bit long-winded. We all set?" she asked.

"Let's ride," Indigo said. "Sitting here in the heat's about to fry my brain."

The other women each gave a thumbs-up.

"Havoc, these vatos were your people once," Fuego said. "Mind taking the lead?"

"Will do."

"¡Órale! Vámonos, muchachas."

They started their bikes and roared out of the parking lot, driving west with the glare of the sun in their eyes. The businesses and houses of Bradshaw City were replaced with evergreens and the occasional stand of aspen, which glowed like posts of polished silver.

Much of her childhood was spent riding these country roads on the back of her father's motorcycle. She recalled the thrill, the freedom, and the joy of being a part of the extended family of a motorcycle club.

She'd had no idea the kind of people they were. No inkling of their racism, their sexism, or their penchant for brutality.

Watching her parents fight on an almost daily basis had seemed normal. Even when Shea's father got physical, her mother assured her it wasn't as painful or as terrifying as it looked. Just a misunderstanding.

It wasn't until the morning her father slashed her mother's throat that Shea understood the viciousness of the one-percenter club.

Shea felt on high alert, leading her sister bikers through the heart of the Confederate Thunder's domain. Despite her familiarity and history with this rural landscape, it was now enemy territory.

When they reached the gate, Shea stopped and raised her visor. A man wearing a Confederate Thunder prospect cut stood guard holding an AR-15.

"Fuck off. This is private property." He had a military haircut, and his bearing made Shea wonder if he'd been an MP at one time.

"We're the Athena Sisterhood MC." She emphasized the initialization. "We're expected."

The prospect called someone on his phone. Shea couldn't hear the conversation, but he nodded and hung up. "Go on up."

Shea gave a signal to the others to follow. They rode up the grassy hill on a narrow strip of pavement toward what had been a Baptist church a century earlier.

More memories flooded her mind. Playing with other kids of patched members. Watching the men get drunk, fight, and mess around with women who were desperate or stupid enough to get involved with outlaw bikers.

But the memory that blazed most prominently was the day she'd run away. The screaming match she'd had with Julia and Monster inside the Church while they begged her to live with them. Her running into the pouring rain, stealing Monster's Harley, and driving into the wet night with nothing but the clothes on her back.

The hardest part had been losing that sense that whatever she faced, she had people who had her back, who would fight for her, who would kill for her.

But she was no longer that broken teenager, vulnerable and alone. She was a defiant warrior with a tribe of her own, ready to wreak justice on their own terms. The Sisterhood had her back in a way the Thunder never would.

They parked in the lot beside the church building.

Lines of Harley Davidson motorcycles of all types and sizes covered the blacktop. Dynas, Streets, Fat Boys, and Road Kings. Every one emblazoned with the Johnny Reb on the tank or a fairing.

The aroma of grilled meat made Shea's mouth water. Country rock blared from speakers mounted on the side of the building. Members of the club and their families wandered the grounds, drinking, eating, laughing, and shouting. A few Thundermen tended large grills made from fifty-five-gallon drums.

Annie slipped off the back of Shea's motorcycle. Shea followed suit and pulled her jacket and cut over the pistol holstered at the small of her back.

Shea turned to Annie. "Let's find Gramma Julia. I think she might be near the playground."

The women walked through the mass of people, ignoring the stares and pointing, following the sound of children's laughter and squeals of delight. They found Julia on the other side of the building, watching the younger kids on the swings and jungle gym. Others cycled in and out of an inflatable bouncy castle.

When Annie saw her, she rushed toward her. "Gramma Julia!"

Julia's face lit up. She stood and crushed out her cigarette on the ground.

It had only been three years since Shea had seen her, but Julia easily looked ten years older. Thinner, if that was even possible. Prison had a way of turning people to gristle to survive.

"That you, Munchkin?" Julia hugged Annie then pulled back to study the lanky twelve-year-old. "Girl, you done grown two feet taller since I seen you last."

"Oh, Gramma. You're so funny."

"Hey," said Shea.

Julia released Annie and eyed Shea. "Hey yourself. Glad you could make it."

"Julia, these are my sisters. Savage, Indigo, Dragon, Raven, and Fuego."

"Welcome to the Church, ladies."

The women gave each other nods. No hugs, no handshakes.

"One-Shot, Bryz, and the others are inside the chapel waiting on you."

"Who the hell's Bryz?" Shea asked.

A shadow passed over Julia's face. "Patch-over from Los Angeles. He and a few others kept the place running while the rest of us were in lockup."

"We ain't walking into an ambush, are we?" Shea asked.

"Far as I know, everything's cool. Long as y'all behave yourselves, you should be all right." Julia paused. "And as long as y'all didn't get us busted three years ago."

Shea locked eyes with her. Julia had known her since she was a small child. For the most part, Julia was a generous, kind-hearted person. But her ultimate loyalty was always to the club.

"You know me better than that," Shea lied without hesitation. "We don't snitch."

Julia held her gaze. "Well, y'all go on inside and meet with the boys while Annie and me catch up. Afterwards, maybe we can share a plate of barbecue."

Shea waved the rest of them inside.

"Anybody else feel we're walking into the lion's den?" Savage asked when they stepped through the front door of the Church.

"More like walking into the middle of a KKK rally," Indigo replied, gesturing to a Confederate flag on a pole just inside the door. "With us as the guests of honor."

"Just keep a cool head, hermanas," said Fuego.

Framed photos of the club at various events covered one wall of the foyer. The opposite wall featured a rogues' gallery of members' mugshots. Some had small Confederate flag stickers in the lower left corner. Shea knew this meant they'd died.

Shea spotted a photo of Hunter, Annie's father. She was responsible for the flag on his photo. During a clash between the Thunder and the Jaguars street gang, he had come after Shea. She put a bullet through his ugly face. Even Annie didn't know the truth, and this haunted Shea.

"Havoc, you coming?" Indigo asked.

Shea shook away the ghosts of the past. "Yeah."

They walked through a double door into what had been the main sanctuary of the church. A bar now stretched along the wall where the altar had once stood, with tables and chairs having replaced the pews. The music was loud, as was the laughter and conversation in the room.

When the doors shut behind them, the conversations and music stopped. The patched members, the prospects, the hangarounds, and the women stared at them in their Athena Sisterhood cuts. Shea had known the older ones, but most of the patches were unfamiliar to her.

"Come on," Shea said, leading her Sisters across the room. "Let's do this."

She stopped outside the solid oak doors of the chapel. Two prospects stood guard outside the door.

"Pull up your shirts and drop your pants," said the prospect on the left, a twenty-something skinhead with a poorly inked Nazi eagle prison tat on his throat.

"Why the fuck would we do that?" Fuego asked.

"We gotta search you for wires."

"And weapons," added the other prospect, a chunky guy with short curly hair cut in a Mohawk style.

"You can search us for wires, but we're keeping our weapons," Shea insisted.

"Like hell you are," said the skinhead. "Bad enough they lettin' bitches in the chapel. But you sure as fuck ain't bringing in no weapons."

The women exchanged glances, then Fuego nodded. "Órale. But we get them back after the sit-down."

Shea and the others surrendered their guns, raised their shirts, and lowered their pants to their knees. This elicited a series of whistles and catcalls from the rabble sitting around the bar. Shea flipped them a bird, refusing to look at them.

The guy with the Mohawk patted down Shea and Indigo, while the skinhead patted down Savage and Fuego. Once the prospects were satisfied they weren't wired or still armed, the prospect with the Mohawk opened the heavy door. The women pulled their clothes back into place and walked into the chapel.

It resembled a corporate boardroom gone to seed. A large version of the Johnny Reb was painted on one wall. Five men sat on one side of an antique dining room table in much need of refurbishing. A United States flag stood in one corner and a Confederate flag in the other.

Shea recognized the six-foot-two president of the club, One-Shot, who sat at the head of the table. He was more muscular than she remembered. A scar now cut across his left cheek. She didn't recognize the other Thundermen.

"Glad you could make it," One-Shot said.

"Yeah," Shea replied.

"Y'all have a seat. We'll get down to business."

Once they were all seated, One Shot introduced the others at the table.

"Case y'all don't know, I'm One-Shot, president of the Cortes Chapter of the Confederate Thunder MC. This is

Hooch, our VP." He gestured to a man with a weathered, tanned face and a circlet of white hair. "Next to him is Bryz, sergeant-at-arms. The big guy at the foot of the table's Titan, our road captain. And the redhead next to him's Snook, club secretary."

Shea stared at Bryz. With his pale-blue eyes and his unkempt, chestnut hair, he reminded Shea of a surfer. His cut was worn, except for the bright new sergeant-at-arms patch. Something about him seemed familiar, but she couldn't place it. She didn't recall seeing him before, and since he was a patch-over from California, she probably hadn't.

Fuego introduced the five of them. "We're here because we're hoping the truce we negotiated a few years back still holds."

"Depends," said One-Shot. "Some of us think your club set us up. That y'all were working with the cops."

"Not true," Raven snapped.

"Bullshit," grumbled Bryz. "Giving the Thunder a shit-ton of drugs and not wanting nothing for 'em? No one does that. You bitches ain't nothing but snitches."

"You weren't there at the time, Bryz, so let me fill you in. The drugs belonged to Bonefish, a wannabe drug queen-pin," Shea replied. "We killed her and her crew. You think we'd be snitching to the cops after that? Fuck no! We don't sling dope, so we used it to stop the fighting between our clubs."

"Your former president firebombed our bar," Hooch added. "Killed several patches and a few old ladies."

"Well, y'all raped and murdered three of our members," Indigo insisted. "And tried to run Savage and me off the road."

The room erupted into shouts and accusations from

both sides. Shea got a sinking feeling that this entire thing was a mistake, one they wouldn't walk away from.

Dragon stood up slowly and extended her arms in a gesture calling for silence. The room quieted, all eyes on her.

"Gentlemen, ladies, too much blood has already been spilled," she said. "How many Thundermen and Athena Sisters have to die before we're willing to put an end to the violence? How does this gang war help the Thunder's business interests?"

"It doesn't," One-Shot admitted.

"Then what say we live and let live."

A heavy silence hung in the room. The Thundermen looked at each other.

"What are the terms?" Titan asked.

"When we see each other on the street," Shea replied, "we leave each other the fuck alone. No harassment, no insults, no catcalls."

"And we're allowed to wear our cuts," added Savage. "Call ourselves a motorcycle club. Do what we need to do in this county to protect the rights of women."

"So long as it don't interfere with our business," Hooch insisted. "But you call the cops on any of us, this truce don't mean shit, and then it's open season on Barbie bikers."

"And if Mackey or any other Thunderman shows up at my place again, I'll put two in the back of their heads." Shea glared at One-Shot.

"Fair enough," One-Shot said.

"You leave us alone," Fuego replied. "We leave you alone."

One-Shot turned to his fellow Thundermen. "All in favor of reinstating the truce with the Athena Sisterhood, say aye." He held up his right hand. "Aye."

Hooch locked eyes with Shea, paused for a moment, and said, "Aye."

Bryz crossed his arms. "Fuck no."

"Nay," Snook said. "This is our territory. No room for Barbie bikers."

Titan didn't say anything at first. It was clear from his expression he was weighing his options. "Fucking bitches."

"What's your vote, Titan?" One-Shot asked.

"Aye."

One-Shot clacked the gavel. "The ayes have it. Motion passes. This meeting is over."

The chairs in the room squeaked when they were pushed back. Shea turned to One-Shot. "We want our guns back now."

"Shank! Poptop! Give these ladies back their guns."

After the two prospects returned their weapons, Shea and the rest of the Sisters walked out past the silent, glaring eyes of the people at the bar.

She was glad that they'd come to an agreement, but she wondered how long it would hold.

17

"I'm glad that's over," Indigo said when they stepped outside.

It felt about ten degrees cooler than when they had gone in. The shadows were growing long, and the trees surrounding the fenced-in property sliced through the streams of golden sunlight spilling on the patchy grass.

"You and me both." Shea put a hand on Indigo's shoulder.

"But will they honor the peace agreement?" Raven asked. "Gotta say I have my doubts."

Fuego nodded. "Either way, best we get the hell out of here while we can."

"Y'all go on ahead," Shea said.

"We can't leave you here alone," Indigo replied. "Not with these animals."

"I'll be fine," replied Shea. "I got history with these people. They're fucking bigots, and I hate everything they stand for. But I should be okay for an hour or so."

Savage clapped her on the back. "Watch your six, Havoc."

"And call us if you get in trouble, hermana," Fuego added.

Raven gave her a quick hug. "I don't live too far. Shit goes down, you give me a buzz. I'll be here."

"Thanks."

Shea watched the five of them drive off then returned to the playground where Julia was watching Annie supervise a game of tag with the smaller children.

"Hey." Shea sat on the bench next to her. "D'y'all come to an agreement?"

"For now. How was lockup?"

Julia shrugged. "You know what it's like. Wasn't my first go-round, though at my age it sure as hell wasn't no picnic. A few women tried to muscle me around." Julia took a long pull on her cigarette. "I showed 'em I wasn't no pushover."

"How'd you hook up with Hooch?"

"We've known each other for years." She sighed. "Ain't nothing like Monster was. For all his toughness, Monster had a gentle side to him. Hooch, he's all business. Likes to make sure I keep in my place. Don't like me riding my own bike. Says it ain't ladylike."

"Sounds like a real charmer. Why'd you hook up with him?"

"With Monster gone, it was that or walk away from the club." Julia stubbed out the cig on the bench and tossed the butt in a nearby barrel.

"You could always join the Sisterhood."

"Girl, I'm too old to be prospecting in somebody else's club. The Thunder, for all its flaws, it's all I know. I was seventeen when Monster and I started dating. These people been my family my entire adult life. Wouldn't know what to do without them."

"You can do better," Shea replied. "As you've pointed out many times, Annie and I are your family. The Sisterhood treats women with respect, not like property." Shea tugged on Julia's cut, which read Property of Hooch on the back.

"Maybe if I were twenty years younger, I'd consider it. But this ol' dog ain't learning no new tricks."

"Suit yourself."

"How about you and me fix ourselves a plate of barbecue?" Julia suggested.

"All right. Annie, come on. We're going to eat."

"Not now. We're in the middle of a game."

"Come on, Shea-Shea. She'll be along when she's hungry."

On their way to the picnic tables, Mackey stumbled into their path, clearly hammered. The side of his face was purple where Shea had smacked him a few days earlier.

"You took my gun, bitch! And I want it back."

"Go sleep it off, Mack," Julia said. "Don't nobody want any trouble this evening."

Mackey pointed his finger at Julia. "What I want is for you to shut your ugly trap, you old cunt, and for this Barbie biker bitch to gimme my gun back. Shit cost me three hundred dollars."

"It's gone, asshole. I tossed it in the middle of the forest where no one will find it."

He lunged at her. Shea sidestepped and stuck out her foot. He tripped and face-planted in the dirt.

"What the fuck's going on here?"

Shea turned to see Hooch striding over and met his eyes. "Your boy trying to start something."

Hooch grabbed Mackey's arm and pulled him to his unsteady feet. "What the hell, Mack?"

"Bitch took my gun. I keep saying. Ain't nobody's listening to me."

Hooch glared at Shea. "You took his gun?"

"A few nights ago, when he threatened me and my niece with it at my house. I tossed it in the national forest south of Ironwood. It's gone."

"Bitch is a rat, Hooch," Mackey slurred. "Fucking goddamn snitch."

"Get him outta here, Hooch," Julia said. "Before he fucks everything up."

Hooch put his arm around the man. "Come on, brother. Let's go inside and leave these women alone."

Shea watched the two of them shuffle into the church. Julia led her to a table spread with food. Shea filled a plate with ribs, coleslaw, and potato salad.

They found a place at one of the long picnic tables where a few others were sitting. When they sat, the people nearby glared at Shea and left.

"Don't take it personal," Julia said. "This is Thunder property. We ain't used to having no one from a rival club be here."

"Suits me fine," she replied. "I'd rather not share a table with them either."

The two of them ate in silence while more memories poured through Shea's mind. As much as Shea enjoyed being part of the Sisterhood, they rarely had gatherings like this. It made her feel nostalgic.

Periodically, Shea caught Julia staring at her, as if she was about to say something. There was a haunted look in her eyes.

"What?" Shea asked.

Julia grimaced. "I...nothing."

"There was something you said we needed to discuss. Something we couldn't talk about on the phone. What was it?"

"It's...it's nothing. Just glad to see you is all."

Shea studied her as the woman across the table from her picked at her food. "Whatever."

Annie still hadn't joined them by the time Shea finished eating.

"I better check on Annie." Shea wiped her hands with a napkin, stood, and tossed her plate in a trash barrel.

"I'll be along in a sec."

The sun had set behind the trees, and the light was fading. Shea found Annie sitting on a swing next to Bryz. All the other kids were gone. Bryz was leaning close to her. His body language had a predatory edge to it, like a wolf about to pounce on a rabbit. Shea's protective instincts roared into overdrive.

"Get the fuck away from her," Shea growled.

Bryz held up his hands in surrender. "I'm just talking to the little lady. She and I have a lot in common."

"Just stay away from her," she barked. "Come on, Annie. We're going home."

Annie looked up. "But I haven't eaten yet."

"Pack a to-go box. You can eat at home."

"But I'm hungry now." Annie looked past her.

Shea turned and saw Julia beside her. "Don't argue with me."

"Shea," cautioned Julia. "Let her stay and eat."

"You had your chance to talk. Whatever it is can wait. We're going. That's final. Annie, say goodbye to Gramma Julia."

"Bye, Gramma. Sorry Shea's being such a bitch."

"Don't sass your Aunt Shea," Julia warned. "She's doing what she thinks best. Now run along. I'll see you again soon. Okay?"

"Yeah." The two hugged.

"Shea-Shea, you call me when you get home."

Shea nodded, but she had no intention of calling. "Right."

Shea led Annie to the picnic tables to fix a to-go box while keeping an eye out for Mackey, Bryz, or any other Thunderman looking for trouble. After Annie closed the Styrofoam box, they returned to the parking lot, neither of them speaking.

"Why are you being so mean to me?" Annie asked when they reached Shea's bike.

"I'm not trying to be mean. I'm trying to protect you."

"From Bryz? He wasn't doing nothing."

"A grown man shouldn't be talking to a teenage girl that way."

"Why not?"

"'Cause a guy like Bryz ain't interested in just conversation."

Annie held Shea's gaze for a moment. "Oh."

"Put on your helmet. We'll heat your dinner when we get home."

"Okay." She put her dinner in the top case on the back.

Shea threw a leg over the bike and started it while Annie strapped on her helmet and climbed on the passenger seat.

"All right, hold on."

They rode through the dark, taking the Ironwood Bypass so they wouldn't have to go through the congestion of the city's streets.

When they finally got home, Annie put her dinner on a plate and stuck it in the microwave. "It's weird."

"What's that?"

"Bryz and me both have a crooked pinky finger." She held up her finger. The end joint was tilted slightly off center. Always had been.

"It happens," Shea said.

"I wonder if we're related somehow." Annie took her dinner out of the microwave, and the two of them sat down in front of the TV.

"You're not." Shea turned on the news. "Hunter was your father. Wendy was your mother. You're not related."

"Could be a long-lost cousin or something. People getting those DNA tests find out they're related to all kinds of folks."

The headline at the bottom of the screen mentioned a local reporter had been found dead following a home invasion. They flashed her picture. Shea's blood ran cold when she saw it was Elia Quinn.

"Shit." Had her confrontation with Connelly led to this? How would he have known Quinn was working on the story?

"What's wrong?" Annie asked.

"Nothing, just eat your dinner."

Shea stepped into her bedroom and called Indigo.

"Hey, girl. You get home okay?" Indigo asked.

"I did. Where's Deirdre?"

"In the guest room. Why?"

"She safe?"

"Of course. Havoc, what's going on?"

"That reporter, the one that put me in touch with Deirdre? She's dead. Home invasion, according to the news."

"You think Connelly killed her?"

"Or had her killed. Some men don't take no for an answer." She didn't want to mention her meeting with the man.

"Should we tell the cops what we know?" Indigo asked.

"Not sure what good it'd do. Connelly is buddies with Sheriff Buzzkill. For now, keep Deirdre safe and your eyes open. I suspect this'll get worse before it gets better."

18

THE NEXT MORNING, Shea stepped through the shop's back door into the service bay.

Lakota was draining dirty oil from a Harley Street. A Honda Magna stood on a lift behind her, with its tank and seat on the floor nearby.

"Morning," Lakota said, rubbing her face with a grimy hand and leaving a black smudge on her cheek. "How was your night?"

"Interesting. Annie and I went to a welcome-home party for the Confederate Thunder." She didn't mention the Sisterhood's sit-down with the Thunder's officers, since it was club business.

When Lakota gave her a what-the-hell look, Shea continued. "Annie wanted to see her grandma who just got outta prison."

"Wow. Did they know you're a member of a rival club?"

"They knew. We kept things civil. When will the Magna be finished?" Shea said, wanting to change the subject.

"Transmission's done. Still waiting on a new regulator. The ones for the V45s are a dime a dozen, but finding one for a V65 is proving to be tricky. Terrance is trying to track one down now."

"Good."

Shea continued on to the shop's office. Terrance sat at his desk, talking on the phone.

"Any other place you can suggest we get a replacement regulator for an '84 Honda V65 Magna? I've tried every name in my book. Even went on eBay and Craigslist. Nothing. Right, tried them yesterday. No luck. Oh, really? Augusta, Georgia? Oh, Augusta, Maine. Got it. Okay, I'll give them a holler. Thanks, man."

"Find one?" Shea asked when Terrance hung up.

"Pete knows a guy up in Maine who collects Magnas. Keeps a dozen or so on hand for spare parts. Might have a regulator for a V65 we can use."

"Good deal."

"Also sold the Flying Tree bike." Terrance beamed like a gold-medal Olympian. "Ka-ching! I love payday."

"Glad to hear it."

"Which means you should start designing something for the upcoming Albuquerque show."

"Okay, I'll brainstorm some ideas and go over them with Lakota." Shea considered the best way to word what she had to say. "Elia Quinn was killed last night."

Terrance stared at her. "The reporter who was here? What happened?"

"According to the news, it was a home invasion. I don't know all the details, but my gut tells me it's connected to the favor she asked me to do for her friend."

"The favor that involved the Athena Sisterhood?"

"Her friend was being harassed by someone—a powerful someone. Quinn was writing a story on it. This someone didn't want it published."

"Who is this someone?"

Shea debated how much to tell him. It was technically club business, but she didn't want Terrance to get blindsided if this mess spilled over into the shop.

"State Senator Joe Connelly."

"Connelly? You think he killed Elia Quinn? Why?"

"He'd had an affair with the woman that the Sisterhood's protecting. He doesn't want it getting out and ruining his campaign."

"Seems extreme, even for him. Don't get me wrong. Connelly's an arrogant asshole. But to murder somebody to cover up an affair? Wow. You have proof?"

"Just a gut feeling for now. But figured you oughta know."

"You think the paper will still run the story Elia wrote about Iron Goddess? It was supposed to run tomorrow morning."

"Seriously, T? A woman was murdered, and you're worried about press coverage for the shop?"

"Sorry, that was crass of me. I should call the paper."

"T..."

"To express my condolences. Not to ask about the story."

"Uh-huh."

"You don't think Connelly will try something here, do you? Since you're involved in this?"

She wondered if Connelly could identify her. "No reason for him to connect the shop to the woman we're protecting."

"Make sure it stays that way. We don't need it affecting business here."

Shea poured herself a cup of coffee and sat at her desk to sketch designs for the new custom bike. But her mind kept drifting back to Connelly and the reporter.

She considered solving the problem once and for all by

taking out Connelly. He wouldn't be the first person she'd killed. But he would be the first that wasn't in self-defense. She wasn't an assassin and wasn't sure she wanted to become one.

Monica stepped into the office. "Hey boss, someone up front's asking to speak to you."

"Me?" A flash of alarm rippled down Shea's spine. "Who?"

"Some skinny old lady. Smells of cigarettes. Wearing Confederate Thunder ink."

"Shit." Not Connelly or one of his thugs, at least. "I'll be right up."

"Should I be worried?" asked Terrance with concern in his voice.

"Doubt it."

As Shea expected, she found Julia standing by the front counter.

"What d'you want, Julia? Annie's at soccer camp."

"You didn't call last night."

"I was tired."

"There some place private we can talk?"

Shea peered through the window to the office. Terrance was on the phone again. Probably calling the *Cortes Chronicle*. There were two service customers sitting in their waiting area. "How about the back parking lot?"

"Yeah, that'll do."

Shea led her out through the service bay to the parking lot. "What's so urgent and secret you have to tell me in private?"

"You weren't wrong about Bryz." Julia sighed.

"What d'you mean?"

"While Hunter and Wendy were dating, Bryz came in for a big gathering of the Southwest chapters. Roadster, who was Cortes president at the time, was getting the chapter into some things that LA and Vegas weren't keen on."

"What kinda things?"

"Not important. The thing is, while the LA boys were here, Bryz..." Julia flinched. "He raped Wendy."

"What? And you're just telling me now?"

"Wendy confided in me, Shea. She begged me not to tell anyone else. Not Hunter, not Monster, just me. But since you're taking care of Annie now, I suppose you oughta know."

"Wendy was only fifteen when she got pregnant. He was what? Early twenties, I'm guessing. You should've reported it."

"To who? The cops? The club never would've allowed it."

"Fuck the club. She was my sister. You were her godmother, for Chrissakes. At least report it to Monster."

"If I'd done that, we would've had a war between the two chapters. Plus, I was afraid that breaking Wendy's confidence would only cause her more sorrow."

"So, he got away with it. Well, next time I see him—"

"Shea, he's a patched member. You can't touch him. You'd start another war between our clubs. You gotta let it go. She's dead and gone. The only reason I'm telling you now is to let you know to keep Annie away from him."

Shea felt herself fuming. This was one of the worst things about outlaw clubs. Women were property. Treated like dirt. Controlled like children.

"Don't worry. I won't let him or anyone else connected to the Thunder anywhere near her. That includes you!"

"Shealene..."

"Don't 'Shealene' me. How many other girls has Bryz raped? How many daughters of patched members? And you've warned no one?"

"Believe me, I hated keeping it a secret."

"Fuck you and your club secrets. Get the fuck out of here." Shea's phone rang. She recognized the number.

"Please don't shut me out, Shea-Shea. We're family."

"Family doesn't allow rapists to go free."

Julia hung her head and disappeared around the building.

"Rios," Shea answered the call on the third ring. "How you feeling?"

"Better. Still hurts to talk." The word *hurts* came out more like *hirsh*.

A swell of emotions rose in Shea, adding to the anger she was already feeling. Shea was in no mood to be social. "You should get some rest then."

There was silence before Rios spoke. "I want to see you."

"Yeah, well, I got a lot on my plate right now. Whatever you need to say, you can say over the phone."

"Thanks for calling."

"What? You called me."

"No. The message on Sunday. Meant a lot. Had lots of CIs over years. Never had one show concern for me."

"I'm not a fan of cops. But you saved my life. Guess I owed you something."

"Still want to see you. Maybe buy you dinner."

"Dinner? A cop wants to buy me dinner? That's new. What's going on, Rios? You doped up on pain meds?"

"A little." Rios sounded hurt.

Shea felt a pang of guilt. She also thought maybe Rios might give her more info on what happened to Elia Quinn. "Look. I'm sorry. You still in the hospital?"

"For now."

"Maybe I'll drop by later today."

"I'd like that. I'm at Cortes Regional on the fourth floor.

Room 468. I'll inform the unis posted outside my door you're coming."

"Okay. See ya soon." Shea hung up.

A little while later, she was ringing up the customer picking up the Harley Street while Monica was at lunch. Dragon walked in wearing her business suit. Her expression was grim.

"What's shakin', Dragon?"

"We need to talk."

"Be right with you. Lemme finish with this customer."

Shea handed the customer her receipt. "Vince will bring your bike around front. Thanks for your business."

She ushered Dragon over to the customer waiting area, which was now empty. The burnt-orange tweed covering the chairs was torn and ratty. The wooden legs bore scratches as if an animal had been sharpening its claws on them. Shea hoped with the sale of the Flying Tree bike, Terrance would spring for something made in this century.

"What's going on, Dragon?"

"Indigo called this morning. Deirdre was freaking out over Elia Quinn's murder. She's convinced Connelly found out she was talking to Quinn and had her killed."

"What's your take?" Shea asked. "You think Connelly's behind it?"

Dragon shrugged. "I don't know. I did a little research. There've been five home invasions in Quinn's neighborhood in the past few years. But this is the first where somebody was murdered. Deirdre asked me to help her get an order of protection against Connelly."

"You think a piece of paper would stop Connelly?"

"No. Connelly will try to quash it before the weekend. But Deirdre was having a panic attack. Getting the order of protection seemed to calm her down for now. There's one other thing."

"What's that?" Shea was afraid of what else Dragon had to say.

"We need a new place for Deirdre to stay. Savage doesn't want her staying with them."

"Why not?"

"She's dealing CBD oil. Savage doesn't want her selling it out of her house."

"Maybe Deirdre should put her side hustle on hold for now."

"I'll pass along the message." Dragon glanced around the showroom. Several women wandered the aisles, searching for supplies or looking at safety gear. "Looks like business is up since you won that award."

"So it seems." Shea recalled her conversation with Julia. "Hey, let me ask you something. If a guy raped a girl, say fifteen years ago, could he still be prosecuted for the crime? Or is there some statue of limitations?"

"You mean statute of limitations. In the case of rape, there's no statute of limitations in Arizona. The challenge would be proving it after all these years. Is the victim just now coming forward?"

"The victim was my baby sister, Wendy. Annie's mom. She's dead."

"Did the alleged rapist murder her?"

"No. She died several years later in a shootout."

Dragon made a face. "Did you or anyone else who's alive witness the rape?"

"No. She told her godmother. No one else."

"I hate to say it, but unless you can get the rapist to confess, it doesn't sound like you have a case. The godmother's testimony would be hearsay. Not admissible in court, I'm afraid."

"I thought as much. Thanks anyway."

"I'm sorry that happened to your sister. Sounds like she had a rough life."

"Growing up with the Thunder has that effect."

"Well, I have to meet with a client in an hour, so I need to hit the road. I'll see you round, Havoc."

"Keep the shiny side up, sister."

19

AFTER DRAGON LEFT and Monica returned from lunch, Shea stepped into the office. Terrence was working on an advertising campaign.

"Hey, T, I gotta go out for a while. Probably won't be back before closing."

"What's going on?"

Shea said, "Gotta see someone."

"Everything okay?"

"More or less."

He pushed away his keyboard and faced her. "I'm worried about you, Shea. You're family. I don't want you hurt."

"Don't get all mushy on me, man. I'm fine. I shouldn't tell you this, but last night, the Sisterhood and the Thunder agreed to a truce. Whatever this thing is going on between Connelly and that woman, it won't land on me or the shop. Okay?"

"All right. See you tomorrow."

She pulled on her helmet and jacket, hopped on her bike, and headed north.

Halfway between Sycamore Springs and Ironwood, Shea came to the large boxy building of Cortes Regional Medical Center. When she got to the ward on the fourth floor, two uniforms were standing outside Rios's room.

The unis asked her who she was. Shea showed her ID and explained that Rios was expecting her. Apparently, they were aware and let her pass.

Rios was sitting up in bed, reading something on her laptop. A bandage covered the left side of her face.

"Hey," Shea said, feeling strangely self-conscious. She told herself it was from being around so many cops at once. "How you feeling?"

"Still sore, but better than I was."

"Surprised they brought you down to Cortes Regional. Andover Monterosa's closer and newer."

"Cortes Regional apparently has a trauma unit. Monterosa's is still under construction."

"What happened exactly?"

Rios winced, took a breath, and sighed. "I was in Ironwood with friends celebrating my twenty-fifth year on the force."

"Twenty-five years? No way you been a cop that long."

"You're sweet. Believe me, it's been that long. I was walking to my car alone when someone called my name and opened fire from the shadows. Caught a couple rounds on the side of my face. Didn't get a good look at the perps, but there were at least two. Got one of them. I guess the other paid you a visit too."

"Mackey." Lying about the pistol weighed on Shea's conscience. She hated protecting the scumbag, but it beat having the two clubs warring with each other.

"You really toss that gun?"

Lying came easy to Shea when needed. But she looked away from Rios. "Why wouldn't I? I got caught with one of his guns before and nearly got sent down for murder. Don't need that kinda trouble." She finally met Rios's gaze. "Bad enough Mackey suspects me of setting them up on the narco bust. I thought you were keeping my identity confidential."

"I have. No one but me knows you tipped us off to the Thunder carrying those drugs."

"But you made me sign those papers. Someone could've got ahold of them."

"They're secured."

"And yet Mackey knows, or at least suspects, it was me."

"If the CCSO had Mackey's gun, we could put him back in prison. He would no longer be a problem."

"Yeah, you put him away, and then the rest of the Thunder comes after me and my club. Last night, we brokered a fragile truce. If that goes sour, this county turns into a bloodbath all over again. Is that what you want?"

Rios held her gaze. "No, that's not what I want. You're saying you tossed the gun in the woods somewhere, right?"

"Yeah. Why?"

"So, who's to say some hiker didn't stumble upon it and turn it in. If we can get a match to Mackey's fingerprints and to the ballistics from the shooting, we get Mackey, and you're in the clear. If we had the gun."

Shea considered this. Rios's explanation could get Mackey off the street without implicating her or the Sisterhood. "All right."

"All right? You can get the gun?"

"Possibly."

Rios's face lit up. Smiled even. "I've missed you."

"Really?" Emotions fluttered in Shea's stomach.

"I shouldn't say this, since you're a potential witness in a case, one involving me, no less. But I've always been attracted to you, Shea."

"You coming on to me, Detective?"

Rios's smile faded for a moment. "Just expressing my feelings, my appreciation for you reaching out and coming forward." But the gleam in her eye told Shea there was more to it than that.

"No offense, but I don't date cops. I don't trust cops. You sure these feelings of yours aren't just 'cause they got you doped up on pain meds?"

"Pain meds may be why I'm expressing my feelings. But the emotions are genuine."

"Like I said, I don't date cops."

"Fair enough. Text me once you've recovered the weapon. I'll have Bello pick the gun up from your house."

"Right." She couldn't help but admit to herself that she felt a little something for Rios too. Even if she was a cop, Shea admired her toughness and persistence.

She was about to leave when a thought occurred to her. "What've you heard about the death of that reporter, Elia Quinn?"

"Haven't heard much. Detectives Morris and Bello are working that case as well. Do you know something?"

Shea had half an inclination to name Connelly. Perhaps it would be better if she got Deirdre to talk directly to the cops.

"Nope."

"I see." Rios didn't look convinced.

"Well, I'll see you around."

"Take care of yourself, Shea. And thanks again."

Shea walked out of the room. Her insides felt like a roiling bag of snakes.

20

When Shea arrived home, it was late afternoon. She sent a text to Rios about the gun shortly before Annie walked in the door, still complaining of cramps.

"Well, crap." Shea shook her head. "You drinking enough water?"

"Until my back teeth float."

"Huh. Did the Pamprin help?"

"Coach took it away. Said I couldn't have any drugs without a note."

"Asshole. All right, I'll get you some."

Shea was returning from the bathroom when someone started pounding on her front door.

Annie looked panicked.

"It's okay. I think I know who it is."

"Who?"

"Same cop who was here before. It's all right. He's expected."

Shea opened the door to find Bello with sweat beading on his forehead and a frown on his face.

"You know, Miss Stevens, I don't appreciate having to

come all the way down here a second time. We could've resolved this before."

"Whatever." She let him inside and shut the door. "Wait here."

She stepped into her walk-in closet to retrieve the weapon from her gun safe. It took her a few tries before she remembered she'd changed the combination to the first six digits of her childhood phone number. When she finally got it open, she picked it up with a pen through the trigger guard and returned to the living room. "Here."

He was waiting with an open plastic evidence bag. "Have you done anything to it? Cleaned it, wiped it for prints, anything?"

She shook her head and dropped it in the bag. "Just took it away from Mackey. I hope he rots in prison for the rest of his life. Just remember, you didn't get it from me. You found it off the side of the road in the woods."

"Right. Whatever you say." Bello sealed the bag. "The Cortes County Sheriff's Office thanks you for your cooperation. You think of anything else that can help, call me." He gave Shea his business card and headed for the door.

She stuffed the card in her wallet, sure she'd never use it in a million years. "Hey, you're investigating Elia Quinn's murder, aren't you? Any idea who killed her?" Since he was here, Shea figured she might as well ask.

He turned and narrowed his eyes. "Why you asking? Did you know the victim?"

Shea saw how he changed things up and regretted bringing up the question. "She was writing a story about my motorcycle shop winning an award. Was surprised someone killed her."

"Do you know of anyone who meant her harm?"

Shea wondered what Bello would do if she shared about Deirdre West's problems with Senator Connelly.

Would he look into it or help cover it up? "Didn't really know her. Like I said, she just did a story about the shop."

Bello studied her as he had before when she'd claimed to have ditched Mackey's gun. "You think of something, call us. Y'all have a good night."

She closed the door after he left.

"Why'd he want Mackey's gun?" asked Annie.

"May've been used to shoot a cop."

"What's Mackey gonna do when he finds out you gave it to them?"

"Let's not tell anyone, and maybe he won't find out. What d'you say to baked fish and steamed broccoli for dinner?"

"I'd rather have mac and cheese."

"We used the last box a week ago."

"I saw a bag of macaroni noodles in the pantry. And there's cheese in the fridge."

"Yeah, but fish and broccoli's healthier."

Annie made a pouty face that gutted Shea's resolve. Since the numbers on her bathroom scale had been creeping up the past several months, she'd attempted to cook less processed food and more lean meats and fresh vegetables.

But since Annie wasn't feeling well, one night of fatty comfort food wouldn't hurt.

"All right. Let me look up a recipe to make it from scratch."

Shea was in the middle of making dinner when her phone rang.

"Hey, Indigo, what's up?" She pressed the phone to her ear while stirring the gooey cheese and pasta in the pot on the stove.

"Deirdre split."

Shea stopped stirring and turned off the burner. "What do you mean she split?"

"I mean she split, as in not here no more."

"Maybe she's meeting one of her essential oils customers."

"No, all of her stuff's gone. Savage and me, we talked to her this morning. That CBD oil she's selling? Savage looked it up. Tests showed that brand, Gaia's whatever, contains THC, pseudoephedrine, and other controlled substances. DEA's been cracking down on people caught with it. Savage could lose her license as a paramedic. Hell, we could lose our home."

"Shit. I never woulda let her stay with y'all if I'd known." She spooned mac and cheese into a bowl and set it in front of Annie at the breakfast bar.

"We told her she could stay but couldn't keep that stuff here. We thought she was cool with it, but now she's bugged out."

"Thanks for the heads-up."

"I'm sorry it didn't work out, Havoc. She seems like a nice lady, and I don't want nothing to happen to her like it did that reporter, but..."

"No need to apologize, Indigo. It's your home. You got a right to set boundaries. I'll track her down and see what we can work out that doesn't put any of us at risk of being arrested."

Shea was tempted to let Deirdre sort out her own mess. But considering Quinn's recent death, the nagging voice of her conscience reminded her that the woman might still face retaliation from Connelly.

Shea dialed Deirdre's phone number. It rang four times and went to voicemail. The outgoing message was chipper with a little self-promo for her business that belied the seriousness of her situation.

"Deirdre, this is Shea. Call me when you get this."

Shea turned to Annie, who'd barely touched her food. "What's wrong? That's what you asked for. Did I not make it right?"

"Just not hungry." Annie looked more miserable than ever. "Sorry."

"Cramps?"

Annie shrugged. "Just don't feel good."

Shea felt Annie's forehead. "You don't feel hot. You want me to make you something else? I think I've got some cans of chicken soup. There's some boxes of Jell-O in the cupboard, but I'm not sure how old they are."

"Maybe later."

Shea gazed at her, trying to decide what to do. She shouldn't leave Annie while she wasn't feeling well. But if Deirdre went back to her condo, she could be in danger.

"What's wrong, Aunt Shea?"

"I'm worried about the woman that the Sisterhood's protecting. She was staying with Indigo and Savage, but she left. I'm afraid the person who's been bullying her will try to hurt her."

"You should go help her."

Annie's concern only piled on the guilt she was feeling. "I shouldn't be more than an hour. You think you'll be all right? I could drop you at Indigo's or Terrance's."

"I'll be okay."

"If you feel worse, call me right away. If you can't get me, call Indigo. Agreed?"

"Yeah, I'll be fine. I might have a bowl of cereal later."

Shea gave a last look at Annie and hustled to the garage.

Once she reached the top of Sycamore Mountain, Shea blazed through Olde Towne Sycamore Springs with her high beams on to make sure she didn't hit any wildlife. She blew past the patrol car sitting just outside the little business district. To her surprise, the cruiser remained on the side of the road. No lights or sirens. Maybe the deputy was taking a nap.

Twenty minutes later, she pulled into Deirdre's condominium complex. She spotted her Kia in her reserved space. A wave of relief washed over her. Thank goodness she was here!

Shea rushed to the door and found it ajar, the doorframe cracked.

Shea's pulse quickened.

"Deirdre! You here? It's Shea." She nudged open the door with her elbow and stepped inside, pistol drawn and ready. "Deirdre?"

She flicked on the living room light. Everything looked normal. No overturned or broken furniture. No abandoned dinner on the table. A thump from upstairs caught her attention.

She backtracked to the front entrance and crept up the staircase, opting not to turn on the upstairs light in case what she heard was an intruder working for Connelly. She continued to hear shuffling sounds but couldn't make out what they were. Possibly someone rooting around for something.

She was two-thirds up the stairs when a high-pitched squeal nearly made her jump out of her skin. "What the f—"

A shadow charged her. She pulled off a shot just before it slammed into her legs, pitching her backward. The handrail slammed hard against her rib cage. She clung to it with a death grip to arrest her fall.

Painfully, she pulled herself to her feet and felt along the wall until she came to the light switch at the top of the stairs. Her right leg throbbed where the animal had rammed her. A ragged tear in her jeans gaped about mid-calf. She lifted her pant leg to find a shallow cut in her leather boots. Fortunately, it didn't go through to her skin.

"Goddamn pig."

She cast a glance downstairs but saw no sign of the pig. It must have run right out the front door. The absence of a blood trail meant her shot had missed the potbellied beast. She wasn't sure whether to be disappointed at her aim or grateful she wouldn't have to explain to Deirdre that her emotional support animal was dead.

Shea reclaimed her gun from where it had fallen. She continued upstairs and checked the guest bedroom and bath before turning to the master bedroom. The bed was unmade. A lamp lay on its side. The drawers were pulled out of a small desk, files and paperwork tossed everywhere. Somebody was looking for something. Possibly the dirt Deirdre had on Connelly.

In the bathroom, she found a foul-smelling puddle of what she assumed was vomit. Nearby lay wrappers, bits of plastic, and other assorted detritus often left behind when emergency medical services showed up.

"Hey!" called a male voice from downstairs. "Whoever's up there better come down now, or I'm calling the cops."

Shea held her pistol at her side as she returned to the top of the stairs. A heavyset guy in a button-down shirt stood at the bottom, holding a wooden baseball bat. "Who the hell are you?" he demanded.

"A friend of Deirdre's."

"Well, she ain't here."

"Where is she?"

"Police showed up a little while ago. Busted in her door. Then an ambulance took her away."

"What for?"

"Hell if I know. She always got those sketchy-looking

people coming round knocking on her door at all hours. You her connection?"

"Connection?"

"Her drug connection. Her supplier. I figured that's what she's doing. Selling drugs. Am I right?"

"Last I heard, she was selling essential oils. And no, I'm not her connection. Just a friend who's worried about her."

"Who you shootin' at? I know a gunshot when I hear one."

"The pig surprised me."

"Ha! I hope you killed that squealin' sonofabitch. Damn thing keeps me awake with all that racket."

"It ran away." She holstered her weapon.

"Too bad."

"You know where they took her?"

"Monterosa Medical, I reckon."

Shea trudged down the stairs. Every step sent lightning bolts of pain up her leg and into her lower back. Her side throbbed mercilessly, making it hard to breathe. The neighbor backed up, a wary expression on his face.

"Thanks for your help." She walked past him and left him standing inside Deirdre's entryway.

She wasn't sure what to do about the pig being loose. Considering what it had done to her, she wasn't inclined to track it down and force it back into the condo. For now, it would have to fend for itself. It was a pig, after all. They'd eat just about anything. With all the landscaping in the complex, it would be all right.

As soon as she threw a leg over her motorcycle, the pain in her ribs intensified. She'd broken a rib before. This wasn't as bad. Probably just bruised. She took a shallow breath and started the bike.

The cool night air helped get her mind off the pain as she drove west to the hospital. Unlike Cortes Regional,

Monterosa Medical Center was a sprawling complex of buildings centered around the main tower.

She parked in the Emergency visitor parking, stashed her weapons in her top case, and walked inside. At the Emergency Department's information desk, she asked the volunteer at the desk, a woman Shea guessed was in her mid-sixties, if Deirdre had been admitted.

The woman typed the name into the system. "We admitted to Emergency a few hours ago and released into the custody of the sheriff's department."

"Sheriff's department? For what?"

"I'm sorry, I don't have that information."

"Why was she here? Was she attacked?"

"Unfortunately, I'm not allowed to give out private health information. You'd have to talk with the patient."

"Who's now in custody. Swell."

"Anything else I can do for you?" The woman seemed sorry.

"No thanks."

"I hope everything works out for your friend."

Shea was on the phone as soon as she was outside.

"Shea?" asked Rios. "I didn't expect to hear back from you so soon."

"I need a favor."

"What kind of favor?"

"A friend of mine's been arrested. I need to know where she's being held and why."

"Who's your friend?"

"Deirdre West. I stopped by her place a little while ago. Neighbor said an ambulance took her to Monterosa Medical. ER said she was released into the custody of your buddies at the sheriff's office. I got you Mackey's pistol. You can do me this one favor."

"Okay, I'll make some calls and see what I can find out."

21

WHILE SHE WAITED for a call back from Rios, Shea texted Annie.
How are you feeling?
The response came at once.

Better. Nuked some chicken soup.

Shea felt a little less guilty.
I may be longer than expected. You want me to call Indigo?

No. How long will U B?

About an hour. The woman got arrested.

Whatevs. I'm going 2 bed.

Get some sleep. I'll be home soon.
Shea's phone rang. "What'd ya find out?"
"Dierdre's been arrested on charges of possession," Rios said.

"Possession of what? CBD oil?"

"No, heroin."

"Heroin? Are you sure?" This made little sense. Shea had been around her share of junkies. She'd even hired a few who were in recovery. For all her drama, Deirdre didn't strike Shea as a dope fiend.

"I'm just telling you what I heard. Patrol was called to do a wellness check. They found her unconscious in her bathtub, a heroin rig nearby, needle still in her arm."

"A wellness check? Who called for that?"

"I'm not at liberty to say, Shea," Rios replied. "Lo siento, but I've already told you more than I should."

"This is bullshit. She's being set up."

A moment passed before Rios asked, "Set up by whom?"

"Senator Connelly. She's got dirt on him. He's trying to keep her quiet. Where is she?"

"She was booked by the Narcotics Division at the District I substation. It's a class four felony. She have any priors?"

"Not that I know of."

"I'll make a call, see if I can get her released ROR."

"Thanks, Rios. I'd appreciate that."

"On one condition."

Shea let out a loud sigh. "What?"

"After I'm released from the hospital, you'll at least have dinner with me. Not a date. Just two friends having a night out. This hospital food is the pits."

"No offense, but we ain't friends, Rios. Don't you have some cop buddies to have dinner with?"

"I'd rather it be you. And please call me Toni."

"Fine, I'll have dinner with you. But first, I need Deirdre out of jail."

"I'll call right now."

"Thanks." Shea hung up and called Indigo. "I found Deirdre. She's been arrested."

"Lemme guess. Possession."

"Yeah, but not for the CBD oil. For heroin."

"Heroin? Shit. The bitch is a junkie? Fuck."

"Did you call the cops for a wellness check at her condo?"

"A wellness check? No."

"Someone did. I think she's been set up. My gut tells me Connelly's involved in this."

"Just saw Connelly on the news. He's been in Prescott at a rally all day."

"Maybe one of his associates. It just feels wrong. I've known a few heroin junkies. Deirdre didn't strike me as one of them."

"Some addicts are better at hiding their disease than others. This thing with Connelly coulda driven her to use."

"Could be. Listen, any chance she can stay at your place a little longer after I get her out of the can?"

"Shea, I know it's the Sisterhood's mission to protect women in trouble, but between the CBD oil and this heroin shit, I don't feel comfortable saying yes. And I think you know what Savage will say."

"Fair enough. Just thought I'd ask. By the way, I turned Mackey's gun over to the cops."

"Hope it doesn't blow back on us. We just got the Thunder to agree to a truce yesterday."

"So far as everyone's concerned, I tossed the gun in the Cortes National Forest. Rios said she'd have the sheriff's office say a hiker found it and turned it in. Besides, if Mackey shot Rios, he needs to go down for it."

"I don't disagree. As cops go, she's all right. Keep me updated on Deirdre's situation. Take care, sister."

"You too, Indigo. I'll let you know when she's out."

When Shea hung up, she saw a text from Rios saying that Deirdre's release was being processed. Shea thanked her and drove to the substation. Inside the lobby, Shea approached the desk sergeant, who sat behind bulletproof glass. A locked door with a card key entry to her left led to the rest of the building.

"Can I help you?" asked the desk sergeant, a tall, square-jawed man with a buzz cut.

"I'm here to pick up Deirdre West. Detective Toni Rios should've called about getting her released ROR."

"Your name?"

"Shea Stevens. I'm a friend."

"Okay, have a seat. Let me see what's going on."

Shea sat down on one of a row of hard plastic seats. She sent a group text to Fuego and Dragon, updating them on the situation.

Thirty minutes later, a buzzer sounded. The door next to the desk sergeant opened. A uniformed deputy stepped through and helped a disheveled Deirdre shuffle out. Shea almost didn't recognize her. The stylish professional had morphed into the stereotype of a junkie. Her eyes were lidded, her clothes and hair disheveled, and her skin pale and clammy. She clutched her purse to her chest as if it were a child.

"Shea? Wha...what're you doing here?" Deirdre asked in an unsteady voice.

"Picking you up."

"How...how'd you know I was here?"

"Made a few calls. How you feeling?"

"Miserable. Every cell in my body hurts."

Shea led her outside into the parking lot. "Be honest with me, Deirdre. How long you been a heroin user?"

She rubbed her face. "Never. I kept telling the cops I never used drugs. The CBD oil's the only thing I use."

"According to Savage, that stuff you're selling contains more than just CBD oil."

"It's not true. Some Big Pharma medical journal published a fake news article trying to keep consumers in the dark about the benefits of CBD oil so they can maximize profits for their own drugs."

Shea didn't want to go down that rabbit hole. "Cops saying they found you doped up with a needle in your arm. Care to explain that?"

"I can't. All I can tell you is I have never bought illegal drugs. Wouldn't even know where to buy them. I'm not that kind of woman."

"So, what happened earlier today?"

"Everything is a blur. I remember I was at home. I heard a motorcycle pull up outside. Thought it might be you or someone else in your biker gang."

"Who was it?"

"No idea. That's where my memory gets fuzzy. A guy, maybe, but I can't recall what he looked like. Next thing I know, I'm on my bathroom floor with EMTs staring down at me. Oh, and I felt horrible. I think I threw up on my carpet."

"You did."

"You were at my house?"

"Indigo called. She was worried about you moving out. I stopped by to check on you."

"They didn't want me running my business out of their house. So, I left."

"I'm told the cops showed up after someone called in a wellness check. Any idea who might've done that and why?"

"Indigo or Savage?"

"Wasn't them. When I got there, your door was busted open. Upstairs, someone had gone through your desk.

Papers and folders everywhere. I'm guessing they were looking for the dirt you have on Connelly."

To Shea's surprise, Deirdre let loose with a maniacal laugh. "Ha! He'll never find it. Got it hidden where no man will look." She paused for a moment. "Wait, d'you say my door was open?"

"Yeah, why?"

Her expression flipped from humor to dread. "Oh, my God! Did Sophie get out?"

Guilt punched Shea in the chest. "She nearly knocked me down the stairs when she ran past me out the front door."

"Oh, oh dear. I have to find her. What if the coyotes catch her?"

Then the coyotes will develop a taste for bacon, Shea thought but then felt bad about it. "Can you ride on the back of a motorcycle?"

"I...I've never ridden on one."

"It's easy. I'll loan you my helmet and jacket. Come on."

They walked through the parking lot to the bike. Shea pressed her helmet onto Deirdre's head.

"It's a little loose." Shea tightened the helmet's chinstrap. "But it's better than nothing."

"I hope it doesn't mess up my hair," Deirdre said.

Shea couldn't help bursting out laughing. "Have you seen your hair?"

When Deirdre sobbed, Shea felt immediately ashamed and hugged the woman. "It's gonna be all right. You just need a good night's rest. We'll go find Sophie and figure the rest out from there, okay?"

Shea threw a leg over the bike, wincing at her sore ribs, and helped Deirdre onto the passenger seat. "Keep your feet on the pegs and watch out for the tail pipes. They'll burn you. Hold on to me and lean the way I do."

"Ugh, I hope I don't get sick."

"Don't you dare throw up on me."

They drove back to Deirdre's condo. The front door was still ajar.

"This is so weird." Deirdre examined her shattered doorframe.

"Weird how?"

"I remember parts of what happened, and yet it's like a dream. I need to find Sophie. Sophie! Sophie, where are you, honeybunch?"

Squeals erupted from a nearby juniper bush. Sophie rushed out and leaped into Deirdre's arms, nearly knocking her over. "Oh, my precious baby, I was so worried. Did you miss your mommy?"

"We should go. Whoever did this might come back."

"You think this was Joe?"

"You said you heard a motorcycle before everything went down?"

"Yes, a loud one."

"Connelly may have the Confederate Thunder doing his dirty work."

"That biker gang?" Deirdre appeared to take a moment to let it sink in. "You think they killed Elia too?"

"I dunno. But based on my experience, they're capable of anything."

"What do I do about my door?" Deirdre stepped inside, studying the damage to the doorframe.

Shea spotted a wedge-shaped doorstop. "You got a back door, right?"

"Yeah. Why?"

"We'll use this to keep it shut from the inside." Shea closed the door and kicked the wedge into the bottom. "Won't keep anyone out, but it won't be too obvious. I'll call

Troll in the morning. She does home repairs and can fix it up better than before."

"Troll? You people have weird names. Havoc, Indigo, Savage."

"Just part of biker culture." Shea smiled.

"Must be nice having people to depend on. Elia was one of my only friends. I have clients, but I wouldn't feel comfortable asking them for favors." Deirdre sighed. "So where should I go now? A motel?"

"You can sleep on my couch for the night. Just keep the pig away from my cat, Ninja. She has claws and won't hesitate to turn Sophie here into bacon slices."

"Thanks, Shea. I'll be sure Sophie sleeps with me. I best grab my suitcases."

"Just leave the CBD oil at home."

"Okay." She started up the stairs but stopped when her gaze fixed on the bullet hole in the wall. She put Sophie down, who squealed in protest. "Did someone shoot at me? I don't remember that."

"No, uh, that was me. I mistook your pig for an intruder when I was looking for you."

"You shot at Sophie?" Again, she picked up the pig and hugged her.

"A mistake. I'll pay for the repairs."

Deirdre sighed. "No, you were just trying to help."

When they reached Shea's place, Shea told Deirdre, "Wait here a moment. I'll go get some sheets and a pillow for you."

But first, Shea crept into Annie's room. Ninja was curled up next to Annie's pillow.

"Hey, kiddo. How you feeling?" She felt the girl's forehead. She felt warm, but that could be from being snuggled with the cat.

Annie rolled over in the dark, the nightlight casting shadows that distorted her face. "Better."

"You still feel nauseous?"

"No, just tired."

"Okay, sorry I woke you. Go back to sleep." Shea walked out and closed the door then grabbed the bedding for her guest.

"Your daughter?" asked Deirdre in hushed tones.

"My niece. Her parents died a while back."

"Oh, I'm sorry."

Shea shrugged. "Tomorrow we can see if another member of the Sisterhood can put you up till this shit blows over. You may need to put your side hustle with the CBD oil on hold for the foreseeable future."

Deirdre looked pained at the suggestion. "Not ideal, but I can live with it. I appreciate all you've done to help me. You and the Sisterhood have gone above and beyond."

"You can thank me once this thing between you and Connelly's over. Get some sleep for now."

22

The next morning, Shea wandered into the living room to make breakfast. Deirdre sat up on the love seat, looking every bit the junkie she insisted she wasn't. She sniffled like she'd come down with a cold and shivered despite the blanket draped over her shoulders.

"Morning. How you feeling?"

"Awful. My body hurts all over. I'm hot one minute, freezing the next. Nose won't stop running. Must be coming down with something. A cold or the flu."

"More likely a side effect of the Naloxone. It flushes the dope outta your system. Makes you feel like shit, but it beats being dead." Shea started the coffeemaker.

"Ugh. Not so sure." Deirdre lay back down on her side and groaned.

"I got a text from Fuego, the president of the Sisterhood. She's trying to find you an alternative place to crash until this thing with Connelly is over. Also, I got ahold of Troll. She can be over at your condo to fix your door as early as eight this morning, if you want to meet her there."

"Right now, I don't want to move from this couch." Sophie snuggled in next to her.

"I gotta go to work, and Annie's heading off to soccer camp." Shea weighed the risks of leaving this woman alone at her place. "I suppose you can stay here for now. I'll give you Troll's number, and you two can decide when to meet."

Annie wandered in wearing her soccer outfit. Her face was flushed, and she looked tired. "Breakfast."

"Working on it," Shea replied and felt Annie's forehead. "You're running a fever. Maybe you should stay home today and keep Miss Deirdre and her pig company. She's not doing so hot either."

"I don't want to stay home. We're playing a scrimmage today. I feel okay."

"Really?" Shea shot her a disbelieving look.

"Well enough." Annie took a deep breath and let it out. "The cramps are better. Sorta."

"All right. But if you get to feeling worse, call me and I'll pick you up. Okay?"

Annie nodded.

AFTER SHEA ARRIVED at Iron Goddess, Terrance showed her the story about the shop on page four. Only Terrance's and her names were mentioned. Shea would've preferred to keep her details out of it, but she couldn't do anything about it now.

An hour later, Shea and Lakota began unboxing the motorcycle parts that had arrived back from the paint and chrome shop. Shea inspected each part for imperfections.

They were using a new vendor after McCullough Chrome and Paint closed its doors. Shea didn't want any complaints from the client. Women paying six figures for a custom bike tended to be picky.

Lakota inspected a ruby-red fender accented with stylized orange-and-yellow flames. "Everything looks good."

"It always amazes me how a painter can turn one of my sketches into something like this," Shea replied as she studied the fuel tank.

Monica poked her head into the service bay. "Yo, boss. Someone wants to see you up front."

"Let Terrance handle it. I'm busy."

"He only wants to talk with you. I think it's personal."

"He?" Not Julia or a member of the Sisterhood this time. Could it be Connelly or a Thunderman?

"He who?" Her gun was locked in her desk in the office.

"Wouldn't give his name. Said you'd know what it was about."

"A biker?" Shea pressed Monica.

Monica snorted. "Doubt it. Guy drove up in a Mazda Miata."

"All right. I'll be right up."

"Everything okay?" asked Lakota.

"Not the way my luck's been going." Shea picked up a dead-blow hammer from a workbench. "Once I'm done dealing with this guy, we can start reassembly."

Shea strolled down the hallway into the showroom. She found a guy in a polo shirt and jeans waiting by the sale counter. "I'm Shea Stevens. What can I help you with?"

The guy handed her a folded piece of paper and took a photo of her with his cell phone. "Shealene Eleanor Stevens, you've been served. The Superior Court of Arizona orders you to take Annie Grace Wittmann to one of the listed labs for DNA testing in pursuant to a paternity lawsuit filed by Lloyd Brzyinski. Failure to comply will be considered contempt of court, resulting in potential fines and/or jail time. Have a nice day." He turned on his heel and walked out the door.

Shea followed him. "Paternity lawsuit? What the hell you talking about? Who the fuck's Lloyd Brzyinski?"

The man climbed into his Miata, the windows rolled down. "It's all there in the subpoena."

He backed out of the lot and took off down the street, while Shea tried to make sense of all the legalese nonsense in the subpoena.

After a moment, she realized Lloyd Brzyinski must be Bryz, the fucker who'd raped Wendy. Was that why he was cozying up to Annie at the Thunder's party? Trying to decide if she was his kid? Hunter Wittmann was Annie's father. Surely Wendy or Julia would have told her otherwise.

She called Julia to get some answers.

"What the fuck's going on? I just got a subpoena ordering Annie to get a DNA paternity test. Bryz claims he's Annie's biological father."

"Shit. I suppose it's possible. Hunter and Wendy were already dating when Bryz showed up. Couple months later, she found out she was pregnant. She and I never discussed whose it was. But when Annie had dark-brown hair and eyes like Hunter's, I assumed she was his."

"So why does Bryz think he's the father?"

"Beats me. Something about the eyes, I suppose. And she's got a crooked pinky like he does."

"And no one noticed this until now?"

"No one cared."

"I'm her legal guardian now, Julia. If he thinks he's getting custody of her after he raped my sister, he's got another think coming. I'll put him in the ground first."

"Shea, I understand you're concerned. But even if he somehow gets partial custody, I'll make sure she's safe."

"Bullshit. That creepy fuck ain't getting nowhere near her. Not so long as I'm sucking air. And you can tell that to whoever you want. This is an act of war, Julia. The Sisterhood won't let this happen. Tell him to back off, or so help me, Thundermen will drop like flies."

"I'll pass along the message. But Shealene, I beg you not to do anything rash. I lost a lot of dear friends when your former prez burned down Bootlegger Bob's. You lost some friends, too, when the Thunder retaliated. I'm sure we can figure out a solution where no one gets hurt on either side."

"I'll do whatever it takes to protect Annie. Especially from a rapist like Bryz. So, if you don't want this to turn bloody, you and your old man better talk him out of this paternity suit."

"I will do what I can. I promise."

Shea hung up and dialed Dragon, explaining the situation.

"I'm truly sorry, Havoc. This is unbelievable. You said your sister was a minor when she conceived Annie, correct?"

"Yeah, she was fifteen. I thought you said we couldn't file because her godmother's testimony would be hearsay."

"We might not prove sexual assault, but maybe we can go with statutory rape. How old was the plaintiff at the time of the rape?"

"Bryz?" Shea looked at the subpoena and found a date of birth for him. "He was born April 10, 1989. Annie's twelve. She'll be thirteen in November."

"Let's see. Born in November, so assuming Annie was conceived in February of that year, the assailant would have been seventeen at the time of the assault. Not legally statutory rape."

"Shit. What can I do? I can't let him get custody, whether or not he's the father."

"Right now, you have the same rights as if you were the biological mother. I can have my investigator look into Bryz's background, see what we can pull up on him. He's a rapist and a long-time member of the Thunder. He's probably got a record. Then again, so do you."

"I also did my time. I've raised her the last four years and am an upstanding citizen and local business owner. I think that should count for something." Of course, upstanding citizen was in the eye of the beholder.

"Which all works in your favor. Comply with the subpoena and have Annie take the DNA test. We'll fight any change in custody."

"Thanks, Dragon. I don't like her having to get stuck with a needle over this prick."

"DNA tests don't require a blood sample anymore. Just a simple cheek swab. Very non-invasive."

"Thank goodness for small favors. Okay, I'll take her to get the test."

23

Rios breathed a sigh of relief while the man from Transport pushed her wheelchair through the hospital corridors, her computer bag in her lap. Deputy Georgia Clark, a uniformed officer in her early thirties, walked alongside, carrying a clear plastic bag containing Rios's paperwork, an incentive spirometer, and a couple changes of clothes.

The stitches in Rios's face had been removed, but her cheek was still sore. The surgeon promised the scarring would be minimal. Her ear was healing but would forever look like something had taken a bite out of it.

"Happy to be getting out, Detective?" Clark asked.

"I'll be happier when I'm back on duty, working cases. Sitting on mi culo with nothing to do but watch telenovelas is for the birds."

"I hear ya. I caught a bullet a couple years ago and was out for six weeks. Got so stir-crazy I was ready to beat my boyfriend with one of his own golf clubs."

As they approached the hospital's main entrance, Clark added, "I'll bring the car around."

"Thanks, Deputy," Rios said unenthusiastically.

"How long have you been a police officer?" the man from Transport asked.

"Twenty-five years."

"Really? Wow! You don't look that old."

"Thanks, I think." She didn't think of herself as old. Not yet forty-three. But since getting shot, she was feeling twice that.

The black-and-white patrol car pulled up to the curb. Clark got out and ran around to help Rios into the passenger seat.

When they were on the road, Clark asked Rios where she lived.

"I'm not going home."

"But Detective, I've got orders..."

"Screw your orders. Take me to District I."

"With all due respect, ma'am, you're on medical leave. And last I heard, SIU is still investigat—"

"Don't make me pull rank on you, Deputy. Take me to the substation. I need to confer with my colleagues."

"I just don't want to get reamed by Captain Andrews."

"If Andrews gives you any grief, tell him I ordered you to."

"Yes, ma'am."

While Clark drove, Rios called Detective Johnson. "Hey, partner. Where are we on the Wolf Ridge Arms hijacking?"

"We've compiled a list of a half dozen Wolf Ridge Arms employees who had access to shipping route information. Special Agent Powell's running background checks. Detective Tolliver and I are interviewing suspects. So far, we got a whole lotta nothing."

"I should be at the station shortly."

"Tolliver and I are on our way to re-interview Wolf Ridge's assistant director of security."

"Text me the address. I'll meet you there."

"Girl, you done lost your damn mind? You need to be home recuperating. Tolliver, Powell, and I got this handled, all right?"

"I'm done recuperating. Those pendejo bikers messed up my face a little, but the rest of me's just fine. I have to get back into the game before I lose my mind."

"Trust me, girl, I hear what you're saying. And I could use your help tracking down these missing guns. But you know Goodman would shit a brick if he knew you were working a case before SIU cleared you."

"Come on, amiga. Don't cut me out."

"Sorry, partner. Hang in there. You'll be back to the grind in no time."

Rios knew it was no use arguing with her. "Yeah, all right."

Rios caught Clark shooting her a glance. "Doesn't change a thing, Deputy. Take me to District I. I need to update one of my fellow detectives on something."

When Rios walked in the door, the desk sergeant, a burly man named Perkins, gave her a big toothy smile. "Like Lazarus from the grave. Welcome back, Detective."

"Not officially back yet, but thanks."

Rios took the elevator up to the Violent Crimes Division and was met with applause and claps on the back.

"Would you guys cut it out? You're embarrassing me."

"How you feeling, Toni?" Detective Elyssa Morris, a barrel-shaped white woman in her fifties, was walking from the adjoining break room with a mug of coffee.

"Better. Any luck confirming this Mackey character was one of the cabrones who shot me?"

"Sort of." Morris set her coffee cup down on her desk and picked up a file. "Most of the fingerprints on the recovered .38 revolver came back a match for Henry McNary, aka Mackey, so that's good. A few were from

Shealene Stevens, the woman who turned the weapon over to Bello."

"But..." Rios injected, knowing bad news was coming.

"CSU recovered nine rounds, two from your vest, three from your vehicle, and four from the nearby wall." She turned a page. "Ballistics confirmed four of the rounds were .40 caliber semi-auto, including the two in your vest. The other five likely came from a .38 special. Unfortunately, those slugs were so damaged from impacting the wall or the vehicle that they could only get a thirty-three-percent probable match to McNary's gun. We can tie him to the gun but not conclusively to the shooting."

Morris looked across the bullpen to where Bello was leading a woman with a tear-strewn face out of interview room 2. "There's my partner now. Woman's a witness in the Quinn homicide."

Bello returned from escorting the woman to the elevators. "Shouldn't you be home doing the whole Netflix-and-chill thing?"

"Screw that. I need back in the game. And I need answers. What's the latest on my shooting?" Rios and Morris followed him to his desk. "I hear Ballistics wasn't able to match the bullets."

"Afraid not."

"Bring in McNary. See what we can get out of him."

"Who's we, Kemosabe?" Morris asked. "You're on medical leave. Bello and I have it handled. We'll question McNary. If we get anything useful out of him, we'll let you know."

"In the meantime, you need to stay far away from the case," Bello added.

She hated to admit they were right, but with these high-profile cases, procedure needed to be followed to the letter. Any whiff of impropriety risked an acquittal.

"By the way," Morris said, leaning on the divider between cubicles, "Sergeant Crider in Narcotics mentioned you'd called him about one of his cases. Why is that?"

Rios's face warmed. "Wellness check turned into a possession charge. I believe the woman they arrested, Deirdre West, was set up. No priors or history of drug use. Crider confirmed she didn't have any old track marks. I asked if he could release her ROR. How'd you hear about it?"

"I bumped into Crider at the gym. He was surprised to have heard from you, considering you were in the hospital. How are you involved?"

"The woman who turned over McNary's gun contacted me. Ms. West is a friend of hers."

"Shea Stevens?" Bello furrowed his brow. "She was asking me about the Quinn case when I picked up McNary's gun. Odd how her name keeps popping up in all these cases."

Rios thought it was odd, too. "As far as I know, these cases aren't connected. McNary assaulted her. Possibly because she's in a rival biker club. Quinn was a reporter doing a story on her motorcycle shop. As for Deirdre West, I assume they're friends."

"Except she lied about ditching McNary's gun. Maybe there's more to these cases than meets the eye. Why would she call you to get West sprung from jail?"

"You two have history? Is Stevens an informant?" Bello asked.

The question made Rios uncomfortable. Maintaining a CI's anonymity was important.

"I saved her life when Edelman and Foster went off the reservation. They kidnapped her niece, killed her sister, and tried to kill her after she exposed their heroin operation. I'll grant you it's odd she's tangentially connected with all three cases, but I don't think there's much more to it."

"Uh-huh," Morris responded, looking unconvinced. "Perhaps you're right. Or maybe Stevens is more involved than you think. She could be harboring a grudge against the department after what happened to her and her family. Doesn't she run a motorcycle shop that hires drug addicts and ex-cons?"

"And she's a member of that all-girl biker gang," Bello added. "Couple of them were slinging dope laced with rat poison a few years back. I'm thinking she's worth looking at."

"I'm telling you, you're barking up the wrong tree. Shea Stevens wouldn't shoot me, and she hates drug dealers."

"In either case, Toni, go home until SIU clears you." Morris put a hand on Rios's shoulder. "Goodman catches you here, he'll wring all our necks. I can have a uni drive you home."

"I can find my own ride. But bring in McNary. My gut tells me he's the one who shot me."

"We'll bring him in."

"And I want to watch the interrogation."

Bello shook his head. "Hey! We know how to do our jobs, Rios."

"He's right, sister. Trust us to do right by you. If he's the other shooter, we'll nail him for it."

"Yeah, yeah." Rios turned to go.

24

SHEA DROVE to the Catalina Athletic Fields. After she pulled off her helmet, she could hear coaches shouting commands to players.

"Go, Wittmann! Hustle!" said one coach.

"Watch her, Langdon. Don't let it get past you," another shouted.

"Atta girl, Wittmann! Put it in there!"

Shea reached the soccer field in time to see Annie launch the ball into the goal just out of reach of the goalie. Her teammates cheered and patted her on the back.

Shea approached Annie's coach. "Excuse me. I need Annie Wittmann to come with me."

The coached looked at her. "And you are?"

"Her aunt and legal guardian."

"Well, we're in the middle of a game."

"I have to take her to a last-minute doctor's appointment." Shea didn't want to explain that Annie was going for a paternity test.

"Now? She's my best player."

His praise should have made her swell with pride. But it

only piled on the guilt. "Nevertheless, I need her to come with me. I'll have her back tomorrow morning."

"See that you do. Tomorrow's the big match. Red versus blue. Just between you and me, I've got fifty dollars riding on it." He winked at Shea and turned back to the field. "Wittmann, come in! Brady, take her place."

Annie spotted Shea, and her head dropped. She walked to the side of the field.

"Superb job, Wittmann." The coach handed her a bottle of water. "I'll see you tomorrow."

"Tomorrow?"

Shea shot her an apologetic look. "We have something to take care of."

"What?"

"I'll explain by the bike."

"Gah! This is so embarrassing!"

"You'll live. Come on."

As they approached the parking lot, Shea took a deep breath and let it out. "You remember that guy, Bryz, who was at the Thunder's welcome-home party?"

"The creepy guy with the crooked pinkie like mine?"

"Yeah. You may have been right about being related." Shea struggled with how best to explain the situation. "He thinks he's your father."

"Father? But Daddy was my father. How could Bryz be my father too?"

"Um, well, I guess we haven't had the talk yet."

"You mean the sex talk? No need. I know all about it."

Shea cocked an eyebrow. "And what do you know exactly?"

Annie blushed. "Gah! You know. Sex is how girls get pregnant."

"Where did you learn all this?"

"Aunt Shea, I'm not stupid."

Shea shook her head. "No, you're not. Clearly. Well, Gramma Julia told me a little secret."

"What secret?"

"While your mom was dating your dad, she and Bryz had a ... well, an encounter." Shea wondered how much to tell her. She didn't want to scare Annie but also didn't want to leave her vulnerable.

"She cheated on Daddy? No way!"

"From what Julia tells me, it wasn't your mom's idea. He...well, he sort of forced himself on her."

Annie looked equally horrified and disgusted. "He raped Mom? Oh, my God! And I was sitting right next to him?"

"Yeah." Shea hated that Annie knew what rape was.

"So, he's my baby daddy? Oh God, could this day get any worse?"

"I've been ordered to take you to a lab in town for a test to determine whether or not Bryz is your father."

"Like a DNA test?"

"You know about DNA too?"

"Hello! Ms. Marquez's science class."

"Damn, when I was your age, I didn't even know how to spell DNA."

"Hilarious. Not." Annie stood there, arms crossed, staring at the pavement. "What happens if it turns out he's my bio dad?"

"I don't know. Right now, I'm your legal guardian, not Bryz. If it turns out he's your biological father, he may try to get custody."

"No! You can't let that happen. Not if he raped Mom. They can't make me live with him. Please. I mean, it's my life. Don't I get a say in the matter?"

Shea put an arm around her. "Let's not get ahead of ourselves. Dragon will help us out if necessary. Okay? Let's just get this test done. Then you can hang out with me the rest of the afternoon at Iron Goddess."

Annie sighed. "Okay."

"Look at me." Shea cradled Annie's face until she met her gaze. "I won't let him or anyone else hurt you, okay? You know that. I don't care if I have to kill every Johnny-Reb-wearing motherfucker to do it, I'll keep you safe. And we ain't alone. The Sisterhood's got our back. And we got Terrance and Jake, too. It's all gonna work out. Okay?"

Annie wiped the tears from her face and hugged Shea hard. "Thanks, Aunt Shea. I love you."

"Love you, too, Doodlebug."

They drove to Canyon State Labs, located in one of the medical offices near Monterosa Medical Center.

Shea approached the counter, showing the paperwork she'd been given. "Annie Wittmann here for this paternity test."

The guy behind the counter, a balding man with wire-rimmed glasses, examined the paper and pulled up the information on his computer. "Okay, just fill out this information, and we will call you."

He handed her a clipboard with several sheets of paper. On the first sheet, it asked for contact information and full medical history.

"Why do you need all this information? This is just a DNA test."

"Sorry. ma'am. Standard procedure. Also, there will be a fifty-dollar copay."

"What? I have to pay for this shit?" A vein throbbed in her temple.

"Ma'am, please. No profanity in front of the child."

"Trust me, she's said worse."

"And I wonder where she learned it."

"I don't understand why I have to pay for this test. We

don't want it. And we don't want this asshole who's claiming to be Annie's father in our lives. If he wants to prove he's the father, he can pay for it."

"I'm sorry, but that's not how this works. If you refuse to pay, we can't administer the test. We will have to report back to the court that the defendant was noncompliant."

"Oh, for fuck's sake. Fine." Shea pulled a fifty-dollar bill out of her wallet and tossed it on the counter. "There."

"We can't accept any denominations over a twenty-dollar bill."

"Are you fucking kidding me? Now who's being fucking noncompliant. This is legal tender. I'm not asking for change. You want to get paid? Here I am paying. You take this or nothing. And if you report us as noncompliant, I'll report you as a goddamn liar."

The guy behind the counter glared at her, took the fifty, and placed it in the drawer in front of him. "Please fill out the forms."

"Whatever." Shea sat down next to where Annie was reading a *National Geographic*.

"What was that all about?"

"The guy at the counter has a serious medical problem."

"What kind of problem?"

"He has an enormous stick stuck up his butt."

Annie laughed, and the sound of it eased Shea's anger and frustration.

After Shea returned the completed forms, a female lab tech wearing scrubs decorated with cartoon cats called Shea and Annie back to an examination room.

"I like your shirt," Annie said when the woman opened the packet.

"Thanks, I like yours. You play soccer?" The nurse

opened a packet that contained four long cotton-tipped swabs.

"I've been going to soccer camp this week. Until I had to come here."

"This won't take long at all. Just open your mouth. I'm going to swab your cheeks. Twice on each side. Okay?"

Annie opened wide. The nurse swabbed the insides of her cheeks. "All done. Now you have a good rest of your day, okay, Annie? Have fun at soccer camp."

"Thanks."

As they were walking out of the medical office, Shea's phone rang. It was Rios. Shea's pulse quickened as she wondered if this would be another request to go out to dinner.

"Detective," Shea said as coolly as she could. "If you're still calling about that dinner date, it'll have to wait. I have other priorities."

"Not about dinner. I was curious why you asked Detective Bello about the Elia Quinn investigation."

"Quinn asked me to help Deirdre West with this shit going on between her and Senator Connelly. She was working on a story about Connelly forcing Deirdre to get an abortion after he got her pregnant."

"And you think Connelly had Quinn killed?"

Shea noticed Annie growing restless, her face a portrait of impatience. Shea unlocked the helmets from the side of the motorcycle and handed the smaller one to Annie. "What do I know? I just build motorcycles for a living. You're the cop."

"Don't be coy, Shea. If you know something about Quinn's death, you need to contact Detectives Bello and Morris. They're working the case."

"All I know is what I told you. The Athena Sisterhood is protecting Ms. West."

"She needs to talk to Bello and Morris."

"And then what happens? I'll tell you what happens. Nothing. Connelly will shut it down, and he'll try again to hurt her, possibly kill her to keep the story quiet. You want to know who killed Quinn, find out who requested the wellness check on West."

Silence filled the line. "Anything else, Rios? I gotta go."

"Anything else you're not telling me?"

"Like what?"

"I don't know. But your ties to three ongoing cases are suspicious."

"I'm not tied to anything. Only reason Mackey came after me was because he figured out I ratted out the Thunder. Quinn and West reached out to me only because of my ties to the Sisterhood, which, as you recall, I'm only a part of because you forced me to be. I'm just trying to build motorcycles, raise my niece, and keep a woman safe from an asshole senator who everyone else bows and scrapes to."

Shea hung up. "You ready to roll?"

Annie nodded without a word.

25

When they reached Iron Goddess, Shea set Annie up at her desk to use her computer and noticed Deirdre had called twice and left a voicemail.

"Shea...Shea, please call me when you get this." Deirdre sounded distraught. Possibly crazed.

Shea returned the call, but after five rings, it went to voicemail. "Hey, Deirdre. It's Shea returning your call."

She debated whether to run home and check on her. But only a few people in the Sisterhood knew where Deirdre was. Rios might have guessed, but Shea didn't think the detective would have disclosed it to anyone, even if she was a cop. She decided instead to focus on getting the Hughes bike ready until Deirdre called back.

In the service bay, Lakota had reassembled the painted and chromed parts and was working with Vince to mount the engine. Shea began working on the wiring.

By midafternoon, they were mounting the gauges when Monica's voice came over the loudspeakers. "Shea Stevens, you're needed up front."

"Oh, for fuck's sake. What now?"

"You're just Miss Popularity today," Lakota said with a grin.

"Lucky me." Shea wiped her hands on a rag and walked into the showroom. Deirdre stood unsteadily by the front sales counter, holding Sophie Bacon over her shoulder like an infant. She looked more miserable than she had that morning. Fever sweat glistened on her pallid face. Her eyes were swollen and red. Did the effects of Naloxone last this long? Or was something else going on?

Shea ushered her and the pig over to the customer waiting area. Deirdre set Sophie down on a chair next to her. When Sophie noticed Shea, she squealed frantically until Deirdre picked her up again, patting her back.

"What's wrong?" Shea asked. "Why aren't you at my place?"

"He killed her, Shea. He fucking killed her. First Elia and now her. How could Joe do that?"

"Who's her?"

"My mother. She...she's dead." Her voice was choked with emotion.

"Aw, fuck. When?"

"Last night."

"While Moon Cat was watching over her?"

"Moon Cat left at eight o'clock when visiting hours ended. They found my mother dead around nine. The staff claims she had a stroke, but that's impossible. She was on blood thinners. Joe did this to her. He killed Elia, got me arrested, and now he's killed my mother! He killed her, Shea." Her voice was now a screech. She looked and sounded frantic. The pig grew restless in her arms.

"Okay, okay, just calm down." Shea handed her a tissue from a box on a nearby table. "How do you know she didn't have a stroke? I mean, it happens. You yourself said she didn't have long to live."

"You think I'm crazy. Don't you?" Tears streamed down Deirdre's face.

Shea studied the woman's disheveled appearance, recalling the events of the past few days. The woman sold and used CBD oil that, at least according to Savage, contained THC and pseudoephedrine.

Was Deirdre really the target of Connelly's malice? Or was she a junkie in the throes of addiction? Maybe that was why she lost her job. Maybe the stories of slashed tires and threatening notes were nothing more than paranoid fantasies. Maybe her mother had died of natural causes, but Deirdre simply couldn't accept one more major loss.

"I don't think you're crazy, just...I don't know. To be honest, you remind me of my sister when she was jonesing for a fix. She had a problem with oxy."

Deirdre erupted into loud, gulping sobs.

Shea immediately felt guilty over the accusation. "Sorry, that was rude. You're grieving over your mom. Naturally, you're not looking your best. I got pretty messed up after my mom died." Shea sighed. "Still, I don't get why Connelly would kill your mother if she was already dying."

"To take away what little time we had left. Joe knew how close we were." Deirdre blew her nose on the tissue and put Sophie down to reach for another. After a moment, her back straightened. "But I won't back off. No, ma'am. I won't let him win. I've been talking to Drew Chambers, Elia's editor. He's still willing to publish my story. If not for me, then to honor Elia."

"I'm sorry we couldn't keep your mother safe. Did you call the police?"

"After getting arrested last night, I'm afraid to. Their loyalty is to Joe, not me."

"I hear what you're saying. Let me see what I can find

out. What was your mother's name, and where was she staying?"

"Her name is … *was* Madelyn West. She was a resident at Kings Ridge Assisted Living. They're on Doc Holliday Road, just north of Antelope Canyon Drive in Ironwood Valley."

"I'll check it out. See what I can get from the staff."

Deirdre smiled through the tears. "Thank you, Shea. That means so much."

"Did you lock up my house before you left?"

"Yes."

"I think I have a spare key in my desk to let you back inside."

Deirdre waved her off. "No need. I'll just go back to my place. Troll messaged me she'd repaired my door. Even rekeyed the locks and left a set with the condo office."

"Deirdre, that may not be the best idea. Connelly could have someone watching your place. You're welcome to stay with me until…until you're no longer in danger. Whenever that will be."

"Maybe you're right. But the proof I have of the abortion is at my place. I'll need to provide a copy to Mr. Chambers at the paper. He won't publish without it."

Shea got an idea. "Wait here, okay?"

Shea rushed to her desk in the office. From the middle drawer, she took out an old burner phone she used occasionally.

Back in the customer waiting area, she handed the burner to Deirdre. "For now, turn your other phone off. Use this instead. It already has my phone number programmed in it and should have a couple hours' worth of minutes on it."

"Why do I need this?"

"Connelly is buddy-buddy with the cops. I don't know if

he'd use them to track you, but let's not put anything past him. And don't use your credit cards anywhere. It's one more way he can track you. Do you need any cash?"

"I have some on me. You think of everything."

"Not everything. Just go back to my house for now. After I look into your mother's death, I can follow you back to your condo to pick up the proof you got against Connelly and anything else you need." Shea walked her to the front door of the shop. "Don't call anyone unless it's an emergency. Don't let anyone else know where you are. Agreed?"

"Agreed. I hate being a burden."

"You're not a burden. Just a woman who's dealing with a lotta bullshit right now. You'll get through it."

Shea watched her drive off and strolled back to the office. Guilt and failure hung heavy on her shoulders. Had they failed to protect Deirdre's mother? Or did she simply die of a stroke? Shea needed answers.

Terrance and Annie were chatting about soccer and how well Phoenix Rising was doing this season.

"Hey, T, you mind looking after Annie a little while? I got something to take care of."

"Again? That custom bike is due to be delivered tomorrow. We incur penalties if we miss the deadline."

"Vince and Lakota got it under control. It'll be ready by end of day tomorrow. I just have something to look into. It's important."

"Fine. Do what you gotta do. Annie'll keep me company."

"When are you coming back?" Annie asked. Concern was written across her face.

"Shouldn't take long."

"Is this about the woman who stayed with us last night?"

Shea was grateful Annie didn't mention the woman by

name. Not that Terrance would do anything to harm her, but it was club business and on a need-to-know basis. "Yeah, her mom died last night."

"Was she murdered?"

"Murder?" Terrance looked at Annie then at Shea. "What's going on, sister girl? Is this about that thing with Senator Connelly?"

"Yeah. The woman the Sisterhood is protecting from Connelly. Her mom died last night at an assisted living facility. I just need to make sure nothing hinky happened."

"Don't let this blow back on the shop. That's all I ask."

"It won't, I promise. I'll be back shortly."

26

AFTER PULLING ON HER JACKET, her Sisterhood cut, and her helmet, Shea looked up the address of Kings Ridge Assisted Living.

Under the glare of the late-afternoon sun, she rode out of Sycamore Springs then picked up Highway 64 east before hopping on I-17 north to the Ironwood Valley exit. Three miles after she got off the highway, traffic came to a standstill, stretching for as far as she could see into the town of Ironwood Valley.

"What the hell?" she said under her breath while the sun beat down on her.

She pulled onto the shoulder and sailed past the long line of vehicles, avoiding any debris that might puncture a tire. Eventually, she reached the source of the tie-up, a collision between two out-of-state vehicles. Three police cruisers with blue lights blazing had all but one lane closed off.

"Tourists," Shea muttered while she nimbly wove between a police cruiser and the traffic, eliciting shouts of protest from the uniformed officers. She didn't care. She had shit to take care of. Dealing with someone else's reckless driving didn't fit into her schedule.

Kings Ridge Assisted Living comprised a one-story brick building with corridors of rooms extending from either side of the front entrance. It reminded her in some ways of a funeral home. The elevator music playing when she marched through the automatic glass doors did nothing to dissuade her of this impression. It took her a moment to realize the song playing was an easy-listening version of Ozzy Osbourne's "Crazy Train."

She approached the main desk, where a fragrant bouquet of tiger lilies and sunflowers sat in one corner. A woman with long dark hair and wearing cartoon cactus scrubs glanced up from behind the desk and smiled. Her name tag read Leslie Drinkwater. "Good afternoon. Can I help you?"

"I'm a friend of Deirdre West's. I understand her mother, Madelyn West, died last night."

A sad smile crossed Leslie's face. "Oh, yes. Miss Madelyn. Sweet lady. Always full of laughter. We'll miss her."

"How did she die?"

"I'm afraid we're only allowed to give that information to family."

"Deirdre was told her mother died of a stroke."

Leslie appeared conflicted. "Yes."

"Deirdre believes somebody murdered her."

"I was the one who spoke with Miss Madelyn's daughter. I've never seen someone look so devastated. She and her mom were close."

Shea recalled her conversation with Deirdre. "Ms. West was on blood thinners, right?"

"I'm sorry, I'm not allowed to give out medical information."

"What's it matter if she's dead?"

"HIPAA applies for fifty years after a person's death."

"So, there's no chance she was murdered?"

"Why would anyone hurt such a sweet woman? She was an absolute joy to be around. Besides, she was dying anyway. It wouldn't make sense to kill her."

"Did she have any visitors yesterday?"

"Visitors? Well, a friend of her daughter's was here. Wore a leather vest like yours. Said she was here to keep Miss Madelyn company. You don't think *she* did anything to her, do you?"

"No. Anyone else besides the woman in the biker vest?"

"Not that I saw. I left at five o'clock. Visiting hours end at eight in the evening." Leslie pulled down a clipboard. "I don't see where she had any visitors after I left."

"Huh." Maybe Deirdre was paranoid. Understandable after all she'd been through. Her gaze drifted to the flowers.

Leslie flipped to another page. "She had a late delivery. Flowers. Came in quarter after eight."

"Flowers? These flowers here?" Shea pointed to the vase of tiger lilies and sunflowers.

"Must be. I don't remember seeing them yesterday."

Shea examined the bouquet closely. There was a tag from Patrick's Foods, a statewide supermarket chain. "Since when does Patrick's deliver flowers?"

"Patrick's? Well, I don't know. According to the sign-in sheet, the delivery person's name was Luca Brasi."

"Shit." A chill ran down Shea's spine. Maybe Deirdre wasn't paranoid after all.

"Why does that name sound familiar?" Leslie scrunched her nose in thought.

"Luca Brasi was an enforcer in *The Godfather*," Shea replied. "An assassin. Whoever delivered these was trying to send a message."

Leslie's eyes went wide. "Seriously?"

"Was there a card with it?" Shea searched among the orange and yellow blossoms but didn't see an envelope or card. "Who was on duty when these were delivered?"

"Angel was working last night. He might have seen the delivery person." Leslie picked up the phone and called for her coworker over the intercom. A few minutes later, a slender man with a goatee approached. He wore pale-blue scrubs.

"You called?"

"Can you describe the man who delivered the flowers?" Leslie asked him.

"I didn't notice. White guy, maybe. Nothing that stood out."

"Clean-shaven? Scruffy?" Shea pressed. "Do you remember what he was wearing?"

"No, sorry."

Shea glanced around the area and noticed a camera mounted near the ceiling. "Could I review the surveillance recording?"

"Are you a police officer?" asked Angel.

"No. But this is suspicious. The guy signed in as Luca Brasi."

"From *The Godfather*?"

"Exactly. In the past few days, someone murdered a friend of Deirdre's and attacked Deirdre herself. Then last night, her mother dies an hour after getting flowers from a guy who signed in as a mafia assassin. Am I the only one who finds this fishy? This killer could come back to tie up loose ends, if you get my drift."

"But Miss Madelyn died of a stroke. Doctor Ferguson said." Leslie's voice rippled with uncertainty.

Shea shrugged and walked back toward the front

entrance. "Believe what you want. But if this guy comes back to kill witnesses..."

"Wait!" Leslie sounded almost frantic.

Shea turned. "Yes?"

"You really think she was murdered?" Leslie's tan skin had turned pale.

"Leslie," Angel admonished, "she's trying to frighten you."

Shea turned to Angel. "Did you see the flower delivery guy leave?"

"Of course I did. I mean, he must have left. We were dealing with a situation in another room. Things were a little crazy."

"And how often are flowers delivered so late?"

Now even Angel appeared uncertain. "Well..."

"Just let me take a peek at the surveillance footage. If I'm wrong and the delivery guy left right away, no harm, no foul."

"But we can only let police in the security room."

"Look, I work with the Cortes County Sheriff's Office from time to time as a consultant. Should I call Detective Toni Rios in the Violent Crimes Division and tell her to stop what she's doing and come down here?"

The two employees looked at each other. "I guess it's okay if you take a quick peek. Let me call Alec. She's in charge of security."

Leslie paged the security guard. Moments later, a burly woman in a security uniform with a scowl on her face approached.

"Alec, this woman is a consultant for the sheriff's office. She needs to check the surveillance footage from last night."

Alec glared at Shea. "You got a warrant?"

"I'm investigating a string of suspicious deaths. I believe Madelyn West was murdered."

"Fine. Show me a badge and a warrant, and I'll show you whatever footage you want."

"But Alec, what if the killer comes back looking to...you know, clean up loose ends?"

"Clean up loose ends? Leslie, you been reading too many of dem crime novels." She pointed to the door marked Security. "Nobody goes in that room without my permission, 'less they have a badge and a warrant."

"Come on, Alec," said Shea, trying to establish a personal connection to the bristly security guard. "I need to confirm who delivered flowers to Ms. West. Then I'm out of here."

"Lady, you have five minutes to leave 'fore I call the police and report you for trespassing."

"Sorry," Leslie said to Shea, looking like a whipped puppy.

Shea sighed. No way she was getting past this woman.

"Fine. It's your funeral."

Shea turned on her heel and marched out of the facility. She would have preferred to identify whoever delivered the flowers, but it looked as if Deirdre's suspicions had substance.

In the parking lot, Shea saw that Deirdre had texted her.

I'm at the Hacienda Motel. Room 167. Don't want to be burden, but scared to go to condo alone. Meet me here to go pick up proof of abortion at my place. Thanks. -D

Shea decided to try one more thing before calling her back. She pulled a business card from her wallet.

"Detective Bello," said a familiar voice from the other end of the line.

"I'm hoping I can trust you."

"Who is this?"

"Shea Stevens."

"How can I help you, Ms. Stevens?" His tone sounded curt.

"I believe someone else has been murdered. It may be connected to Elia Quinn's death."

"Who was murdered?"

"Madelyn West. Deirdre West's mother. She died at Kings Ridge Assisted Living last night. Everyone thinks it was natural causes, but Deirdre suspects murder, and I agree with her."

"Any evidence to support this claim?"

"Someone delivered flowers to her an hour before she died. But the flowers were from Patrick's Foods. They don't deliver. And whoever dropped them off signed in as Luca Brasi."

"An old lady dies, and your evidence of murder is a bunch of flowers and a delivery guy with a *Godfather* fetish? Ms. Stevens, with all due respect, that sounds awful thin."

"Look, Detective, I gave you the gun Mackey used to shoot Toni, er, Detective Rios. I'm asking for a favor. Senator Connelly is trying to keep Deirdre West from going public about an abortion he forced her to have. I believe he murdered Elia Quinn. Then he broke into Ms. West's home and made it look as if she'd overdosed on heroin. Now he's murdered her mother."

"You think Senator Connelly killed these women?"

"Or had them killed."

"That's a serious allegation, Ms. Stevens. And one that makes no sense. If this so-called killer wanted to silence Ms. West, why didn't he murder her instead of her mother?"

"How the hell should I know?"

"Senator Connelly is a respected elected official. We

need more than conspiracy theories and speculation to go after him."

"So, you're going to bury it?"

"No, I'm not. I'm interested in arresting Ms. Quinn's killer. And if someone murdered Deirdre West's mother, as you claim, I'd be interested in prosecuting them as well. Tell you what. Come down to the substation and share what you know with my partner and me. We also need to speak to Ms. West, if you know how to reach her."

Shea didn't want to talk to the cops any more than she had to. And she sure as hell wasn't going to risk Deirdre's safety by giving this bozo her location. "Check the surveillance recording for the Kings Ridge Assisted Living Facility where her mother was staying. I'll bet you a box of doughnuts it shows a fake flower delivery guy going into the woman's room and killing her."

"I'd need a warrant, and for that, I'll need probable cause. Do us both a favor. Come down to the sheriff's office and make a formal statement. With that, I'll put together the affidavit myself. Deal?"

This was one of the many reasons she hated cops. Always the runaround, always some excuse to delay instead of doing what needed to be done. "I was wrong to trust you. Just forget it. I'll handle this myself."

"Ms. Stevens, don't do anything—"

Shea hung up. It was almost six o'clock. The shop would close soon. She needed to pick up Annie and go home. But first she needed to check in with Deirdre.

The call to the burner phone went straight to voicemail. Shea was sure she had turned it on before giving it to Deirdre. Maybe she'd turned it off. Or maybe something was wrong.

Deirdre's text said she was staying at the Hacienda Motel, room 167. Shea would stop by and then escort her back to the condo. She messaged Terrance that her errand was taking longer than expected and to take Annie home with him. She'd pick her up in a little while.

She zipped up her jacket, pulled on her helmet, and rode west to the Hacienda Motel.

27

Twenty minutes later, Shea found the Hacienda Motel between a Denny's restaurant and a Walgreens pharmacy. It was nicer and smaller than the national chains. The landscaping had a more personal style. More flowers, fewer overly manicured shrubs. The lot was three-quarters full, mostly tourists escaping Phoenix's more intense summer weather.

She parked around the back of the motel, knocked on the door to Deirdre's room, and waited. And waited. After a minute, she knocked harder.

"Deirdre, open up. It's Shea."

Still no response.

Shea ticked through the possibilities. Maybe she was taking a bath, listening to music on earbuds. Maybe she was taking a serious shit. Maybe her withdrawal from the heroin had gotten the best of her and she'd scored some dope and gotten loaded.

But if Deirdre was here, wouldn't the pig make some noise when Shea knocked on the door? That damned beast was always squealing.

She pulled her cell out and called the burner phone. It again went straight to voicemail. She dialed Deirdre's cell phone. Shea could hear it ringing inside the room.

"Shit."

The door had a traditional keyed lock rather than an electromagnetic one many chain motels used these days. She glanced around the parking lot. With no one in sight, she pulled out a narrow leather case and retrieved a lock pick and an L-shaped tensioner. Soon the tumblers aligned, the cylinder turned, and the door opened. The sharp smell of blood sent a wave of fear through her.

Shea drew her pistol and flicked on the light switch with her elbow. The comforter on the nearest queen bed was rumpled, but the bed didn't appear to have been slept in. A suitcase lay open on the other bed next to Deirdre's regular cell phone, the display still on from Shea's recent call. Clothes, papers, and belongings were scattered everywhere. The lamp on the nightstand was overturned, its shade bashed in. On the floor near the smashed flat-screen TV, a pizza box from Gino's gaped open. A small veggie lover's.

Just outside the bathroom, Sophie Bacon lay motionless in a puddle of blood soaking into the carpet. Two gunshot wounds to the swine's head, one in the back. Shea's gorge rose at the sight of the dead pig, and she barely kept from throwing up.

Shea checked the bathroom, the closet, and under the beds. No sign of Deirdre or the burner phone Shea had given her.

"Motherfucker."

She knew she should call 9-1-1. And at one time, she might have. But she was done trusting the cops. She called Fuego instead.

"Hola, VP. What's up?"

Shea filled her in on the situation.

"They killed her pig? What the fuck? You think they killed her too?"

Shea's eyes wandered over to the deceased emotional support animal. "Beats me. The situation's fucked up."

"You call the cops?"

"Hell no. Connelly's close with Sheriff Buzzkill. I don't trust them."

"Mierda. You need backup?"

Shea didn't want to put anyone else at risk, but she felt out of her depth. "I won't say no."

"Sit tight, hermana. I'll make some calls and be there pronto."

"Gracias, Fuego."

"De nada."

Shea sat on the bed, staring at the dead pig. Her chest constricted and throbbed, making it difficult to breathe. All her snarky thoughts about Deirdre's emotional support animal came flooding back in waves of shame. Pigs had never been anything but a food source. Until now. Tears stung her eyes. She wiped her face with the inside of her arm. "Goddamn pig."

Outside, the rumble of motorcycle engines approached and went silent. Fuego had arrived sooner than expected. Shea opened the door and stepped out into the growing gloom.

Two motorcycles sat a few rows away in the parking lot, though it was hard to make out details at this distance. A streetlight on the far side of the lot flickered on in time to reveal a biker raising a gun in her direction. Shea ducked behind a parked car a split second before a barrage of bullets peppered the motel room door.

"Fuck!" she cursed under her breath.

Shea popped up to return fire then duck-walked along the sidewalk, using cars for cover. Glass from exploding windshields rained down on her. When she reached the building's corner, she rose and fired off several more rounds.

Only one of her assailants was visible, and he was too far away for an accurate shot. He looked like Mackey, but she couldn't be sure. She wasn't sticking around long enough to confirm.

Shea took off running, trusting to luck and the growing darkness to protect her. When she reached a six-foot chain-link fence, she made a running leap with enough momentum to swing her legs over and land on the other side. As bullets flew past, she raced on at full speed, using what cover she could find.

After passing behind the pharmacy, a bank, and a Kwik Mart, Shea realized the gunfire had stopped. She hunkered down behind the far side of a liquor store, her heart thundering in her chest, her lungs burning for air. The Glock's slide was locked back. She was out of ammo. She had more, but it was in the top case on the back of her bike.

As she stood up, she caught movement out of the corner of her eye. Someone plowed into her like a charging rhino, slamming her onto the ground. Shea rolled, punching and kicking with all her strength. Her attacker did the same. His bearded face was familiar. She glimpsed a Johnny Reb tattoo on his bicep while they grappled and exchanged blows.

A knife appeared in her attacker's hand, its blade flashing toward her. Shea raised her left arm to protect her throat an instant before the blade sliced through her leather jacket and bit into her flesh.

The knife came at her again, but she grabbed the guy's

arms and twisted. He held onto the knife and tried to head-butt her until another gunshot rang out. When he raised his head toward the shooter, Shea wrestled the knife from him and was about to stab him, but he took off running into the dark.

Shea rolled to her feet when two more gunshots shattered the night. Fuego rushed toward her, gun pointed in the direction where the Thunderman had disappeared.

"You okay, homita?"

Shea's forearm felt like it was on fire. She winced when she pulled off her jacket. She pressed her hand against her arm, which was slick with blood.

"Hold still." Fuego wrapped a bandana around the wound.

"Ugh. Fuck, that hurts," Shea said through gritted teeth.

"Don't suppose you want me to call 9-1-1, eh?"

"Not really." The words were barely out of her mouth when the wail of sirens made the question irrelevant. "You hit him? The asshole who attacked me?"

"No se." Fuego studied Shea's arm. "Blood's still seeping through. I better get Savage down here and have a look at it."

"Yeah, okay."

While Fuego placed the call, Shea glanced back toward the motel. Deirdre's pig was dead. But Deirdre wasn't in the room. Was she still alive? Was she on the run? Had someone kidnapped her? Shea hadn't noticed whether her car was in the lot.

Fuego hung up. "She and Indigo'll be here in ten. You recognize the vato who attacked you?"

"Seemed familiar, but don't know his name. Had a Johnny Reb inked on his arm. Other guy may have been Mackey. All happened so fast." She wiped the Thunderman's blade on her jeans, folded it, and stuffed it in her pocket.

"What the hell are the Thundermen doing here? And why attack you? We had a truce."

"Dunno. Maybe they found out I turned over Mackey's gun and tracked me down somehow. How'd you find me?"

"Saw you run off when I pulled behind the motel. Raced down the street to intercept."

"Lucky you did."

Fuego helped her to her feet and led her to the front of the liquor store, where Fuego's Kawasaki Vulcan sat under the glow of the store's outdoor lights. Blood stained Shea's shirt, jeans, and jacket.

"Mierda, Havoc. That cabrón got you good."

"Coulda been worse. He was going for my throat."

While they waited for Savage and Indigo, several customers coming into the liquor store stopped and asked if they were okay. The clerk came out shortly thereafter. Fuego thanked them but told them that help was coming.

Savage and Indigo arrived in their Jeep. Savage removed the bandana, which stuck to the wound, causing it to start to bleed again. Savage rewrapped it, tighter this time, making Shea choke off a cry of pain.

"Havoc, this needs stitches."

"Not going to a hospital." Shea gave Savage a "don't argue with me" glare.

Savage sighed. "All right, VP. I suppose I can patch you up at my place."

They helped Shea into the back of the Jeep.

"Where's your bike?" asked Indigo.

"Back of the Hacienda Motel." Shea pointed with her uninjured arm in the direction she'd come.

"Got your keys?"

Shea fumbled in her pocket until she came up with the keys to her bike.

Indigo took them, hopped into the front passenger seat, and turned to her wife. "Drop me off next to Havoc's bike. I'll drive it home."

"Roger that."

Fuego threw a leg over her bike and followed them back to the motel, but the rear lot was blocked off by police vehicles. Their flashing lights washed the scene in alternating shades of blue and red.

"Well, that's not gonna work." Savage stated. "Unless you wanna spend the next few hours explaining to the boys in blue what happened."

"Shit," Shea muttered through gritted teeth.

She had done nothing wrong except defend herself from the Thundermen. But her fingerprints were in the motel room with the dead pig, the one with the bullet-riddled door. Her motorcycle was in the lot. Wouldn't take them long to zero in on her as a person of interest. But she wasn't in the mood to deal with all that right now.

"Let's get outta here," Shea said, the defeat heavy in her voice.

"Hold up." Indigo jingled Shea's keys. "I can get the bike."

Shea shook her head. "Not worth the risk."

"I'm the police liaison for the Lambda Resource Center. I know a lot of the deputies assigned to this area. I can get your bike."

Shea wasn't so sure. "Watch your back, sister."

"See you ladies back home." Her black-and-sapphire-blue braids swung while she dashed out of the Jeep.

"I love that woman." Savage pulled around the front of the motel, out of eyeshot of the cops who were scouring the back lot. "But sometimes I wonder if she's lost all sense."

They waited for what felt like hours but was closer to twenty minutes. Finally, Indigo cruised around the building and gave them a thumbs-up.

"Let's get outta here," Shea said from the back of the Jeep.

"You got it, VP." Savage pulled out of the lot with Fuego and Indigo following behind them.

28

AT SAVAGE and Indigo's house, Shea sat on the toilet in the master bathroom while Savage examined the cut on Shea's left forearm. Indigo and Fuego talked in the living room, though the pain made it hard for Shea to make out what they were saying.

"It's a clean laceration, but deep. Could be muscle or nerve damage. You sure you don't want to go to the ER, have a surgeon look at it?"

Shea flexed her fingers and swallowed a scream while fire ran the length of her arm. "No. Still got feeling. And movement. Don't need to be spending the next several hours having some doc poking at me."

"Okay, I'm closing the wound with Dermabond, basically a medical-grade superglue. Should hold, but won't fix any damaged nerves or muscles."

"Got anything for the pain?"

"Ibuprofen, acetaminophen, or aspirin. Or your choice of beer, bourbon, or rum. What's your pleasure?"

"Nothing with a little more kick?"

Savage offered a sympathetic smile and bandaged the

wound. "Sorry, no. They don't give us paramedics any of the fun drugs."

"Bourbon's fine."

After Savage treated and dressed the wound, they joined Indigo and Fuego in the living room.

"Cops give you any hassle?" Shea asked Indigo.

"No. Deputy Cruz was in charge of the scene at the moment. He's cool. Asked if I knew anything about the shootout or anyone staying at the motel. I told him I'd just eaten at Denny's next door and had parked behind the motel because the restaurant's lot was full. He seemed to buy it."

Savage brought Shea a tumbler of bourbon. Shea took a sip. Smoky, not too much of a burn. She resisted the urge to chug it.

"Those pendejos violated our truce," Fuego said. "I've left a message for One-Shot to call me and make this right, so this situation no se va a la chingada."

"Where's Deirdre?" Indigo asked.

Shea shook her head. "Best guess, Connelly's got her."

"You think that hijo de puta's involved in this?" Fuego asked.

"I think he or his cronies tracked Deirdre to the motel somehow. Killed her pig. No doubt trying to get rid of the proof they had an affair and an abortion."

"What do we do now?" Savage looked at Shea then Fuego.

"Dunno. I'm hurt too much to think right now." Shea glanced at her watch and remembered Annie. "Fuck! I gotta pick up my niece from Terrance's."

"You okay to drive, chica?" Fuego asked.

"Long as no one else tries to stab or shoot me."

Fuego put a hand on her arm. "I'll follow you. I'm

headed that direction anyway. I'd hate to see something else happen to you tonight."

"Thanks, Prez."

Shea thanked everyone and drove off with Fuego at her four o'clock.

Every time she pulled the clutch to shift gears, pain lanced up her arm. Once they were on the open road, things settled down. She tried to make sense of the night's events, but the pain turned everything into a jumble. Had Mackey and the other Thunderman followed her to the motel? Surely, she would have noticed. No, she remembered hearing the motorcycles pull up right before she walked out of the motel room. Were the Thundermen working with Connelly?

When they drew close to Terrance's neighborhood, Fuego pulled ahead of Shea, waved, and drove off. Shea turned into the neighborhood and was soon knocking on Terrance's front door. His husband, Jake, opened the door and gasped. "Oh my! Is that blood all over you? What happened?"

Shea shuffled in. "Long story." She followed him to the living room, where Annie, Terrance, and his twenty-year-old son, Elon, were watching television.

Terrance's eyes nearly bugged out of his head. "Jeez, is that your blood or someone else's?"

"Aunt Shea?" Annie sat up on the love seat.

"I'm okay. Just a minor cut on my arm."

Terrance approached her and met her gaze. "What's going on, sister girl? This got to do with that woman you've been protecting?"

"Yeah, she's missing."

"What about Sophie?" Annie asked.

"Who's Sophie?" Jake asked.

"Her pet pig. Is Sophie Bacon okay, Aunt Shea?"

Shea felt a tightness in her chest. "'Fraid not, kiddo. Sophie's in hog heaven. I mean..."

"She's dead? Why?" A tear streamed down Annie's face.

"I don't know." Shea gingerly wrapped her good arm around her. "Come on. It's been a rough day. Let's head home and get some sleep. You got your big game at soccer camp tomorrow."

"I don't feel like going to soccer camp tomorrow."

Shea pulled away and looked at her. "Cramps again?"

Annie nodded and wiped the tears from her face.

"She was running a low fever earlier, too," Jake added. "We gave her two acetaminophen. Hope you don't mind."

"You feel better?" Shea asked.

"A little."

"Did, uh, you-know-what start?"

"No."

"Huh." Shea felt her forehead. It was warm. "Hold on a sec."

She pulled out her phone and called Savage.

"Havoc? What's wrong? Did the wound reopen?"

"No, but I need to know what the symptoms for appendicitis are?"

"Generally, pain in the lower-right abdomen, but sometimes it can be elsewhere. Why?"

"Annie's had cramps the past few days. I thought she was getting her first period, but it hasn't started yet. Wanted to make sure I wasn't missing something more serious."

"Any other symptoms?"

"Low fever, nausea, constipation."

"Could be PMS. I had it bad for more than a week before my first period. Every woman's different. Then again, it could be appendicitis. Do this. Press gently on her lower-right abdomen, then release. If it's appendicitis, it should be painful."

"Let me press your belly." Shea did and released. Annie winced a little but didn't otherwise react.

"That hurt?"

"A little."

"What do you think?" Shea asked Savage.

"Might be helpful to take her to the ER for a CT scan. Appendicitis can turn deadly fast. Better safe than sorry."

"Shit. All right. Thanks, Savage."

"How's the arm?"

"Hurts, but still works. Thanks for the patch-up job."

"Happy to help. Let me know how things turn out."

Shea hung up. "Guess we're taking you to the ER. Just to make sure it's not something serious."

"Sister girl, let us drive you," said Terrance. "You look like death warmed over. You shouldn't be driving."

"What a coincidence. I feel like death warmed over. But we can manage."

"Shea," said Jake, "if she has appendicitis, she shouldn't be bouncing around on the back of the bike. Come on. Let us help."

Shea took a breath, wanting to curl up and go to sleep. But she didn't want to risk Annie's health.

"Yeah, okay."

Shea climbed in the back seat of Jake's SUV, and Annie lay on her lap. She let her mind go numb as she stroked Annie's hair, wondering where the hell Deirdre was. The cops didn't seem to care. And Shea couldn't think of anything else to do.

Next thing she knew, Jake opened the sliding door of the SUV. "End of the line. Everyone out."

The four of them shuffled into the emergency room, went through the usual procedures of getting vitals checked, and waited for an hour before being called back. Shea told Terrance and Jake to head home, promising to update them when she knew something. They refused.

"Sister girl, we family. I'm not going nowhere," Terrance insisted.

"What happened to you?" the nurse asked Shea while they got Annie situated on the bed.

Shea held up her bandaged arm. "Cut myself shaving. I'm not the patient, though. My niece is."

After going through the preliminaries, a familiar woman walked in. "Hi, I'm Doctor Sossamon." She looked at Shea. "Have we met before?"

"A few times. You treated me for road rash once. And treated Annie here after some asshole cut her ear off."

Sossamon nodded and turned to Annie. "I remember you, young lady. You're looking much better than the last time you were here. Still have both ears, I see. What brings you in tonight?"

Shea repeated to her the symptoms that Annie had been experiencing.

Sossamon poked and prodded Annie's abdomen, asking if it hurt. "Something's going on, but I'm not sure what. I'm ordering an abdominal ultrasound. Okay?"

"Will it hurt?" Annie asked.

"Not at all. You hang in there." Sossamon left the room.

For two hours, Shea tried to sleep, while Terrance and Jake searched for coffee and vending machine sustenance.

Transport arrived and took Annie to have the ultrasound. Then back again to wait for another three hours.

"We have good news and bad news."

The sound of Sossamon's voice jarred Shea awake. "What's the good news?"

"She doesn't have appendicitis."

Shea's head throbbed. "So, what's the bad news?"

"She has an infection of some type. We're admitting her.

We'll administer some antibiotics and see how she responds. I've also ordered a CT scan, but it may be tomorrow morning before we can schedule it. One of our machines is down, so we're a little backed up at the moment."

"I have a big game tomorrow," Annie said.

"What big game?" asked Sossamon.

"At soccer camp. I'm the team's forward."

"Well, my dear, I'm afraid you will have to miss it this go-around. But I'm sure there will be plenty more games in your future. But we have to make sure you're healthy. Okay?"

"Thanks, Doc," Shea said, trying to wake up.

"No problem. I'll be in touch."

29

SHEA WAS DOZING in a chair in Annie's hospital room when her phone rang. Morning light burnished the room in shades of gold. Sharp prickles of pain stung her hand when she answered the call. "Yeah."

"I'm looking for Shea Stevens," an unfamiliar male voice said.

A thrill of fear ran down her spine. Who the hell was this? The cops? One of Connelly's guys? Shea glanced at the phone's screen, but the caller ID read Unavailable. "Speaking."

"Ms. Stevens, I'm calling from Canyon State Labs for Annie Wittmann. We need her to come back and provide us with another sample."

Her fear morphed into anger. "Another sample? What the fuck for?"

"I'm afraid there was an unfortunate mix-up. Somehow her sample got switched with someone else's. We do apologize, but she needs to come in today."

"Well, that ain't happening. She—"

"Ms. Stevens, I realize it's an inconvenience, but the court order requires—"

"Fuck you and your court order. My niece is sick with an infection at Monterosa Medical. We gave you a sample. We complied. End of story."

"I realize that. But without another sample, we can't conduct the paternity test."

"Not my problem."

"It will be your problem if you're held in contempt of court."

Shea hung up and tossed the phone on the windowsill next to her.

"Who was that?" Annie rolled over in her bed.

"Asshole at the lab. Wants you to come down and give another sample. I told him to stick it up his ass. How you feeling?"

"Better, I think."

"Good."

"What time's breakfast?"

"Hell if I know. Cafeteria's probably open downstairs. You want something?"

The nurse walked in and started the blood pressure monitor. "Morning, sunshine."

"I'm hungry," Annie complained.

"I'm sorry. The doctor's ordered no food by mouth until they've run the CT scan."

"When's that supposed to happen?" Shea asked.

"I'm not sure. Shouldn't be too long." The generic hospital answer which could mean anything from an hour to a few days.

"I've heard that before."

The nurse smiled. "I promise we'll try to get it as soon as possible."

When she left, Annie asked, "Aunt Shea, can you please get me something to eat?"

Shea glanced toward the door. "I wish I could. But I don't want to cause any problems with them running whatever tests they got planned."

"I'm gonna dry up and blow away."

"No, you're not. But I promise not to eat anything until you do."

Terrance, Jake, and Elon walked in. Jake held a couple of bags from Nola's Diner, while Terrance carried a tray of hot beverages. The smell of coffee and sausage made Shea's mouth water.

"Who's hungry?" Jake asked in a singsong voice, waving a grease-stained bag. "I got Nola's breakfast biscuits."

"Shit." Shea stood up, eyeing a cup of coffee on the tray. "Annie can't eat anything right now. They're still running tests."

Elon was already digging into the bag. "But it's all right if I eat, ain't it?"

"*Isn't* it," Terrance corrected. "And if you must, do so in the waiting room. Poor Annie doesn't need to watch you stuff your face when she can't have any."

Elon shot Annie an apologetic expression. "Sorry, girl. I'm starving." The tall young man took two breakfast biscuits from the bag and disappeared out of the room.

"You mind if I have some coffee, at least?" Shea asked Annie, feeling pangs of guilt.

Annie shrugged, and Shea picked up a cup.

Terrance set the beverage tray on the counter and sidled up next to Annie's bed. "How you doing, girl?"

"Hungry."

Shea sipped her coffee and filled the guys in on the latest.

"Don't you worry," Terrance said. "You'll feel better in no time."

Shea turned on the TV. A news reporter was standing in front of the Hacienda Motel. "...reports of gunfire. When police arrived on the scene, they discovered a grisly scene. The body of a pig was found shot to death in a room rented by a local woman, thirty-six-year-old Deirdre West."

Deirdre's mugshot appeared on the screen. "We've discovered that Ms. West was recently fired from her job at an Ironwood marketing firm. Days later, she was arrested for possession of heroin and released on bail."

The shot cut to a male news anchor in studio. "We also spoke to one of Ms. West's neighbors, who had this to say."

The neighbor Shea had encountered in Deirdre's apartment with the baseball bat appeared on screen. "That lady's crazy. I'm always hearing strange animal sounds coming from her condo. She's got people knocking on her door at all hours. Everyone around here thinks she's dealing dope. Doesn't surprise me one bit she killed the damn pig and took off. She's a menace who needs to be locked up."

"Police say they are trying to locate Ms. West and question her in regards to the incident at the motel."

Shea turned off the TV. "Shit."

"Is that the woman you and the Sisterhood are protecting?" A worried look crossed Terrance's face.

"Were protecting, but yeah."

Jake cradled the bag of breakfast biscuits in his lap. "She crazy like her neighbor says?"

"I honestly don't know what to believe at this point. I do know she loved that pig. So, whatever happened at that motel, I hope she's okay."

∼

A LITTLE AFTER NINE O'CLOCK, a woman from Transport wheeled Annie a few floors down for the CT scan. Annie complained about the warm feeling when they injected her with the contrast media, but Shea assured her it would pass soon.

Shea's phone rang on the way back to Annie's room.

"Hey, Dragon. What's up?"

"Indigo told me what happened last night. You okay?"

"I'll survive."

"I've been researching the overturning of the Confederate Thunder's conviction. Turns out that Connelly belongs to the same fraternity as two of the three appellate justices who threw out the case. And both justices attended a Connelly fundraiser a week before the ruling."

Shea blew out a breath. "And they say justice is blind. You think the Thunder's doing Connelly's wet work?"

"I don't have any direct evidence, but it's possible."

"The good old boys' network just never dies, does it?"

"Have you heard from Deirdre?" The concern in Dragon's voice was clear.

"I've left messages on the burner phone I gave her, but I suspect the Thunder took her. Killed her pig, turned her motel room upside down looking for the dirt on Connelly, then grabbed her when they couldn't find it."

"So much for our truce. Where would they take her? The Church?"

"That would be my guess."

"Shit. We need to have an officers' meeting. Decide on a course of action."

"I can't. Annie's in the hospital with an abdominal infection." Shea brought her up to date on Annie's situation. "But I can call Julia Mueller. Maybe I can get some answers."

"Let me know what you find out. And give Annie my best for a speedy recovery."

Shea hung up and called Julia.

"Shea-Shea, what in blazes is going on? Police picked up Mackey to make him confess to shooting that cop. They had the gun you took off him. You working for the cops now?"

"Don't get all high and mighty with me, Julia. I told you to get that rapist motherfucker to back off this paternity shit. And last night, the Thunder attacked me and kidnapped an innocent woman. Where are they holding her?"

"I don't know nothing 'bout that."

"Bullshit. You pretend you don't know shit, but you hear everything, no matter how hush-hush them boys try to keep it. Senator Connelly got you all sprung, and the club's helping him cover up an affair he had. So, where are they hiding her?"

Julia didn't reply right away. "Shealene, you need to leave this one alone."

"The Sisterhood protects women, Julia." Shea walked down the corridor so Annie couldn't hear. "Listen up, bitch. You ever wanna see Annie again, you'll tell me what I need to know."

"Shea-Shea, you can't mean that. She's my grandbaby. I helped Wendy raise her."

"Help me find Deirdre West, and we'll talk."

"I'll keep my ears open. But you have to understand, Hooch is a lot more secretive than Monster ever was."

"That's the deal. Take it or leave it."

"Fine. I'll see what I can find out. Is she there? I want to talk to her."

Shea glanced in Annie's direction. She considered telling Julia about Annie being in the hospital, but the last thing they needed was for Julia to show up, possibly with Thundermen in tow. "Not at the moment."

Shea hung up.

While they headed down the corridor toward the elevators, Annie asked, "Can I get something to eat now?"

"Dunno. We'll see what the nurse says. May have to wait for the doctor to look at the results of the CT scan."

"Shit."

Shea grimaced at Annie's profanity. "You really shouldn't curse."

"Does Gramma Julia know I'm here?" Annie asked when they boarded the elevator.

Shea sighed. "Uh, yeah. Not sure when she'll be able to stop by. She's busy."

"But I could be dying."

"You're not dying. The doctor says you have an infection."

"So, I'm not having my period?"

"Not yet. But it'll happen. I didn't have mine until I was thirteen."

Shea's phone rang as they exited the elevator.

"This is Shea."

"Ms. Stevens, I'm Detective Lacey Olsen with the Cortes County Sheriff's Violent Crimes Division."

"Shit," Shea muttered under her breath.

30

"Your fingerprints were found last night at a crime scene in the Hacienda Motel. We have questions for you about what happened."

Shea drifted back while the guy from Transport pushed Annie's gurney through the maze of hallways leading back to the room. "Right now's not a good time. I'm with my niece in the hospital."

"I'm sure her parents can look after her while we speak."

"Her parents died years ago. I'm her legal guardian."

"Which hospital are you at? We can come to you, if it's easier."

Shea could see them detaining her for hours, leaving Annie alone and afraid in the hospital. She wouldn't let that happen. "I ain't talking to no one but Rios," she said instead.

"You know Detective Rios?"

"I do, actually."

"Then you probably know she's on medical leave."

"I tried to get you people to protect Deirdre West and

her mother, and you ain't done shit. Now her mom and that reporter are dead, and Deirdre's missing. Probably dead too, thanks to you people. That's all I got to say." She hung up.

When she reached the room, Annie was back in bed, flipping through channels on the television. Terrance sat beside her. Jake leaned against a wall, bathing in the sunlight coming through the window.

"Everything okay?" asked Terrance.

"It's fine. Where's Elon?"

"Caught an Uber back home. He's working an internship at a law firm in town. I called Lakota. She's opening up the shop for us."

"Good. The nurse come back? Can Annie eat yet?"

"Still waiting to hear from the doctor."

"What if it's cancer?" Annie said glumly.

"It's not cancer," Shea reassured her.

"Or one of those diseases only one in a million kids gets, but I'm that one."

"I'm sure it's not. Probably a nothing burger. You're already feeling better after a night of antibiotics. Maybe they'll let you go home once the doc checks out the results. Then you can eat whatever you want."

"Like a whole pizza?" Annie's eyes grew large in anticipation.

Shea laughed despite her exhaustion. "Sure."

She settled into a chair on the other side of Annie's bed and was dozing off when her phone rang again. "Son of a bitch."

The caller ID told her it was Rios. She wasn't in the mood to be playing games with cops. But this was Rios. Toni. The woman who'd risked her badge to save Shea's life once. The woman who got her involved with the Athena Sisterhood, even if it was originally as a snitch. The woman who Shea was attracted to, despite all the reasons she shouldn't be.

She let it ring three times, debating whether to answer it, before tapping the accept button and stepping into the bathroom for some privacy.

"What's going on, Shea?"

"Don't start with me, Rios. I'm not spending the next several hours in some goddamn interrogation room. I ain't done nothing wrong. It's Connelly you people should be looking at."

"How's Annie?" The genuine concern in Rios's voice took Shea by surprise.

"She's got an abdominal infection. Why?"

"I hope she gets to feeling better soon."

"Thanks, I guess."

"You're welcome. Understandably, she's your primary concern. At the same time, we both want Deirdre West found. So do Detectives Olsen and Cohen. They're looking into the shooting last night at the Hacienda Motel. Any idea where Ms. West might be?"

"So you can help Connelly frame her on some other bullshit charge?"

"My loyalties are to the people of this county, not to some loud-mouthed politician."

"What about your fellow detectives? I told Bello to look into Deirdre's mother's death. But I haven't heard anything back. And nothing on the news. So, I ask you, where do their loyalties lie?"

"I…I'd like to think they're the same."

"But you're not sure, are you?"

Rios didn't answer.

"I'll work with you, Rios, to find Deirdre and nail Connelly. I'm not talking to any other cops."

"Shea, I'm on leave. I can't work any cases, much less ones assigned to other detectives."

"Then we got nothing else to say to each other. And you can forget about that dinner date."

"Shea, wait. ¡Dígame! Were you at the Hacienda Motel last night?"

Shea hesitated. "I stopped by Deirdre's motel room. Found it trashed and her pig dead. When I stepped outside, two Thundermen shot at me. I ran. One caught up to me and sliced open my arm before he ran off again. That's all I know." Shea left off mention of any other Sisters' names. Didn't need them dragged into this mess any further than they already were. "My guess is Connelly used the Thunder to grab Deirdre."

"Can you ID the shooters?"

"One of them may've been Mackey, but it was dark. Hard to be sure. The other one, I didn't recognize. Full beard, dark hair, Johnny Reb tattoo on his left bicep. About six foot one, two hundred pounds."

"Bello and Morris are questioning Mackey about the shooting that put me in the hospital. I can let them know you suspect he was involved in last night's incident at the motel. I can also hook you up with a sketch artist. See if we can't ID the other shooter at the motel."

"Not interested."

"I'm trying to find your friend to make sure she's safe."

"If the Thunder's got her, they're probably holding her at the Church. I gave her a burner phone. If she still has it, you can use it to confirm her location." Shea glanced out of the bathroom door toward where Annie, Terrance, and Jake were chatting about something on the TV. She was safe for now. No immediate danger. "Once you locate the phone, tell me where it is, and I'll check it out."

"You? You're a civilian. I can't give you the phone's location. I'm not even sure I can get that information with me being on medical leave. But give me the phone number anyway. I'll ask my partner, Detective Johnson, to run it for me on the DL."

"You trust Johnson to keep her mouth shut?"

"Implicitly." No hesitation in Rios's voice.

Shea gave her the number. "Call me back when you got a location."

She stepped out of the bathroom. "Any word from the doctor?"

Terrance shook his head. "Nope."

"I don't understand why I can't eat," Annie whined. "They done run all the tests."

"You want us to sneak you something?" asked Jake. "I'll do it."

Shea studied Annie's pouting face. Following the rules was never Shea's thing. And yet her gut told her to wait. "Let's hold off till we hear from the doc."

"But I'm hungry."

"I know. I'm sure they'll let you eat soon."

Annie switched through channel after channel of talk shows and commercials until she turned it off with a huff. Shea felt bad for her.

"I could bring your laptop. You can stream something on Netflix or play a video game."

"Better than nothing, I guess. Since I'm *starving*!"

Shea's phone rang again. Rios calling back. "Hold that thought." She stepped outside the room. "You found Deirdre?"

"I have a GPS location on the phone. It's not at the Thunder's clubhouse."

"Where the hell is it then?"

"A flophouse in Ironwood's southside barrio. Not exactly a place where Thundermen hang out."

Shea considered the implications. Maybe Deirdre was a junkie. "What's the address?"

"I'll send a couple of black-and-whites to check it out."

"You promised this would stay between us. Tell me where she is. I'll check it out."

"Shea, I can't involve civilians in this investigation."

"First, I'm already involved. Deirdre trusted me to keep her safe. If she's there, I owe it to her to get her out. Nothing you say will change my mind."

"This is the CCSO's responsibility."

"Tell me something. You ask Bello if he's looked into Deirdre's mother's death?"

"I asked. The doctor ruled it natural causes. She was a dying woman."

"Bullshit! Someone delivered her flowers and signed in as Luca Brasi. Did Bello bother looking at the surveillance footage?"

"Not as far as I know." Rios sounded defeated.

"You can either help me save her or help Connelly cover up his crimes."

"Mierda," Rios whispered over the line before giving Shea the address. "You're going to get me fired. You know that, chica?"

"Oh, please! You're a decorated detective. Blue protects its own."

"Meet me outside the flophouse in thirty minutes."

"Make it twenty."

Shea hung up and returned to the room. "I'll go fetch your laptop. Be back in an hour."

"Sounds like you're planning more than that," Terrance replied, giving her a knowing look. "Is this the time to be gallivanting off to save damsels in distress? Can't your biker gang take care of that?"

Shea met his gaze with a "don't judge me" expression

and turned to Annie. "It's Deirdre. She may be in big trouble. You'll be okay for now. You got T and Jake to watch over you."

Annie nodded. "If I don't starve to death."

"If you do, I promise to say nice things at your funeral."

Annie rolled her eyes. "Gee, thanks."

Terrance followed Shea out of the room. "You sure about this, sister girl?"

"I'm sure. I'm working with the cops on this," Shea exaggerated. "Believe me, I'd rather just be with Annie. But the shit's really hit the fan on this. I won't be long."

31

SHEA ARRIVED at the address Rios had given her, a house with peeling paint, a yard overgrown with three-foot-tall weeds and littered with trash. Graffiti was everywhere—on buildings, trees, curbs. Many of the tags belonged to the Barrio Kings, a local gang that had claimed the area after the Jaguars street gang had been all but wiped out by the Thunder years earlier.

Rios hadn't arrived, but Shea didn't feel like waiting. If Deirdre was here, Shea would pull her out and figure out a way to get her clean.

Two junkies dozed on the front porch. Neither of them stirred when Shea pushed her way through the front door, Glock in hand. The reek of the place took her breath away. Urine, feces, mold, body odor, and a sweet chemical haze from a cocktail of weed, crack, and meth. The graffiti on the walls reflected a range of styles and skill levels, some quite impressive.

Power was out, no surprise. The house looked long abandoned, probably lost to a bank during the recession and never sold again. Why had no one torn it down? Maybe the cost of demolition was more than what the property was worth in this devalued neighborhood.

In the kitchen, a few people lay unconscious on the floor amongst a nest of glass pipes, needles, and garbage. Deirdre was nowhere to be seen. Shea turned down a hallway to her left.

Three twin mattresses lay scattered in a bedroom, two of them occupied. Black garbage bags taped over the windows made it too dark to make out anyone's features.

"Deirdre?"

"Shut the fuck up," groaned a guy on a mattress.

Shea considered telling him to go to hell, but she wasn't here to make trouble. She was here to find Deirdre.

She took out the knife she'd taken from the Thunderman who attacked her and cut a slit in one of the bags covering the window. A beam of sunlight blazed into the room. Two of the junkies shielded their faces from the sudden brightness, hissing like vampires. Shea half expected them to burst into flames.

After she confirmed none of the people in the bedroom were Deirdre, Shea continued searching the house.

In a back bedroom, plywood covered the window. Shea used the light on her phone to check the denizens for Deirdre. She came up empty. She checked the living room, closets, bathrooms. No sign of Deirdre. Where the hell was she?

She kicked herself for not thinking of it sooner. She dialed Deirdre's burner. She heard a distant ring and followed the sound through the house until she returned to the first bedroom and found it ringing amidst some garbage next to an empty mattress.

Shea ended the call and picked up the phone. "Where the hell are you?" she whispered to herself.

"What the fuck you doing with my shit?" A large

bearded man dressed in a plaid flannel shirt and tattered jeans charged toward her.

Shea backed away. "This phone belongs to a friend of mine."

"Hell it does. Give it back to me, bitch, 'fore I beat you bloody."

Shea raised her pistol, but the guy was faster than he appeared. He knocked it out of her hand and landed a glancing blow to her jaw. She saw stars but grabbed hold of his shirt and used her body as a counterweight to fling him across the room.

While she searched for her pistol, the guy came at her again. He drove her to the hardwood floor, sending pain radiating from her back into her arms and legs. She blocked his blows the best she could, but he pummeled her with the ferocity of a rabid animal.

Without warning, he sat up and tensed, his face a mask of agony. A fwap-fwap-fwap sound and the scent of ozone filled the air. Her attacker collapsed next to her.

Rios appeared, holding a Taser. Shea struggled to her feet while Rios cuffed the guy.

"You okay?" asked Rios.

Shea's face and torso felt like she'd gone ten rounds with a heavyweight boxer. The cut on her arm burned. She pulled off her jacket and found the wound seeping through the dressing. She pressed against it to stop the bleeding. "I'll live. Thanks for the assist."

"Why didn't you wait for me?"

"Because my niece is in the hospital, and I didn't have all day to wait for you. Your cop buddies know you're here?"

"No. I'm here on my own. To help you find your friend. What happened to your arm?"

"A Thunderman sliced it open last night. It was fine till asshole here reopened it."

The man groaned and rolled onto his side. "Jesus fucking Christ. What the hell?"

Shea bent down and grabbed him by the collar. "Where the hell's Deirdre?"

"Fuck you, bitch."

Shea kicked him in the crotch. "Where is she, you piece of shit?"

"Shea..." Rios cautioned.

"Gungh! Fuck. Don't know no Deirdre. Jeez, that hurts."

"Where'd ya get the phone?"

"Some guy tossed it on the floor and left, all right? Finders keepers."

"What guy? What'd he look like?"

"A guy. A guy. Some white guy."

"Tall? Short? Old? Young? Bald? Hairy?"

"Don't remember."

Shea kicked the side of the head. "Try."

"Shea." Rios pulled her away. "He doesn't remember. Deirdre wasn't here. And you can't assault people."

"No, *you* can't. I have my own rules."

"Shea, I may be on medical leave, but I'm still a cop. I will arrest you if you assault this man again."

"Whatever." Shea retrieved her gun.

Shea stormed out of the flophouse. Fresh air never smelled so good. Her phone rang when she approached her bike. "What's up, T?"

"We heard from the doctor. They're taking her in for surgery soon. You need to get back here."

"On my way." She hung up and pulled on her helmet.

"Shea, where you going?" Rios called after her.

"They're taking Annie into surgery."

"For what?"

"No idea." She threw a leg over the bike and started it up.

"What can I do to help?"

"Find Deirdre and arrest Connelly."

SHEA RUSHED THROUGH THE HOSPITAL, twice nearly colliding with people coming around a corner, then forced her way into a crowded elevator.

Her fear was that the medical staff would take Annie to surgery before she could talk to her and find out what was going on.

"Hey!" She burst into the room. Annie was still in her bed with Terrance and Jake next to her. "Got here quick as I could."

"What happened to your face?" Terrance asked.

"Got into a disagreement with a junkie about personal property. I'm okay."

"You're bleeding again," said Jake.

Shea felt her arm. She'd almost forgotten about it, despite the persistent stinging. Blood had smeared all over her shirt. But the wound had finally closed again.

"I'm all right. What's going on with Annie?"

"I got an angled hernia," Annie replied. "Whatever that is."

"An inguinal hernia," Terrance corrected. "Doc says it's a minor procedure, but she'll have to stay in the hospital for a few days afterward."

"You feeling okay?" Shea asked her.

Annie shrugged. "'Bout the same."

"Hello, Annie," said someone behind Shea coming in the door. "Remember me?"

Shea turned and recognized the female tech from Canyon State Labs. She carried a plastic case and wore a collared shirt embroidered with the lab's logo instead of scrubs.

"What the hell you doing here?" Shea stepped in front of Annie.

"I'm here to collect a fresh DNA sample since the last one was contaminated."

"No, you're not. We fulfilled our part. Get the fuck out."

Terrance and Jake stood beside her, forming a wall between the tech and Annie.

"I don't know why you're making a big deal about this. It's just a cheek swab. And the court requires me to get it."

"Not gonna happen, lady," Shea insisted.

"Gentlemen?" the tech called to someone out in the hall.

Two male uniformed officers—one white, one black—walked in.

"Shea Stevens, you're under arrest," said the white cop, while the black one cuffed her.

"What for?"

"Refusing to comply with a court order," the white cop said.

Shea felt the black cop pull the Glock from her holster at the small of her back. "And for illegal possession of a concealed weapon in a hospital."

"Aunt Shea? What's going on?" Annie's voice grew more distant while they frog-marched Shea out of the room. She'd been in such a rush to check on Annie that she'd forgotten to leave the gun in her bike's top case.

"I have a right to carry concealed," Shea insisted.

"Not in a hospital, you don't. Weapons are prohibited except for law enforcement and security."

"This is absurd. She's my niece, assholes. I'm her legal guardian. I get to say what medical procedures she has."

"The court says otherwise," the white cop said. "They ordered a DNA test. You refused."

"I didn't refuse. She provided a sample. Not my fault they mixed it up with someone else's."

"Tell that to the judge."

"What about my niece? She's about to go into surgery. I need to be there for her."

"Department of Child Safety has been called. They'll send out a social worker to see to her for now."

"Child Safety? This is bullshit."

Shea wanted to tell them all to go to hell. She wanted to kick their asses. But it wouldn't help Annie. Cops would be cops, enforcing the most minor infractions on people who couldn't fight back while letting people like Connelly get away with murder and kidnapping.

32

Shea sat on the holding cell's bench and debated who best to call when given a chance. Would Rios help her out of this? Probably not. Her best option was Dragon.

Detective Bello walked into the holding area alongside a stocky white woman. Both wore dark-blue suits and weary expressions.

"Shea Stevens?" The woman carried a clear plastic bag containing Shea's belongings.

"I get my phone call now?"

"On the contempt charge? We're willing to drop it if you'll talk with us about another matter."

"What other matter?"

"The shooting last night at the Hacienda Motel. I'm Detective Alyssa Morris. I believe you've already met Detective Bello."

"I thought some other detectives were working that case."

"They were. Detectives Lacey and O'Brien turned it over to us when shell casings found in the motel room matched those found after Elia Quinn was murdered."

"I'll make it simple for you. I was the one being shot at."

"What happened to your face? And why is there blood on your shirt?"

"A Thunderman jumped me outside the motel room." No need to mention the guy in the flophouse.

"Do you require medical treatment?" Morris gestured to Shea's shirt.

"I'm all right."

Morris beckoned a uniformed officer, who came over and unlocked the cell door.

Shea remained seated on the bench. "Maybe I should call my lawyer."

"You are free to do so, but you are no longer under arrest. I have your personal belongings right here, minus your gun and knife." Morris held up the overstuffed manila envelope.

"We wanna know what happened last night," Bello added.

Shea studied the two of them. "What about my niece? Cops who arrested me said DCS was taking her into their custody."

"That's something you gotta take up with DCS," Bello said.

"She still in surgery? Is she okay?"

"We can make some phone calls and see what we can find out, okay?" Morris offered. "In the meantime, can you help us out?"

"I still want my lawyer."

"Fair enough. Let's talk in one of our interview rooms. They're more comfortable than the holding cells."

Shea followed the two of them out of the holding area, up an elevator, and into an interview room in the Violent Crimes Division.

Detective Morris returned a few minutes later with a

bottle of water and a vending machine sandwich. "Hope you like ham and cheese. I'll be right back." She left again.

Shea had been in this room and others like it several times before. They'd put in carpeting since she'd been here last. The wooden table had the same metal ring mounted in it for securing handcuffs, but they'd replaced the garage-sale castoffs with more comfortable chairs.

Still, it was an interview room lined with acoustic tiles, a camera mounted in the corner near the ceiling, and a pervasive sense of looming trouble.

Shea took her phone out of the manila envelope and called Dragon.

Dragon walked in two hours later.

"Jesus, Havoc. The detectives do that to you?"

Shea shook her head. "That Thunderman from last night. And some asshole in a flophouse. I'll live. Any word on Annie?"

"Still in surgery, last I heard. No complications I'm aware of. But she remains in DCS custody for the time being."

"Dragon, that's bullshit. I'm her legal guardian."

"True, but because you refused another DNA sample, the judge brought in DCS."

"Dragon—"

"Relax. One of my associates specializes in custody cases. She's working on it as we speak, okay? Let's focus on what these detectives want to discuss."

Shea shared about the previous night's incident, leaving nothing out. She also recounted what happened at the flophouse.

"Sounds like you're in the clear regarding the motel. I'd keep quiet about your excursion to the flophouse with Detective Rios."

Shea nodded. Dragon called the detectives in, whereupon Shea told them what had happened at the motel. Bello and Morris questioned her, asking her to tell the story backward and forward, no doubt looking for inconsistencies.

"Why didn't you call the police when you found the dead pig in the room and Deirdre West missing?" Morris asked.

"You serious? For all I know, you cops are in on it."

"Shea. Not helping." Dragon put a cautioning hand on her arm.

"This entire thing points back to Connelly. He's been harassing her for a while. Slashing her tires. Leaving her threatening notes. Getting her fired from her job. And when that didn't work, he murdered Elia Quinn and her own mother, then tried to discredit her by making her look like a dope fiend."

"Why would he do that?" Morris asked.

"So she wouldn't expose him for the womanizing, sleazebag hypocrite he is."

Bello leaned back in his chair, arms crossed. "You got any evidence to prove these allegations against Senator Connelly?"

"No, but she does. That's why he kidnapped her. And maybe if you'd gotten off your fat ass and looked at the surveillance video at Kings Ridge Assisted Living, you'd know he also killed Deirdre's mother."

Morris turned to her partner. "Kings Ridge? What's she talking about?"

Bello waved her off. "Some paranoid conspiracy theory Deirdre West concocted. Claims Connelly murdered West's mother, even though she only had a month or so to live."

"Why then would someone deliver flowers to her and sign in as Luca Brasi? What kinda sick fuck does that?"

Shea exchanged a glance with Dragon. "Now Connelly's got the Thunder and you guys working for him."

Bello stroked his goatee. "Why would a respected politician like Connelly have anything to do with an outlaw biker gang?"

Shea snorted at the word respected. "To do his dirty work. He got them sprung from prison."

"How do we know this isn't a gang war between your lady bikers and the Thunder?"

"We had a truce. At least until they broke it last night."

"Where do you think Ms. West is now?" Morris asked. "Where would Connelly or the Thundermen take her?"

Shea studied them. Morris at least seemed on the up and up, but Shea had trusted cops before and gotten burned. "Ask Mackey. I heard you arrested him for shooting Rios. He was at the motel last night, too. Or better yet, ask Connelly."

After another half hour, Morris stood up. "Okay, Ms. Stevens. We appreciate your time answering our questions."

"You gonna find Deirdre?" Shea and Dragon rose to their feet.

"We will do everything we can to locate her."

"What about Connelly? You gonna bring him in and arrest him?"

"If we find he's broken the law, we'll deal with him."

Shea scoffed. "So that's a no. Got it. His kind always skates free. What about my niece? You said you were going to check to see how she's doing?"

"Wait here. I'll make some calls." Morris followed Bello out of the room.

Shea sat down and glanced up at the camera. The red light blinked off, no longer recording.

"This is all such bullshit." Shea buried her head in her arms.

"What do you mean?" Dragon asked.

"Everything points to Connelly, but they refuse to bring him in for questioning. Innocent women have been murdered, but even the murder cops are more worried about protecting this douchebag."

"It's frustrating, I know."

"Well, I'm not letting that fucker get away with it. I don't care who he is."

"Havoc, you can't—"

"I can't? I'll tell you what I can't. I can't sit on my hands while that dirtbag gets away with everything."

"We did everything we could to protect Deirdre and her mom."

"It wasn't enough, Dragon. And I'm not going to throw in the towel just because these fucking idiots refuse to do their goddamn jobs. Deirdre is out there. Maybe she's alive. Maybe she ain't. But I'm going to find her. And then I'm going to make sure that those responsible for all this shit pay for what they've done."

Dragon sighed. "Do what you have to do, sister. But leave me out of it."

Morris walked in with a piece of paper in her hand. "I spoke with DCS and the hospital. Annie is out of surgery and expected to make a full recovery."

"When can I see her?"

"That's up to DCS. Temporarily, they've given custody to Annie's grandmother." Morris checked the piece of paper. "A Julia Mueller."

Shea choked from shock. "Julia fucking Mueller? She just got outta prison. Her old man is the Confederate Thunder VP and also just got outta the joint. And as if that isn't bad enough, the Thunderman claiming to be Annie's biological father is a rapist. These are the people DCS thinks she's safe with?"

"I'm sorry, Ms. Stevens."

"Fuck you and your sorry. My niece has been placed with violent criminals. Meanwhile, you people are protecting a man who just murdered two people, maybe three. Whose side are you on?"

Dragon lifted Shea to her feet. "Let's go before you get yourself locked up again."

"What about my gun and knife?"

"They are evidence in an ongoing investigation."

"Gee, thanks," Shea replied without enthusiasm.

Shea and Dragon walked out of the room and made their way downstairs and out to Dragon's car. "You need a ride?"

Shea's concern for Annie hung heavy on her conscience while she tried to remember where her motorcycle was. "Take me to Terrance's house. Left my bike there last night."

"Just remember, don't go back to the hospital. You can't see Annie until we work out this DCS situation."

"Yeah, yeah."

Shea climbed into the passenger seat and checked her phone. Rios had sent a text message.

Shea, it's Toni. We found Deirdre West's car. Call me.

Shea dialed Rios's number. "You found Deirdre? Is she alive?"

"A patrol officer found her Kia Soul crashed off the side of the hill at Cooper's Vista in the Cortes National Forest. No bodies recovered."

"Connelly has her. Or the Thunder does."

"Bello and Morris have put out a BOLO on her."

"I was just talking to them. Why didn't they tell me?"

"You have to understand, as law enforcement trying to solve crimes, our job is to collect information, not give it out."

"Will they bring Connelly in for questioning?"

"It's a delicate situation, Shea."

"Delicate situation, my ass. He's behind this. I'm telling you."

"We're working on it." There was a lengthy pause. "How's Annie?"

"Just got outta surgery to repair a hernia. But I'm not allowed to see her. Fucking DCS stepped in because a member of the Thunder claims he's her baby daddy. Gave custody to her grandmother, who just got outta the can."

"Shea, I'm sorry. That's not right. You want me to look into it?"

"Don't bother. I got my lawyer on it. Someone who gives a shit about my family." Shea hung up.

"Who was that?" Dragon asked while they drove through Ironwood's Downtown District crowded with summer traffic.

"Detective Rios."

"Ah. Don't worry about Annie. We'll get her back with you soon, okay?"

"I hate that I can't be there for her."

An idea occurred to her, and she made another phone call.

"You goddamn fucking bitch!"

"Shealene Eleanor Stevens, how dare you call me that," Julia replied.

"You're the reason the fucking social workers took Annie out of my custody. You and that fucking rapist, Bryz. What would Wendy think of what you're doing?"

"Shea-Shea, I had nothing to do with this."

"Bullshit. I refused to let you see Annie, so you fucking sent DCS after me."

"I swear to God Almighty, I didn't do this. I'd never side with Bryz over you, no matter how inconsiderate you been toward me."

"Yeah, right."

"They're placing her with me until this paternity mess gets worked out."

"Get him to drop it."

"I tried. I begged Hooch. He told me to stay out of it. I swear, sweetie, I did everything I could. Right now, she's in the hospital, recovering from her surgery."

"You're there now?"

"I am."

"Why would they give you custody? You just got outta prison."

"You'd rather they put her in some home with strangers where God-knows-what could happen to her?"

"I'd rather she be with me where she belongs. Bryz is a rapist, Julia. What d'you think he'll do to her if he gets custody?"

"That's not up to me. But I'll keep her safe for now. You have my word on that."

"The way you and the Thunder kept Wendy safe? My mother's last advice to Wendy and me was to get out while we could. She swore we'd end up dead or in prison if we didn't. Damn if she weren't right. I went to prison, and Wendy got raped and then killed. I don't want that for Annie."

"Take it down a notch, Shea-Shea. I'll keep her away from the Thunder for the time being. Okay?"

"How you gonna do that? You live with their vice president."

"Trust me, sweetie."

"Trust is earned." Shea took a breath. "Where's the Thunder holding Deirdre West?"

"I don't know. That's the God's honest truth. The MC's looking for her, but last I heard, they hadn't found her."

"They got her, Julia. I need you to find out where. Or we will unleash holy hell to find her."

"I'll see what I can find out."

"See that you do." Shea's fury subsided a smidge. "How's Annie doing?"

"In recovery. I'm in her room waiting. They should be bringing her in within the next half hour."

"Are Terrance and Jake still there?"

"That black homo and his boy toy? No, they're not family."

"Bullshit. They're as much family as you are."

"Shea..."

"What are the doctors saying?"

"They say the surgery went well. Don't know much beyond that. I'll call you when I hear more, okay?"

"Fucking better."

"Shea, I'm on your side."

"Bullshit. You're a Thunderman's old lady, through and through. You say we're family. But when push comes to shove, the MC always comes first, family a distant second."

"That's not true."

"We'll see."

Shea hung up.

"How's your niece?" Dragon asked. They drove past a series of medical offices that surrounded the hospital.

"Julia says she's out of surgery. No other details. I hate that I won't be there when she wakes up."

"I'm sorry, Havoc. She'll get through this. She knows you love her. Besides, look at yourself. You're covered in blood and look like you went ten rounds with Mike Tyson. You want her to wake up to that?"

Shea laughed despite herself. "Nah, suppose not."

"Go home. Get yourself cleaned up. I'll work things out on the custody end."

33

AFTER DRAGON DROPPED HER OFF, Shea drove out of the parking lot and headed for home, trying to figure out what to do next after she got herself cleaned up. She wanted, more than anything, to see Annie, to be there when she woke up. But it would be a fool's errand. As much as she distrusted Julia and her ties to the Thunder, she could only assume Annie would be safe in the confines of the hospital.

That left Deirdre. Shea was sure the Thunder had her somewhere, since her body wasn't found at the scene of the car crash. Odds were they were holding her at the Church. Rescuing her from the Thunder's clubhouse would be risky, if not impossible. But there was another angle she could play.

After a quick shower and a fresh bandage on her arm, Shea made a few phone calls, pulled on her gear, and rode out once again.

At quarter to five, she pulled into a public lot a few blocks north of Ironwood's Downtown Square. Traffic in the area was moderate—tourists and locals heading to and from nearby restaurants and art galleries.

Her parking spot afforded her a view of the back of Connelly's local office. His dark-blue Mercedes SUV sat parked next to the building's back door.

A few minutes later, Indigo, Fuego, Raven, Brillo, and Rah-Rah arrived on their motorcycles.

Raven lifted the front of her modular helmet. "What's the game plan, Havoc?"

"I talked with Connelly's wife. He's speaking at a fundraiser in Scottsdale at eight. He'll be leaving his office anytime now. My guess is he'll take the I-17 south. There's a dead zone a mile past the Highway 169 exit with no cell coverage for five miles. We trail him, then when I give the signal, we force him to pull over and tell us where he's holding Deirdre."

"Why not confront him here?" asked Rah-Rah.

"Too many people walking around," Shea replied. "Rather not have any witnesses if things get rough."

"What if he won't pull over?" asked Brillo, a redhead with pale, freckled skin. "Or refuses to tell us where Deirdre is?"

Shea held out a compact mustard-yellow Ruger 9mm. "Trust me, he'll stop." She stuffed it in the front of her waistband, ready for a left-handed draw. "And if he won't tell us where he's keeping Deirdre, I'll motivate him to do so."

"You sure about this, hermana?" Fuego asked. "This is going all in."

"Honestly, Prez, I'm already all in. This man murdered two women, maybe Deirdre as well. Cops won't even question him, much less arrest him. If we don't stop him, who will?"

Fuego looked at the others. "You all up for this, amigas? No disgrace if you aren't."

"Shit yeah," said Indigo.

"Ready when you are. Let's put the screws to this douchebag," Rah-Rah added.

Brillo and Raven nodded their assent. Those not wearing helmets pulled bandanas over their faces to keep from being identified if things went sideways.

One by one, Connelly's campaign staff walked out of the building and drove off. Shea wondered if the not-so-good senator had left early and taken someone else's car.

It was five thirty when Connelly walked out with the guy in the Harry Potter glasses—Harrison, Haroldson, Hair Man, something like that.

The headlights of the car flashed when Connelly unlocked the car, and the two men got in. The car turned onto the street. Shea and the others waited a moment before following at a distance.

The sun was riding the hills of the western horizon when they pulled onto the highway. The glare made it harder for Shea to keep her eye on the blue SUV. Swarms of bugs splattering on her visor didn't help. On the plus side, southbound traffic was light.

After they passed the Highway 169 exit, Shea gave the signal and pinned her throttle. She zoomed past a panel van and caught up to Connelly, who was doing eighty in the right lane. Indigo and Fuego pulled ahead and positioned themselves in front of the SUV.

Shea boxed Connelly in on the left, with Rah-Rah at her seven o'clock. The others maintained the perimeter in back of the car. When everyone was in position, Indigo and Fuego slowed. The panel van they'd passed earlier zoomed around them.

Connelly's horn blared above the roar of the wind. Shea chuckled at Connelly shaking his fist, while Indigo and Fuego slowed further. This was where things would get tricky.

Connelly tailgated the bikers in front of him, riding on their rear wheels until Shea gave his door a solid kick. He glared at her. When Shea gestured for him to pull over, he flipped her off and jerked the Mercedes SUV toward her bike. Shea swerved out of the way just in time.

Wanna play hard to get, huh? Shea thought.

She drew the Ruger with her left hand. She was right-handed, but her bike didn't have a throttle control. No way to maintain speed and shoot right-handed. Firing left-handed made for an awkward shot, but Shea was close enough that it didn't matter.

She aimed at the truck's front wheel and pulled the trigger, trying not to flinch when the spent shell ricocheted off her visor. The SUV shuddered when the tire lost pressure. Shea eased away from the car in case it veered toward her again.

Rather than slow, Connelly accelerated, again getting dangerously close to Indigo and Fuego. Shea put a second round into the car's front tire. Sparks burst from the rim grinding into the pavement. The SUV slowed and pulled onto the weed-riddled shoulder.

Shea rolled in front and stopped next to Indigo. Her heart thudded in her chest from the adrenaline rush. "Y'all all right?"

"Shit, that was crazy," Indigo replied, her voice muffled from her helmet. "Fucker got a little close for my taste. But I'm a'ight."

Fuego gave her a thumbs-up, her eyes wide above her bandana.

"You two keep an eye on the nerdy guy riding shotgun. I'll deal with Connelly."

"No problema," Fuego answered.

Shea tossed her helmet onto her seat and sidled up to Connelly's door, the Ruger now in her right hand. She tapped the window with the muzzle of the pistol. Both front windows lowered with an electronic hum.

Connelly sat with his hands still at ten and two, glaring at Shea. His passenger with the geeky glasses stared straight ahead, his sport coat folded on his lap.

"Hello, Joey," Shea said in a mocking tone.

"You again. Should've figured. Miss Stevens, isn't it? Shea Stevens? Served several years in prison for grand theft auto."

Shea didn't answer.

"I was curious after you visited my home, so I researched the name you gave. The real Laura Bullion was the last surviving member of Butch Cassidy's Wild Bunch gang. Clever, I thought. But then I saw your photo in yesterday's paper and remembered Deirdre calling you Shea. Maybe not so clever after all."

"Where the fuck's Deirdre West?"

"I'm sure I don't know. I've had no direct contact with her. As we agreed."

"No, you had the Confederate Thunder abduct her instead. After they murdered her mother."

"Oh please. Deirdre West is a desperate woman with a serious drug problem. She was recently arrested, in fact, for heroin possession. Very sad, if you ask me." His lower lip jutted out in a mocking pout. "Doesn't make for a reliable witness, does it?"

"Kidnapping her won't keep the truth of your affair and the abortion from getting out," Shea growled.

"Kidnapping? Are you insane? I have no reason to kidnap her. The woman is a paranoid, delusional drug addict. She belongs in a mental hospital. If I had her, that's where I would put her. But as I said, I've had no contact with her since that night you saw me talk to her at her condo. I am too busy running for the U.S. Senate to bother with a silly woman like her."

"Which is why you hired the Thundermen to do your dirty work for you."

"The biker gang? Really, Miss Stevens. Now you're delusional."

"Just so you know, she gave me a copy of all the documentation proving your affair and your insistence she get an abortion. Sort of an insurance policy." It was a lie, but Shea was running out of options short of shooting these guys. "So, you best tell me where the Thundermen are holding her. Or I'll send copies to the *Arizona Republic* and the *Cortes Chronicle*. And then I'll send proof of your financial shenanigans to the feds."

"If you do anything to harm the senator's reputation," Connelly's toady growled, "I swear on all that is holy, we will destroy you."

"Easy, Harriman," Connelly said. "Honestly, Miss Stevens, I have no idea where Deirdre is. Send your so-called evidence to whomever you like. Who do you think people will believe? A respected state senator fighting for the rights of the people or a junkie whore and a car thief?" He said it with a taunting smirk. "Now if you'll excuse me, my campaign manager and I have a tire to change before we get back on the road."

"Don't think so, asshole," Shea snapped. "Not until Deirdre is safe."

The barrel of a large-caliber pistol, possibly a Smith & Wesson 1911, poked out from beneath Harriman's jacket, aimed at Shea's chest. "You and your fellow lady bikers best be on your way." His voice had more steel in it than Shea expected.

On the far side of the car, Fuego pressed a revolver against the man's temple. "Drop it, pendejo!"

Harriman sneered at Shea and tossed the gun outside the car. It clattered on the gravel.

"Where'd the Thunder take her?" Shea pressed Connelly.

"I don't know what—"

She smacked the butt of her gun hard against his nose. He fell back against the seat, his hand to his face. Blood dripped onto his starched white shirt.

"Fucking bitch!"

"Gonna do worse than that unless you give us answers."

"I told you. I don't know where she is. I didn't kidnap her."

"I suppose you didn't murder her mother, either."

"Her mother? Of course not." He pulled the pocket square from his breast pocket and held it to his nose. "Why would I kill a dying woman?"

Shea opened his door and pressed the muzzle of her Ruger to his knee. "Enough of your bullshit. You have three seconds to tell me where Deirdre is before I put a forty-caliber slug through your kneecap."

"I don't know. I swear." Abject terror replaced Connelly's swagger.

"Three."

"You can't do this," shouted Harriman. "This man is an Arizona state senator."

"Two."

"I swear if I knew..."

"One."

"Wait! Wait! The Thunder."

"What about them?"

"I asked them to retrieve the evidence she had on me. Never told them to hurt her."

"You're fucking lying again." Shea wrapped her finger around the Ruger's trigger.

"Please, I swear on Jesus Christ and all the saints, I do not know where she is. They told me she got away when they broke into her room. If they have her, they're lying to me, too. Why would they do that?"

Shea studied the man. The primal fear in his voice convinced her he was telling the truth for once. "This ain't over. We will find her. And if she's dead, I'll fucking kill you myself, and will take my time doing it. Don't give a shit who you are."

Shea slammed his door shut and huddled with the other Sisters next to their bikes in front of the car. The Mercedes's engine remained quiet, and neither Connelly nor Harriman attempted to get out.

"That went well," said Rah-Rah sarcastically.

"You believe he's telling the truth?" asked Raven.

Shea replied, "More or less."

"You think Deirdre's on the run?" Indigo glanced back at the car, the colors of the sunset reflecting off her visor. "After what happened at the motel, she might not trust us to keep her safe."

"I doubt it," Shea replied. "Someone dropped her burner in a barrio flophouse. I doubt anyone who owns a fancy condo like hers would know where to find a shithole like that. Someone's got her. My money's on the Thunder."

"What now?" Brillo looked from Shea to Fuego.

"We confront the Thunder," Fuego said. "Pinche cabrones violated the ceasefire. Unless they want things turning bloody again, they'd do best to surrender Deirdre."

Shea nodded. "Let me talk to Julia. See what I can find out from her."

"Sí," replied Fuego. "Vámanos before these hijos de puta try to run us over."

34

THE HOUSE FELT empty when Shea walked in the door. As annoying as Annie's defiant pre-teen attitude had been, Shea missed the snarky remarks, the eye rolls, and her endless capacity to be embarrassed by anything Shea said or did. She worried about the girl lying alone and hurting in the hospital bed without her there to comfort her.

Ninja sauntered out of Annie's room, yowling. Shea set out some treats for her on the kitchen floor, but the cat only sniffed at them and continued to yowl.

"Yeah, I miss her too."

Shea pulled out a bottle of vodka from the freezer and took two hard pulls, then called Julia.

"How's Annie?"

"Sleepy and sore, but doing okay all things considered." The tone in Julia's voice suggested more to the story. "There's something you need to know."

"Something about Annie?" A chill ran down Shea's spine. Had something happened during the surgery?

"Yes. I...I want to explain this in person. There's a diner

called Molly's around the corner from the hospital. I can meet you in half an hour."

"Fine. Is Annie with you now? I want to talk to her."

"Shea-Shea, I don't think that's allowed. Not until this custody—"

"Since when do you follow the rules, Julia?"

"Okay, hold on." There was a pause. "Annie, Aunt Shea's on the line."

"Shea?" Her voice was groggy.

"Hey, Doodlebug. How're ya feeling?"

"Tired. Hurts when I move. Wish you were here."

Annie's words felt like daggers in Shea's chest. "Wish I was there too. But I'll see you soon, okay?"

"Okay. I love you, Aunt Shea."

"Love you too, Doodlebug."

"Shea?" Julia returned to the line.

"Yeah, I'll see you in thirty."

Shea hung up. Ninja yowled again. "We'll get her home soon. I promise."

Shea packed Annie's laptop into her computer bag, raced off into the night, and arrived at Molly's All-American Diner thirty minutes later. Shea had been there before. The prices were high for a diner, but the food was decent, and the servers left you alone.

Inside, Donovan was singing about his runaway girlfriend over the sound system. Most of the booths were empty. Julia sat in the back corner, nursing a cup of coffee.

Shea sat down opposite her, handing her the computer bag. "Here's Annie's laptop for when she's feeling better. Now what the hell's going on?"

"What can I get you?" asked a perky server with teal hair.

"A little privacy," Shea said a little more harshly than she intended.

When she left, Shea turned back to Julia. "Spill."

"After the surgery, the doctor came in and explained that Annie has, well, she may have a condition called..." Julia consulted her phone and read from it. "Complete androgen insensitivity syndrome."

"What the hell's that? Is it fatal?"

"Not fatal. It means that technically she's a boy."

"Excuse me?"

"Well, not exactly a boy. Doc says she's intersex. What people used to call a hermaphrodite. Though I'm told that word's not considered respectful no more."

Shea had heard the term "intersex" before, though she didn't know much about it. "That's impossible. Annie's a girl."

"So we all thought. But the hernia was caused by her..." Again Julia consulted her phone. "Her gonads never developed."

"Gonads?"

"They should've developed into testes. If she'd been a real girl, they would've become ovaries."

"They didn't develop?"

"Just enough to cause a weakening in some abdominal wall. I don't understand it. They didn't exactly teach this stuff when I was in school."

"I don't get it. What makes her a boy? I've seen her naked. She doesn't have a penis."

"It's her genetics. She's got XY chromosomes. Her gonads produce testosterone, but her body doesn't respond to it. Doc doesn't know why. It just happens. He says she's got a vagina like a girl, but her breasts won't develop much. Not unless they give her estrogen."

Was this why the lab thought they had the wrong DNA sample? If the results came up with XY chromosomes, they must've assumed a mix-up had occurred, even if it hadn't.

"Has anyone talked to Annie about this?"

"Not yet. She's still groggy."

"Don't. I'll do it. And not a word to anyone else. Not to DCS. And especially not to anyone in your MC."

"If Bryz is her biological father, he's gonna find out."

"And what d'ya think he'll do to her when he does?"

Julia's face paled, but she didn't answer.

"There's another matter we gotta discuss."

"Deirdre West." Julia sighed. "You shouldn't be involved in this mess."

"I was already involved. She is or was an innocent woman under the Sisterhood's protection."

"Not so innocent. She's been blackmailing a powerful man working with the Thunder."

"I swear to God, the Sisterhood will turn this county red with Thunderman blood until she's safely returned or every member of your club is dead or in prison. You think what happened at Bootlegger Bob's was bad? Just wait."

Shea could see the hurt in Julia's eyes as she recalled the horror of the Bootlegger Bob's firebombing that had claimed the lives of several people affiliated with the Thunder, including patched members and old ladies.

"I overheard that the senator asked the club to fetch proof about an affair he had with that woman. But I ain't heard nothing about no kidnapping."

"They also murdered Ms. West's mother. Did you know about that? She was an innocent old woman. They fucking murdered her. For all I know, it was Hooch who did it."

"Hooch wouldn't do nothing like that."

"You sure about that?" Shea glared at her. "The Sisterhood is calling for another meeting with the Thunder's officers. And on neutral ground this time. Or we're gonna start using Johnny Rebs for target practice."

"I'll pass along the word you want to meet. But do yourself a favor, sweetie. Don't push too hard. These boys don't play. They won't cut you slack just 'cause you're girls."

"Women." Shea stood up. "We ain't asking for slack. We're demanding they surrender Deirdre and honor our agreement."

35

When Shea got home, she researched complete androgen insensitivity syndrome, or CAIS as it was called, watching videos on YouTube from people who had the condition and reading medical journal articles and anything else that might help her understand what Annie was dealing with and how best Shea could help her.

At midnight, she dragged herself to bed. For the first time in years, Ninja snuggled up next to her, no doubt because Annie wasn't home.

As much as she tried to sleep, her mind refused to rest. When she finally succumbed, she kept dreaming of trying to rescue Deirdre West, but someone kept dragging her away.

It was only the pounding on her front door and the incessant ringing of her doorbell that got her up. The clock read nine.

"Who the fuck is it?" Shea shouted while she shuffled through her living room, wearing a T-shirt and sweatpants. She grabbed a baseball bat kept by the door for emergencies.

"It's Toni. Open up. We need to talk."

Shea put down the bat and opened the door. Rios was dressed in a clingy gray T-shirt and tight jeans. She looked good, despite her usual no-nonsense cop expression. The bandage on her cheek seemed smaller than the day before.

"You find Deirdre?" Shea asked.

"No." Rios handed her a folded sheet of paper. "I'm sorry to do this, but Shealene Eleanor Stevens, you are hereby ordered to maintain a minimum of five hundred feet away from Senator Joseph Timothy Connelly. You are forbidden from contacting him by any method, including by phone, mail, or any other electronic means. Nor are you permitted to have anyone contact him on your behalf. Failure to comply with this court order could result in fines and/or jail time. Do you understand?"

"What the fuck? You're serving *me* with a restraining order? I knew it. You're just like all the rest of them bastards. Protecting Connelly, no matter what he does. Never shoulda trusted you." Shea started to shut the door, but Rios caught it.

"The sheriff himself pushed this through, Shea. Detective Morris knew that you and I are...well, friends. She asked me to do it. Thought it'd soften the blow."

"Friends? Friends don't pull this kinda shit. Doesn't surprise me that Sheriff Buzzkill and Morris are Connelly's little bitches. So, what's that make you? Morris's bitch?"

"This is serious. Connelly's claiming you and your friends forced him off the road while en route to a campaign rally. His campaign manager was a witness. You're lucky you're not behind bars. You need to stay away from him."

"He's murdering innocent women. But you're serving *me* with a restraining order?"

"Not my choice. Believe me."

"Is anyone bothering to look for Deirdre? Or doesn't she matter so long as Senator Con Job is happy?"

"Bello and Morris are looking for her. Based on your description, the Thunderman who slashed your arm is a two-time loser named Peter Barbera. Goes by the nickname Basher. Served two years for assaulting a sex worker outside Vegas, then another six for stabbing someone down in Tucson. There's a BOLO out on him and Mackey."

"Mackey? I thought Mackey was already in jail."

"Sheriff Keeler ordered him released due to lack of evidence when we couldn't prove his gun was used to shoot me."

"Sheriff Buzzkill, huh? Why am I not surprised? Have you questioned Connelly?"

"It's a delicate situation. His attorney refuses to bring him in to talk with us. We'll need some serious probable cause to force his hand."

"Funny how the standard for probable cause is much higher for people like him than the rest of us."

"Shea, I appreciate you're frustrated, but if Connelly is behind these crimes, this investigation has to be by the book, or he'll skate on a technicality. Just cool your heels. We'll find her."

"We? You've been reinstated?"

"I meant Bello and Morris."

"Figured. We done here?"

"One other thing. I shouldn't be telling you this, but... things being what they are, I feel I owe it to you. The Vehicular Evidence Division has been going over Ms. West's car. They found an open beer bottle and a small bag of heroin inside. It appears she may have been driving while intoxicated at the time of the crash."

"Bullshit. Deirdre doesn't drink beer. She's allergic to it. The entire thing's a fucking setup."

"I did not know that. The techs in VED also noted that her yellow Kia Soul swapped paint with another vehicle—a dark-blue vehicle, most likely a German or British import. We can't confirm yet whether this other vehicle forced her off the road or she hit it accidentally. But it's a lead."

"A dark-blue German vehicle? You mean like Connelly's Mercedes SUV?"

"Bello and Morris are looking into it. But like I said, it's a delicate situation."

"Have you looked for Deirdre at the Church?"

A confused expression settled on Rios's face. "What church?"

"The Thunder's clubhouse."

"I can talk to Bello about getting a search warrant."

Shea crumpled the order of protection and threw it on the floor. "Yeah, you do that."

"Don't forget, I helped you find Deirdre's burner phone. And I Tased that junkie who attacked you. But you're still questioning my loyalties?"

"Thanks for the save, Detective. Have a nice life."

She slammed the door, shuffled back to her bedroom, and called Julia.

"How's Annie?"

"She's doing well. Nurses say she may go home today. Not sure when."

"You tell her about her condition?"

"No. You can trust me, Shea."

"You talk to the boys about sitting down to meet?"

"I talked to Hooch, and he spoke with One-Shot. What with Mackey getting arrested, the bottom line is that the Sisterhood needs to forget this woman. No negotiations. It's Thunder business."

"Bullshit. Deirdre West was under our protection. Also,

Mackey and Basher violated the truce by attacking me. The Thunder needs to make this right."

"You knew it was Basher?"

"Yep, and so did you, obviously."

"I'm begging you, Shealene. Let this one go before you or anyone we care about gets hurt."

"We will find Deirdre. And we'll punish anyone and everyone who hurt her."

"Don't forget, I still have Annie."

"Goddamn bitch! You gonna use her like she's your pawn? I will fucking end you."

"Don't you dare threaten me, young lady. I may not be the VP of my own club, but I've been in this life a whole lot longer than you."

"You call that a life? The Sisters protect women. You're just some asshole's property. The back of your cut says so."

Shea hung up and called Fuego.

"Hola, VP. Any word on Annie?"

"Doing okay, or so I'm told. Still can't see her." She decided not to bring up Annie being intersex. Not until after she talked with Annie herself.

"What about meeting with the Thunder?"

"They told us to fuck off. Truce or no truce. Claim that Deirdre is Thunder business."

"Mierda! Now what?"

"Dunno. To top it off, I got served a restraining order to stay away from Senator Con Job. We need to meet in the chapel and discuss this."

"Okay. I'll let everyone know and will be in touch."

36

THE NEXT MORNING, after a quick shower, Shea found herself staring at a plate of bacon and eggs she'd made for herself. The aroma of the crispy strips of pork belly set her mouth watering, but her stomach soured in revulsion. The memory of Sophie's bullet-riddled body blazed in her mind.

Annie was recovering from surgery in the hospital. Deirdre was probably in a shallow grave somewhere. But it was the image of that damn potbellied beast lying in a pool of its own blood that filled her with the most grief. Her eyes pricked with tears until she tossed the food in the trash and pulled on her biker gear.

When she arrived at Iron Goddess, Terrance informed her that Clarissa Hughes had been delighted with her new custom bike.

Shea gave him the latest on Annie, including what she'd learned about Annie having CAIS. "How do I tell her she's intersex, T?"

"Be honest with her," Terrance replied. "Let her know it doesn't change who she is. She's the same person she was before. It doesn't define her. Reassure her you don't see her any differently now. She'll need your support to accept this aspect of herself."

"Thanks. I'll do that when I get custody back. If I get custody back."

Terrance clapped her on the back. "Why don't you head home. We got no more custom orders. Vince and Lakota have all the service tickets covered. You deserve some 'me time.'"

"'Me time'?" Shea snorted. "Geez, when did you get all woo-woo, T?"

"Sister girl, have you looked in the mirror lately?"

"I try not to if I can help it."

"Please know that I mean this in the most loving way possible, but you look like shit. Your face is so bruised it has more colors than the Pride flag. You've been raising Annie, running the shop, and doing God-knows-what for the Sisterhood. You're burning yourself out. Gotta take some time off, or you will end up six feet under."

"So, I should do what? Go get a facial and a massage? Maybe a makeover and a mani/pedi?"

Terrance guffawed in response. "I'd pay good money to see you getting all dolled up."

Shea couldn't help but laugh along with him. Femme was the last thing she was. Or wanted to be.

"Do something that makes you happy. Get some serious wind therapy. Take the big loop around the Mogollon Rim, past Lake Mary up to Flag. Then snake back down Oak Creek Canyon through Sedona and Jerome to Prescott."

"Shit. Been years since I rode that loop."

"Nothing like getting out of the heat and racing through a bunch of twisties to get your mind off stuff," Terrance reassured her.

She checked her watch. "I think you're right. I'll see ya 'round, brother."

After gearing up, she picked up the highway heading east, breezed past I-17 at Camp Verde, and put on some serious speed through the sweepers along the Rim. The views of the lower desert were hazy but still spectacular.

The air temperature dropped as she turned left onto Lake Mary Road and rose up past the campgrounds and the cluster of manmade lakes. The cool, pine-scented air and sapphire-blue sky cleared her mind of all concerns.

When she reached Flagstaff, she stopped to top off her tank and grab a fast food lunch. She ignored the looks of concern from the people around her and ate in peace. Terrance had been right. She needed this.

Once on the road again, she crossed over I-17 once again and wound her way south through the hairpin turns following scenic Oak Creek Canyon. A few miles before Slide Rock State Park, a popular tourist attraction in the summertime, a long line of cars stretched to the park's entrance, blocking all southbound traffic. The road had only one lane each way, and the shoulders were narrow and treacherous.

The afternoon sun began to make itself felt on the back of her neck while she waited for the cars in front of her to move. After fifteen minutes with very little progress, Shea decided to take a chance and pulled into the oncoming lane, hoping that if she encountered any vehicles, she could duck between a couple of southbound cars.

She was almost to the park entrance when an RV the size of an aircraft carrier approached. The end of the traffic was roughly halfway between them. She pinned the throttle, keeping as close to the median as possible.

The driver of the RV laid on its horn but didn't appear to slow. Shea's heart pounded as the gap between them narrowed. Memories of the Sons of Anarchy finale flashed through her mind.

An instant before the RV flattened her, it veered unsteadily off the road. She flew by it like a bat out of hell and swerved back into her lane as she passed the end of the traffic jam. Her body screamed with adrenaline as she hurtled on toward Sedona.

The rest of the trip was more relaxing, even as the afternoon heat built up. The only other congestion she encountered was along the twisty streets of Jerome, but once past that, it was smooth sailing past Mingus Mountain, around past Prescott, and on to home.

After spending hours in the heat and winding through countless twisty mountain roads, Shea walked in the door exhausted and dehydrated but still restless. The wind therapy had helped, but it didn't fill the emptiness left by Annie's absence. She tried to watch television but ended up pacing the living room like a caged tiger. Ninja's incessant yowling didn't help. Her food bowl was full, and the dish of treats Shea had set down was barely touched.

She found herself in the garage staring at her stable of motorcycles. More than a dozen, several of them with a layer of dust on the gas tanks from lack of use. Cruisers, touring bikes, café racers, adventure bikes, and crotch rockets. She remembered creating each one. Cutting and shaping the metal, welding the tanks, assembling the frames, installing the electrical systems, adding the fluids, and taking them for the thrilling first ride.

Learning to build custom motorcycles had given her life meaning after serving eight years for grand theft auto. She owed it all to Lenny Slater, the shop's original owner, who had given her a second chance. He had been the father figure she needed after her own father betrayed her so long ago. She missed Lenny as much as she missed her mother.

She pulled the old tarnished lighter from her pocket and flipped the lid open and closed. He'd given it to her on her one-year anniversary at the shop. It no longer had lighter fluid, and she no longer smoked. But it was a memento of her new life.

And where was that life now? For the past few years, her old life had intruded on her passion for building custom bikes. All the chaos disrupting the zen simplicity of turning raw metal into roaring, racing works of art. Now she was a parental figure, though she wasn't sure for how long. And a member of a motorcycle club. Was it all worth it? *Weird how things had a way of circling back to where you were.*

She walked over to an old cruiser she'd named the Black Swan. One of her first custom bikes. She hadn't ridden it since the clutch wore out a few years back. The replacement parts sat in the corner, still in the box.

She picked up the new clutch kit, grabbed a few tools, and began disassembling the Black Swan's transmission. This was the work that brought her joy.

Her phone rang what seemed like moments later. A glance at her watch told her she'd been at it for hours. She wiped her grimy hands with a shop rag and answered the call without looking at the caller ID.

"Yeah?"

"It's me, Aunt Shea. Annie."

Shea nearly dropped the phone. "Oh my God, Annie! How are you feeling?"

"Sore. It hurts to walk, and it's hard to get comfortable in this stupid bed."

"You still at the hospital?"

"No, I'm at Gramma Julia's. She's being stingy with the pain pills. Says she don't want me getting addicted."

"Much as I hate to agree with her, she's right. Your

mama had a problem with them." Shea regretted the words immediately. She never wanted to talk bad about her sister in front of Annie. "Hang in there best you can, kiddo. You'll feel better soon."

"Wish I was home with you."

"Me too."

"Why'd I have to have that operation, anyway? No one will tell me. I'm not stupid."

"I…" Shea didn't want to have to explain over the phone to Annie about her being intersex. "Something in your belly got torn and needed stitching up. Happens sometimes."

"You still looking for Deirdre?"

"Yeah. Why?"

"I mighta heard something."

Shea's pulse quickened. "Heard something? When? Where?"

"Little while ago. After Gramma Julia and Hooch drove me home in his truck. He and Bryz and Basher were talking in the hallway. Musta thought I was sleeping. They said they caught the bitch and were holding her in the back room at the Church, trying to make her talk."

"Oh, you smart, smart girl. Thanks for telling me. Does Julia know you know this?"

"I ain't told her. She doesn't know I'm calling you."

"Good. Don't tell nobody else, okay?"

"What are you gonna do?"

"I will get her back."

"When will you get me back?" Shea could hear the hurt and fear in her voice.

"Soon, baby. Real soon."

"Okay. I miss Ninja."

"She misses you, too. She's been howling like a coyote day and night, missing you."

"No shit?"

"No shit, kiddo. You hang in there. I'll see you soon. I love you."

"Love you too, Aunt Shea."

Shea hung up, her throat tight with emotion. She wanted to forget about Deirdre and bring Annie home. But if she did, the cops and DCS would show up and throw her back in jail.

She chucked the ratchet wrench she'd been using across the garage. It banged against the door, leaving a dent. She picked up her phone again and called Fuego. It rang three times, and she worried it would go to voicemail.

"Havoc, hey! I've spent all day trying to get in touch with the officers. Everybody's been out and about. But we're meeting at the clubhouse at six to figure out what to do about the Thunder."

"Great! Annie just called. She overheard some Thundermen say they're holding Deirdre at the Church, trying to find out where she's hiding the evidence of her affair with Connelly."

"We'll get her back, hermana. Those hijos de puta won't know what hit 'em. See you at the clubhouse at six."

"Thanks, Fuego. That's the best news I've had all day. See ya shortly."

SHEA WALKED into the Athena Sisterhood clubhouse in Downtown Ironwood. Indigo and Savage met her as she entered the chapel.

"How's the arm?" Savage asked.

"Still hurts like a fucker, but it's not bleeding." Shea pulled off her jacket and showed it to the other two women.

Savage studied the wound. "No signs of infection, so

that's good. It'll leave a scar, but chicks dig scars, right?" She winked at Shea.

"And yet somehow I keep running them off."

"Yeah, too bad about that bounty hunter chick. She was all right. Can't believe her fiancée returned from the dead. Talk about awkward."

Shea shrugged. "Story of my life."

"Don't worry," said Indigo, putting an arm around her wife. "You'll find someone."

Rios's face popped into Shea's mind, and she laughed. "Yeah, right. I'll probably end up some lonely old biker bitch with too many cats."

They walked into the chapel where the others were seated. Fuego called the meeting to order and asked Shea to update the group.

"The Thunder refuses to meet with us about them breaking the truce. And they're telling us to forget Deirdre West."

"Screw that!" Raven replied. "I thought we were protecting her."

"We were. Or at least trying to," Shea admitted glumly.

"Are we sure they have her?" Dragon asked.

"Annie called me. She overheard a few Thundermen confirm it. I'm willing to sneak in and rescue her."

"Not alone, you're not," Indigo replied. "If you're going, I'm going with you."

Raven nodded. "Me too. I'll be damned if I'll let those bastards abuse her."

"Same here," Brillo added. "If you need me, I'm there."

Fuego said, "All in favor of rescuing Deirdre West from the Thundermen's clubhouse, say aye."

All but Dragon replied aye enthusiastically.

"Opposed?"

"I could be disbarred if I got caught," Dragon said. "I'm

sorry, but I can't take part. Bad enough I know about it in advance."

"No problema, Dragon," Fuego replied. "You help in other ways."

"Should we bring more of the Sisters?" asked Indigo.

"No, this needs to be a tactical rescue, not an all-out assault," Fuego replied. "Get in. Find Deirdre. Get out. Quick and precise. Let them assume she escaped."

"Agreed," Shea said. "There's a Forest Service road that runs close to the Church. We can take that north about a mile, then hike in from there. We'll need flashlights. And a four-wheeled vehicle, in case Deirdre's too weak to ride on the back of my bike. That dirt road can get gnarly in spots."

"I can run by the house and pick up our Jeep," said Savage. "Should be able to handle it."

"I have four LED flashlights in my top case," Brillo said.

"Why so many?" Raven asked. "Isn't one enough?"

Brillo shrugged. "Don't want to get stuck somewhere and the first three don't work."

Fuego winked and held up her phone. "I got an app for that."

"Let's go get our girl," Shea said.

37

SHEA LED the way up the rugged Forest Service road. As a kid, she'd explored the woods and the labyrinth of intersecting roads and trails via dirt bike, four-wheeler, and on foot.

The route started out as graded gravel, but after a sharp incline, the surface grew rugged with exposed rocks and crater-like potholes. Dancing shadows created by multiple headlights bobbing back and forth didn't help. Shea struggled to navigate the uneven ground. At one point, Raven's bike toppled over, forcing the group to stop and help her right it again.

Eventually, Shea recognized an eight-foot granite monolith standing at a fork in the road. A Johnny Reb and other graffiti had been spray-painted on the boulder.

She pulled to the side of the road and killed her engine. The side stand sank an inch into the sandy soil. She turned to the others, shielding her eyes from the glare of their headlights until all but those from Savage's Jeep went dark.

The six of them gathered at the edge of the road, each

with a light in one hand and a gun in the other. The steady drone of crickets and cicadas filled the summer night air like a high-pitched lullaby, punctuated by the occasional trill of a screech owl.

"You sure we're in the right spot?" Indigo looked warily at the dark pines looming over them. "All these trees look alike."

"It's changed over the years, but I know that rock." Shea remembered making out with Heather Eriksson at the base of it when she was fourteen. "The Church is a mile east of here."

"Think they heard our engines?" Fuego asked.

Shea shook her head. "No chance. I could scream at the top of my lungs. No one inside or outside the Church would hear me." As Heather Eriksson had proved.

"Everyone ready?" Fuego looked at each of the women. They all nodded in turn. "Shea, lead the way."

"Follow me."

Even with the trail, their movement was slow going. The dense forest pressed in around them like a wall of black. Shea's flashlight only penetrated so far. She stumbled twice on roots and stones hidden amongst the carpet of pine needles.

After ten minutes, Shea froze with her light focused on a pile of whitish brown scat in the center of the path. Bits of fur and tiny bones were visible among the round lumps. Next to it, a set of paw prints vanished into the woods.

A chill ran down Shea's spine. She scanned the looming darkness for the fiery gleam of eyes but saw nothing but the inky forest.

"What's wrong?" Savage whispered somewhere behind her.

"Puma scat. Fresh from the look of it." Shea took a

calming breath. "Hopefully, the cat that left it won't mess with the group of us. But they are ambush hunters, so keep an eye out."

Points of light appeared in the distance that could only be the Church. She turned to the group and put a finger to her lips. As they drew closer, Shea turned off her flashlight, navigating by the moonlight and the yellow glow from the Church's outdoor security lamps.

They reached a locked gate in an eight-foot-tall security fence topped with razor wire. A sign warned that the fence was electrified. Another read, "Trespassers will be violated."

Shea recalled the time when she and a few of her fellow Thunderlings made a game to see who could touch the fence the longest before the tingling sensation became unbearable. The longest Shea lasted was five seconds. The club turned off the juice after a kid with a congenital defect died. The warning signs remained to scare away trespassers.

Beyond the fence, patchy grass surrounded the old church building. Long shadows cast by the security lights gave the playground a haunting look, an eerie reminder of childhood lost.

Music thrummed from inside the building. The distant parking lot held a half dozen motorcycles. No people in sight.

Shea pointed to the back of the building. "That's where we gotta go. There's a storage room, a laundry room, and two bedrooms in back—both fairly soundproof. If they got her, she's most likely in one of the bedrooms."

"How do we get past this?" Raven pointed at the sign warning of the electrified fence.

"The juice got shut off years ago." Shea put a hand on

the fence to make sure, grateful when there was no sting of electricity. "As for the lock, I have a key." She held up the leather case of lock picks.

"Someone should wait here as lookout," said Fuego.

"I will," replied Brillo. "I have excellent night vision."

"Text me if you see anything," Fuego said.

"Will do."

"Okay, here's the plan," Shea explained. "First door on the right is an old storage room. Indigo, you take that one. Raven and Savage, take the second door on the right. Should be one of the bedrooms. If the door's locked, use this." Shea handed Raven a small metal rod.

"What if someone's in there?" Savage asked. "Other than Deirdre, I mean."

"Do whatcha gotta do," Shea replied soberly. "Quietly, if you can."

She turned to Fuego. "First door on the left is a laundry room. I doubt they'll keep her in there, but take a peek just in case. Then follow me to the second bedroom on the left. If any of you find Deirdre, come get the rest of us and we'll reconvene here. Got it?"

Everyone nodded.

"Let's go."

Shea set to work on the padlock with her picking tools until the hasp released with a quiet snick.

Could they rescue Deirdre without being detected? She wasn't sure.

"Let's go get Deirdre."

They hustled across the open expanse between the woods and the back of the building, trying to muffle their footsteps as best they could in their leather boots.

Once they reached the door, Shea tried the handle and found it locked. "Crap."

Running on adrenaline and fear of being caught, she

picked at the lock's pins until the cylinder turned and the door opened. A Blake Shelton tune echoed down the hallway from the old sanctuary, accompanied by the sounds of men's voices and drunken laughter.

Shea rushed to the second door on the left, flicked on the light, and gasped at the battered woman tied to a chair. But it wasn't Deirdre.

"Shit. Rios!"

The detective's head drooped on her chest, a bloody rag wrapped around her mouth. She was topless except for a bra.

"Rios," Shea said in an urgent whisper. "You alive in there?"

Rios groaned. One swollen eye opened. "Shea..." Her voice was hoarse and weak.

"We're getting you outta here." Shea holstered her gun and used a jackknife to cut through the zip ties binding Rios's wrists.

"Dios mio," Fuego muttered from the doorway. "You found her?"

"Not Deirdre. A cop I know. Come on, give me a hand." Shea slipped her jacket over Rios and zipped it up. "Can you walk?"

"Not sure."

Shea and Fuego shouldered Rios to her feet and turned to leave. When voices approached from the hallway, they quietly shut the door and turned out the lights.

"Can't wait to sell that truckload of guns," said a harsh male voice. "Old lady's been bitching about money again. Telling me her fag brother's got a job opening down at a fucking warehouse down in Ironwood. As if."

"I hear ya, dude. Money from this job'll help me pay off a few debts," replied a higher-pitched male voice.

Their footsteps passed the door. "Hey! Who the fuck are you?" asked the first voice.

"Go," Fuego told Shea. "We'll be right behind you."

Shea rushed into the hallway to find Shank and Poptop, the two prospects who'd previously guarded the Thunder's chapel, standing just inside the storage room.

Shea pressed her gun against the back of Shank's shaved head. "Get in the room, or I'll blow your fucking heads off."

He uttered a low growl but obeyed. Poptop shot her a worried look and shuffled inside.

The place smelled of bleach. Cases of booze were stacked next to a shelving unit full of cleaning supplies. Indigo stood in the corner with her gun at the ready.

She marched them to the opposite wall before ordering them to turn around. She figured a patched Thunderman had sent the prospects to grab more booze or for some other menial task. Wouldn't be long before somebody wondered what was taking them so long. Fuego helped Rios shuffle into the room, followed by Raven and Savage, who closed the door.

"Where's Deirdre West?" Fuego asked.

"Suck my dick, you wetback cunt," Shank snapped.

"Wrong answer, puto." Fuego smacked him across the face. "Where is she?"

The skinhead grinned with blood in his teeth. "Never heard of her."

Shea took a step toward Poptop. His eyes flashed fear. "How about you, asswipe? You hearda her? Skinny redhead with a pet pig. The one Connelly hired y'all to kidnap."

"W-we didn't kidnap her," Poptop stammered.

Shea aimed her pistol at his crotch. "I'm counting to three. If you don't tell me where she's at, I'm gonna blow your nuts off. One."

"Please don't shoot me. I don't know where she is. I swear."

"Bullshit. Two."

"Shea," Savage cautioned. "Don't do this."

"Don't you say nothing, Poptop," the skinhead warned.

"Thr—"

"Wait, wait, wait! I'll talk." A wet spot spread down Mohawk's pant legs. "M-M-Mackey and Bash tried to grab her at the motel, but she got away. Honest."

"Motherfucking pussy." The skinhead spat blood on the floor.

"Sorry, Shank. I...I couldn't help it."

"Where'd she go then?"

"I dunno. I'm just a prospect. They don't tell me shit."

"Let's roll, Havoc, before we get more company." Savage whispered.

"Hold up." Rios pulled a gun from Shank's waistband and a phone from his back pocket. "I'll be taking these back, pendejo."

"Shoulda killed you, goddamn beaner cop!"

Rios shuffled toward Poptop, pressing her gun to his eye. "Where'd you dirtbags get that truckload of guns?"

"Don't you say shit," Shank growled. "I'll fucking gut you myself."

"Y-y-you d-do what you g-gotta do," the heavyset prospect said, despite the sweat dripping down his face.

"Your funeral." Rios pulled back the hammer on her pistol.

"Wait, wait, stop. We jacked a Wolf Ridge Arms truck, okay? Just trying to make some scratch for the MC after they got outta the joint."

"That's what I thought," Rios replied. "Who's the buyer?"

"Border Patriots."

"Figures," Shea snorted.

The Border Patriots was a paramilitary white nationalist organization operating out of southern Arizona. Most of the members were middle-aged men who liked to dress up like soldiers and carry high-powered weaponry, all in the name of keeping America safe from brown people.

Rios lowered her weapon but maintained eye contact with the prospect. "When's this deal taking place?"

"Monday night at six at the old laser tag place in Bradshaw City."

"Gibb's Lazer Palace?" Shea asked. "The one that shut down a few years back?"

Poptop nodded. "Yeah. That's the place."

Shank spit at her. "I shoulda fucked you while I had the chance."

Rios coldcocked him with her gun. He slumped to the floor, a trickle of blood running from his temple. "Chinga tu madre, cabrón!"

Shea couldn't help but smile. Rios looked like she'd been through hell, but she could still kick a little ass.

"Where the fuck's that beer, prospects?" a familiar voice shouted from the main room. "I'm thirsty. Goddammit!"

"Mackey." Flames of anger erupted inside Shea. She took a step toward the door, but Indigo grabbed her arm.

"Not now. Sounds like there could be a dozen of them down there."

Shea knew Indigo was right. She turned to Rios. "You able to run?"

"Sí."

"Hold up!" Fuego held up her phone. "Brillo says someone's out in the parking lot."

"Shit! We gotta get outta here," Raven muttered.

Shea glared at Poptop and pressed her gun against his wet crotch. "Answer him. Tell him you're on your way."

"Be right there, boss!"

"Mackey! We got some Barbie bike—" Shank started to shout before Rios gave him another smack, then turned her gun back toward Poptop.

"What was that?" Mackey yelled.

"N-nothing, boss!" Poptop answered. "Beer's on the way."

"Coast is clear," Fuego said. "¡Vámonos, hermanas!"

Shea punched Poptop in the gut, knocking the wind out of him, then kneed him in the crotch. He doubled over and collapsed onto Shank.

The Sisters rushed out the back door, where Brillo was waiting for them by the gate. Shea re-locked it once they were through and helped Rios down the path, checking from time to time to see if they were being followed.

They were halfway to the vehicles when angry voices echoed through the woods behind them. The beams of flashlights flickered in the direction of the Church.

"Go, go, go!" Shea shouted. "They're coming."

Rios groaned and grunted on shaky legs. Shea put an arm around her to help her move faster. She could no longer see the rest of the group ahead of them.

A shadow crossed the path in front of her. Fiery green eyes blazed in the dark. Shea raised her light. The tawny, muscular form of a puma stood in the middle of the trail. It growled, revealing killing teeth.

Shea was too pumped to be afraid. "Get the fuck outa our way, you goddamn cat!"

The beast hunched its shoulders, ears back, eyes locked on Shea. She was about to reach for her pistol when the crack of gunfire echoed behind the puma. The cat leapt into the darkness with another fierce growl.

"Come on, Rios. Let's get the hell outta here."

Shea was practically dragging Rios by the time they

reached the vehicles. Savage pulled Rios into the back seat of the Jeep, and they took off. The others followed on their motorcycles. Shea brought up the rear as they raced toward the main road.

38

Once they hit the main road, the group drove south, away from the Church. At a remote gas station fifteen miles away, they pulled around to the far side so as not to be seen from the road.

Shea rushed over to the Jeep and poked her head in the open driver's window where Indigo sat. Savage was in the back with Rios lying on her lap.

"How's she doing?" Shea's eyes adjusted to the darkness of the back seat.

Rios lay on her side. "Hurts."

"She may have a mild concussion," Savage added. "Multiple contusions and lacerations. We should take her to the hospital."

"No." Rios forced herself into a seated position. "If it gets out that I broke in there without a warrant, it's my badge. Please just take me home."

"You sure? Not sure you should be alone," Shea said. "How about you come back to my place? You can stay in Annie's room."

Rios's eyes met Shea's. "I'd like that."

"What about Deirdre?" Fuego asked when she and the others walked up. "Didn't see any sign of her at the Church."

"I don't know. But we can't risk going back. We'll have to deal with that another time."

"Agreed. We'll be in touch." Fuego patted her on the back. "Buen trabajo, chicas."

Shea turned to Savage. "Follow me back to my place."

It was after nine o'clock when Shea pulled into her garage and helped Rios climb out of Savage and Indigo's Jeep.

"Can you walk?" Shea asked Rios.

"I think so." Rios sounded a little stronger, though her voice was still shaky and hoarse. She turned to Savage and Indigo. "Thanks for the rescue."

"You got it, my friend," Indigo replied.

"Let's go inside and take a look at those wounds," Savage said.

"Okay."

"Shea, we got a problem." Indigo drew her gun and pointed toward the front door.

Shea followed her gaze and felt punched in the gut. The front door was ajar, the frame cracked. "Shit. Savage, wait here with Rios. Indigo, you mind coming with me?"

"Not at all."

Shea drew her Glock. Something crunched underfoot when she stepped inside. She flicked on a light. The place had been ransacked. Furniture overturned, flat-screen TV shattered, cushions slashed. Books, record albums, and DVDs pulled from shelves. Her baseball bat lay on the floor next to what had once been her glass coffee table. In the kitchen area, the cabinets and the fridge were open, dishes smashed, boxes of food emptied onto the floor.

Shea nodded toward Annie's room. "Check there. I got the master bedroom."

She found her room similarly trashed with the bed overturned, clothes from the closet scattered across the carpet, drawers pulled out of her dresser. The laptop on the desk next to her bed was smashed, its display ripped apart from the keyboard. "Motherfucker."

She met back up with Indigo in the living room.

"Assholes really did a number on the place," Indigo offered.

"Yeah, ya think? Savage, it's safe to come in."

Savage led Rios inside and helped her onto the one upright stool at the breakfast bar. "Wow. Can't believe they smashed the flat-screen. Probably could've made some cash selling it."

"They broke my laptop in half, too. I don't think they were here to rob the place. More likely looking for the evidence of Connelly's affair. Of course, I lied about having it. Stupid move on my part."

"Shea," Rios said wearily, "you're supposed to stay away from Connelly."

"This was before you served me with that stupid restraining order. I'll be right back." She waltzed into her mess of a bedroom, picked up a T-shirt, and returned to the living room. "Not sure how well it will fit. I'm taller, but you're a bit...bustier."

Rios accepted it with a sad smile. "Thanks. I can call Detective Morris. Report the break-in. It's got to be tied in with this situation with Deirdre West."

Shea scoffed. "And what will that accomplish?"

"Every shred of evidence is one step closer to making a case against Connelly."

"Sheriff Buzzkill's protecting Connelly, and you know it.

Me reporting the break-in won't change that. Besides, how would you explain you being here looking all messed up?"

Rios didn't respond.

Shea leaned against the counter. "I need a drink. Can I get anyone anything? Not sure what's left that isn't smashed. Might be some vodka in the freezer."

"Water's fine," Rios whispered.

"Let me grab my bag from the Jeep," Savage replied. "And take a look at the detective's wounds."

Shea found a plastic cup, filled it with reverse osmosis water, and handed it to Rios.

Indigo clapped a hand on Shea's shoulder. "I'll help you fix the door."

"Thanks."

Savage took Rios into the guest bath to treat her wounds. Meanwhile, Shea and Indigo used glue, wood screws, and some old two-by-fours to reinforce the doorframe. It wouldn't keep out a determined intruder, but it would at least hold the door shut.

They then separated the debris from what they could salvage. Shea would have to take the shattered remains of her laptop to JuJu, a member of the Sisterhood who was a whiz at repairing computers, to see if she could recover the data.

When they were done, it was nearly midnight. A pile of debris and trash bags lined the front porch. Shea walked Savage and Indigo to their Jeep to thank them.

"Y'all gonna be all right?" Indigo asked. "I can stay and keep a lookout in case whoever broke in comes back."

Shea shook her head. "Doubt they'll return. As far as they know, they destroyed what evidence I claimed I had."

"Keep your head on a swivel," Savage said. "And if Detective Rios starts vomiting or experiencing any other neurological symptoms, call 9-1-1 or take her to the ER. Even if she objects. Could save her life."

After they left, Shea returned inside and sat on her duct tape–patched love seat next to Rios.

"How'd you end up at the Thunder's clubhouse?" Shea asked.

Rios didn't answer for the longest time, staring blankly across the room. "You were frustrated by the sheriff's office's lack of action on the Deirdre West case. I was, too, despite knowing why Morris and Bello were proceeding with caution. So, I ignored my years of training and experience, not to mention my commitment to the law, and broke into the Thunder's clubhouse, hoping to find her or at least uncover something, anything incriminating. Instead, I probably tainted whatever case Morris and Bello may have had while putting myself and my career in jeopardy. Dios mio, I was so stupid."

"So, what happened?"

"I didn't find her, obviously. Didn't see evidence she'd ever been there. I was almost out of there when a guy named Hooch caught me. Him, Mackey, and a few others, they...they did what they could to get me to say who tipped us off three years ago about the drug bust. Hit me. Cut me. Burned me with a cigarette. Other stuff. I didn't tell them shit."

Shea recognized the trauma in Rios's eyes, knowing too well the ruthlessness of the Thundermen. Guilt punched her in the gut. Rios endured all that to protect her.

"Did they sexually assault you?"

"No, thankfully. But that guy Bryz. He had a look in his eyes like he would have if I'd stayed there much longer."

"I'm sorry." Shea's words felt trite and inadequate when Shea said them.

"Nothing to be sorry for. How'd you find me, anyway?"

"My niece overheard some Thundermen saying they had a woman prisoner. Assumed it was Deirdre. Found you instead."

"Thank God you did."

"You gonna report it?"

Rios met Shea's eyes. "Can't. At least not what they did to me. I broke in without a warrant." She grew quiet again before saying, "Gracias por todo, Shea. I mean it."

"De nada." Shea shrugged it off.

Rios stood and grabbed Shea's wrist, pulling her close. Her touch was warm and soft but strong.

The vulnerability in Rios's warm cocoa eyes melted the wall Shea had maintained for years around her feelings for the detective. "Stuffy in here. Bastards musta messed with the thermostat."

"Shea..."

"I...I can't." Shea pulled away and stood, forcing the walls back in place. "You're...you're a cop."

"So? You're attracted to me. I can tell."

"Maybe, but I don't date cops. And you sure as hell don't need to be dating...someone like me."

"Someone who's willing to fight for what she believes in? Who'll risk everything for the people she loves?" Rios asked.

"Someone who served eight years in the can and will probably end up back there one of these days. Someone who lost custody of a child for refusing a court order. Not to mention all the shit I can't tell you about."

"I may not always agree with your methods, but I've always admired your motives. You've got a good heart."

All of this praise made Shea all the more uncomfortable. "I'm gonna crash. You need anything, holler."

"Yeah." Rios stood, the disappointment evident on her

face, and disappeared into Annie's room, shutting the door behind her.

On her way to her room, Shea realized she hadn't seen Ninja since she'd been home. She grabbed a bag of kitty treats and began shaking it while walking around the house. "Here, kitty, kitty, kitty! Ninja, where are you?"

Shea looked under furniture, behind curtains, inside cabinets, and everywhere Ninja would hide when guests showed up. But there was no sign of her. Shea opened the front door and peered out into the night. Stray cats didn't last long out there. Coyotes, bobcats, raptors, and other predators roamed freely and frequently.

"Ninja? You out here?" She shook the bag of treats. A low caterwauling came from behind the sage bushes in front of the house. Shea flipped on the porch lights. Ninja's eyes glowed green from the shadows. She yowled mournfully.

Shea picked up the cat, who was covered in leaves from the sage bush. "Poor baby. Must be outta your furry mind. Well, don't worry. You're safe now."

Once inside, the cat hustled to Annie's door and began scratching and crying. "Ninja, no. She's not in there."

When Ninja yowled louder, Shea picked her up again and carried her back to her own bedroom.

39

THE FOLLOWING MORNING, Shea did a double take when she found Rios sipping a cup of coffee at the breakfast bar before she remembered the bizarre events of the night before. *At least I'm wearing a T-shirt and shorts*, Shea thought. *Could've been awkward.*

"Good lord, there's a cop in my house."

"Funny," Rios replied. "I hope you don't mind—I made coffee."

"Won't hear me complaining." Shea poured some coffee into an old mug she hadn't used for years, one of the few left intact. Leaning against the counter, she asked. "How're you feeling?"

"Numb. Don't worry. I'll be out of your hair soon enough. I left a message for Detective Johnson, asking her to pick me up. I'll let her know about the Thunder's involvement in the Wolf Ridge Arms hijacking and the upcoming deal with the Border Patriots."

"And what'll you say when she asks how you learned about it?"

"Tip from a CI."

"Close enough to the truth, I suppose."

Shea felt a tugging in her gut. "You don't have to go. It's Sunday. Stay and recuperate. I'll...I'll take care of you. Then I'll give you a ride wherever you need." What the hell was happening to her? Since when did she say such things to a cop?

"No, I...I need some time to process all this. Please don't think I'm ungrateful, Shea." Their eyes met.

Her entire body grew hot. "No, no, I get it. You've...you've endured a lot. I'm just...worried."

Life flickered into Rios's eyes. "Gracias, but I can take care of myself. Most of the time, at least. When I'm not doing something stupid like breaking into a biker clubhouse without a warrant or backup."

"The Thunder's probably looking for you." Shea realized she was scrambling for excuses to keep Rios close. "Maybe you can't file charges against them, but as far as they know, you could bring down the whole club with what you learned about the arms hijacking. They were willing to kill you once. Doubly so now."

"I'll be fine. I'm a cop. Remember?" Rios drained her coffee cup and stood up, wincing as she did so. "But thanks for being concerned. It means a lot." Her phone rang. "Hola, compañera. Sorry I didn't call back sooner. I'm safe. I'm...I'm at the home of Shea Stevens. Long story. Yeah, that'd be great. Gracias, Ebony."

When Rios hung up, Shea asked, "Your partner?"

"She's on her way to pick me up. Patrol spotted my car where I'd parked it off the side of Pinellas Parkway. They ran the plates and discovered my badge inside. When they couldn't reach me, they towed the car to the District IV garage and put a BOLO out on me."

"You gonna tell her what happened?"

"More or less. She'll be pissed at me for trying to play

the hero. But she's my partner. I trust her to keep her mouth shut."

"Yeah."

"Muchas gracias to you and the Sisterhood for all your help. I...I'll be in touch. I still owe you dinner. A whole shitload of dinners."

Shea was going to say that Rios didn't, but a flurry of emotions left her tongue-tied. Thirty minutes of awkward silence stretched out painfully, interrupted at last by a loud knock at the door. "That'd be your ride. I know a cop knocking when I hear one."

Without thinking, Shea kissed Rios hard on the mouth, and Rios reciprocated. When they finally pulled away several minutes later, Shea's heart was racing, her mind a muddled mess.

"Muchas gracias, mi querida amiga." Rios disappeared out the door without another word.

Shea sat there stunned and stared at her living room while a hurricane of emotions raged inside her—longing, fear, anger, hope, grief.

Her gaze drifted to the empty spot where the coffee table used to be. Duct-tape repairs to the love seat and sofa. The TV stand with no TV. The sanctity of her home had been violated, her possessions destroyed. Annie was homesick and recovering from major surgery. Deirdre was still missing.

And to top it off, Shea had kissed a cop, of all people. What the fuck? Feelings she'd ignored for years were rising to the surface. She wanted to be with Rios. With Toni. But it was wrong for so many reasons. The world was fucking upside down.

She found herself in her garage, sitting on a creeper stool, staring at the collection of gleaming motorcycles. At least no one had messed with her bikes. The Black Swan still lay open, the clutch plates and cover needing to be replaced.

Shea grabbed her tools and put the bike back together with the new clutch. When she tried to attach the cover plate, the bolts wouldn't thread right. She tried over and over, but they kept jamming after half a turn.

In frustration, she threw the screwdriver across the room and kicked the bike over with all her fury. It collided with the motorcycle next to it, causing a domino effect until five bikes lay on their sides.

"Goddamn, motherfucking, bastard, fuck!"

Waves of anger rippled off her like heat from pavement on a summer afternoon. She wanted to hurt someone. She wanted to see Bryz and Mackey and Hooch and Julia screaming in agony. She wanted to bash their heads in until their brains were nothing but smears of gelatin.

She picked up a hammer and pounded her workbench repeatedly until her arm ached and she collapsed on a bench, sobbing. She felt alone. Didn't matter that Fuego and Indigo and Savage and all the members of the Sisterhood loved her, that they were her family. She worried about Annie with such intensity that her chest felt like it would collapse from the weight.

After her ex-girlfriend Jinx went back to her ex-fiancée, Shea figured she'd be alone forever. To die a crusty old diesel dyke with a dozen cats.

And yet here was this thing with Rios out in the open. Shea knew she shouldn't get involved with a cop. Too risky. She'd get hurt all over again. Whatever feelings were emerging between herself and Rios...Toni were fleeting. In the past few weeks, the detective had been shot and kidnapped. She was emotionally vulnerable and clingy. Once she was back to her normal cop self, she'd lose interest in Shea.

When Shea had cried herself out, her mind drifted back to Deirdre. Where was she? Was she still alive? If the Thunder didn't have her, who did?

Maybe Deirdre had gone to ground. Maybe her friends in Camp Verde were back in town, and she was staying with them. But wouldn't she have called? Shea was determined to learn what had happened.

The Thundermen had insisted Deirdre had gotten away from the motel room. And this story seemed consistent with her car being found near Cooper's Vista. Perhaps the crash site still held a clue. Something the cops missed, but which she would recognize because she knew Deirdre. She pulled on her gear, hopped on Sweet Betsy, and rode north.

40

The sky was clear and the air warm while Shea flew past a cluster of small towns with names like Burns Ranch, Dry Harbor, and Blood Creek. Towns that weren't much more than a gas station and maybe a restaurant or a junkyard.

Towering ponderosas replaced grasslands as she entered the Cortes National Forest. She lifted the visor on her helmet and allowed the pine-scented wind to whistle past her ears and through her hair. Granite outcroppings rose skyward on the far side of the road. To her right, the ground plunged two thousand feet into the valley below, her eyes level with the tops of trees growing along the slope.

Sweeping turns tightened into twisting mountain hairpins. Her hand eased off the throttle while the foot pegs scraped the pavement in the corners. The roar of the wind quieted to a whisper, and cicadas trilled above the hum of her engine.

She'd ridden this road so many times her body retained the muscle memory of each turn, knowing instinctively how fast she could take each one and what awaited around the bend.

Eventually she reached the familiar Cooper's Vista overlook. A CAUTION - PULLOFF CLOSED stood in a small gravel parking area bordered by a shattered stone wall. A gap in the trees offered a spectacular view of the distant hazy mountainscape.

Shea ignored the sign and parked. Yellow hazard tape stretched across the large jagged hole in the wall. Below that, a ten-foot-wide strip of cleared undergrowth plunged down at least a hundred feet. No doubt the place where the cops found Deirdre's car. How could anyone survive that? If Deirdre did survive, where could she be now?

Did the asshole who ran her off the road grab her? Did she crawl back up the hill and flag down a passing car? There was no way to know.

A glint of something shiny below caught her eye. A glimmer of hope cut through the questions. Maybe the crime scene techs missed a piece of evidence. Something that would point her to where Deirdre was.

She edged around the end of what remained of the wall and stared down the slope. Her stomach leaped up into her throat. Damn, it was steep. But she was determined to find this woman.

Bit by bit she eased her way down the mountainside, wishing she had a rope or anything to hold onto other than the sheared trunks of small trees. Leaves and loose rocks made the precarious incline more dangerous.

She was halfway to the spot where the tire marks ended at a three-foot-wide pine tree when a rock underfoot gave way. Her body tumbled and rolled until she slammed into the tree, the wind knocked out of her.

"Ungh, fuck me." Her face stung where branches had

slashed it, and a lump was forming on the back of her head. Her armored jacket had protected her against most other damage. She groaned while she pulled herself painfully to her feet.

Sap glistened where the car's impact chewed up the bark of the large pine. She staggered to where something had been reflecting the sunlight. It was a faded aluminum soda can. Too old and faded to be from the crash. Just a piece of garbage someone had pitched from the vista above.

But something next to it caught her eye. She picked up a brass lapel pin from among the carpet of twigs, leaves, and pine needles. Unlike the can, the pin showed no signs of weathering or discoloration. It had been dropped recently.

On the front of the pin, an enameled white star and the letters LSC in blue were set against a red field. She'd seen the design recently but couldn't place it. Who had the initials LSC? No one came to mind.

She pressed the sharp back of the pin into a loose piece of pine bark and slipped it into her pocket, then scanned the area for more clues. A piece of paper, a thumb drive, anything. But anything else of importance had been taken by the cops.

"Hey! You down there! Come up here. Now!" A uniformed deputy with close-cropped hair and a cheesy seventies-era mustache stood at the top of the outlook.

"Shit." Had he seen her pocket the pin?

Shea slowly pulled her way back up the hillside, glancing around, hoping to spot a clue. But nothing remained to be found.

When she reached the top, the deputy offered her a hand and pulled her onto level ground. "Can I see some ID?"

Shea was tempted to tell him to fuck off, but was too winded and tired to argue. She pulled out her wallet and gave him her driver's license.

"What were you doing down there, Ms. Stevens?"

"Such a nice day," she said between gulps of air. "Thought I'd go for a hike."

"Well, you'll have to hike elsewhere. This overlook is closed due to damage. It's not safe."

"I'm looking for the woman whose car was found crashed here."

"What's your interest in the case?"

"She's a friend of mine. Senator Connelly kidnapped her."

"Senator Connelly?" His face grew stern. "Ma'am, I suggest you be on your way and leave the investigating to the sheriff's office."

"So you boys can protect Senator Con Job's fine reputation, no matter who gets hurt. I'm trying to save a woman's life."

"Clearly, she's not here. Please move along, or I will cite you for trespassing and interference in an investigation."

"Fine." Shea turned her back to him and approached her bike. There was no use arguing. "Keep on protecting that rich scumbag. But I will find Deirdre West. And when I do, whether she's dead or alive, the people who did this to her will pay. Every single fucking one of them."

She pulled on her helmet, started her bike, and drove off, leaving the deputy standing in a cloud of dust.

As she fell back into the rhythm of leaning into the curves, her subconscious mind continued working on the problem. Where was Deirdre? Did Connelly get the evidence of the affair, or was it still out there? And who the hell was LSC?

By the time she reached Ironwood, she had an idea. It wouldn't tell her where Deirdre was, but it might provide leverage. She drove east to Whispering Oaks Estates.

41

SHEA CHECKED the parking lot to make sure no one was watching when she approached Deirdre's front door. First, she rang the bell a few times and waited. But as expected, there was no response.

Shea pulled out her lock picks and was soon inside the door. When Deirdre got out of jail, she'd said she kept the evidence of the affair where no one would look. Wait, not no one. Where no *man* would look. Where would no man look? An idea came to her.

She hustled up the carpeted stairs, her eyes drawn to the hole in the wall where she'd accidentally fired at Sophie. Sadness squeezed her heart while she remembered the pig's bloody corpse in the motel room. But she pushed through the emotion, determined to find the evidence she was looking for.

In the bathroom, she emptied the cabinets. Makeup, medications, hair product, a blow-dryer, toilet paper, cotton swabs. Where would Deirdre hide it? She checked the medicine bottles but found nothing except the pills indicated by the label. She sifted through the makeup, opening lipstick cases and containers of face powder and skin creams. Nothing. Shit.

Her eyes zeroed in on a box of tampons. *Where no man would look.* One wrapper was open. She pulled out a plastic object shaped like a tampon. The end popped off to reveal a flash drive. She fell on the floor and laughed until tears streamed from her eyes.

"Fuck, yeah. Where no man would look. No shit."

She needed to check the contents of the drive before she did anything else. Her laptop at home was destroyed. Even if JuJu recovered the data from her hard drive, that could take days or weeks. She didn't have that kind of time.

She made a quick phone call, then slipped back out the door and drove until she pulled into Indigo and Savage's driveway. The front door opened before she knocked. Both Indigo and Savage welcomed her inside.

"You get into another fight?" Savage led her to a chair in the living room. "Your face is all scratched up."

"Had a disagreement with a tree."

"How's Detective Rios?" Indigo pressed.

Shea shrugged, trying not to remember Toni's kiss and the emotions it unleashed. "She seemed better this morning. Her partner picked her up. Haven't heard from her since. Right now, I'm more interested in finding Deirdre. Do either of you recognize this?" She pulled the lapel pin out of her pocket and showed it to them.

Savage took it from her and examined it. "Where'd you find this?"

"Where the cops found Deirdre's car off Cooper's Vista. It must belong to whoever ran her off the road. But I can't think of anyone with the initials LSC."

Indigo looked closer at the pin. "It looks familiar, but I can't place it."

Shea held up the flash drive. "One other thing. I need to borrow your computer."

"By all means." Savage led her over to a wooden rolltop desk in their Arizona room. She raised the top and opened a laptop. "Is that a thumb drive shaped like a tampon?"

"Yep. I found it in Deirdre's bathroom." Shea plugged the drive into the USB port and searched through the files. "Holy shit! This is the motherlode. Screenshots of texts. Receipts. Doctors' notes. Hospital records. Aftercare instructions."

"Wow, she wasn't kidding," Indigo replied. "This is volatile stuff. No wonder Connelly didn't want it getting out."

"What are you going to do with it?" Savage asked.

"Send a copy to Drew Chambers, Elia Quinn's editor. Maybe they'll still publish the article." Shea opened a browser, pulled up the *Cortes Chronicle*'s website, and searched until she found the page listing the staff and the newspaper's physical mailing address. "You got a spare thumb drive and an envelope?"

Indigo pulled another thumb drive out of a desk drawer and inserted it into the computer's other USB port. While the files copied onto the new thumb drive, Shea wrote out a note.

Elia Quinn was about to publish a story detailing an affair between Senator Joe Connelly and Deirdre West. Ms. West has gone missing, but she wanted you to have these documents. They prove Connelly forced her to get an abortion after he got her pregnant.

A concerned citizen

When the files had finished copying, she slipped the note and the duplicate thumb drive into an envelope.

"Thanks. I'll drop this at the information desk at the *Chronicle*."

"Any clues where Deirdre might be? Or if she's even still alive?" Indigo asked.

Shea sighed. "She may be staying with a friend over in Camp Verde, but if she was, I woulda thought she'd have called me. Cops supposedly got a BOLO out on her, but I'm not holding out hope. That lapel pin is the closest I have to a clue."

"We tried." Savage put an arm on her shoulder. "I'm sorry I made her feel unwelcome here. It's just…"

"You did what you had to do." Shea held up the envelope with the USB drive. "I hope this will be enough to ruin Connelly's campaign after what he's done. It won't bring Deirdre or her mother back, but it might provide a little justice."

It was late afternoon when Shea drove toward home. A blanket of black clouds was drifting up from the south, matching the growing darkness in her mood. She pushed her speed, hoping to reach home before the rain started. Driving down the side of Sycamore Mountain was okay in dry conditions. But riding twisties on slick, winding mountain roads with monsoon winds blowing was suicidal.

By the time she cruised past the traffic cop outside of Olde Towne Sycamore Springs, the southern sky was pitch black. Forks of lightning rippled across the gloom. The first fat drops hit her visor when she made the first sharp turn into the switchbacks. The drizzle quickly turned into a chilly downpour, soaking her while she eased down the mountainside.

Water streamed down the slope and across the road, bringing with it sand, rocks, and other debris. She kept her right hand away from the front brake, checking her speed with gentle pressure on the rear brake.

She was two-thirds of the way down when large rocks and mud cascaded across the road in front of her. Out of instinct, she hit both brakes and the clutch. The bike wobbled, tires slipping one way then another, drifting perilously close to the edge of the road. She skidded to a stop where a three-foot-deep layer of earth, rock, and plant matter now blocked her way.

"Holy fuck."

She considered driving over the earthen roadblock, but it didn't look stable. She turned the bike around and headed back up the mountain. When she reached the spot directly above the mudslide, she saw that half the road had given way. Only a foot-wide ribbon of pavement remained for a stretch of ten feet. The ground underneath it had partially eroded away.

"Shit."

She considered her options. Either way could be disastrous.

She turned around again, headed back downhill. When she came to where the mudslide blocked the road, she pinned the throttle. The engine roared and the bike shot forward, bucking like a wild bronco over the debris, and slammed hard back down on the pavement on the other side.

Her heart thundered with the rush of adrenaline while she skidded around the final hairpin turn and hit the open road at the bottom of the mountain.

By the time she arrived home, she was soaked to the bone and shivering. She pulled off her sopping-wet clothes and slipped on a green terrycloth bathrobe.

Ninja yowled desperately to be fed.

"All right, all right, all right, ya damn cat." She grabbed the bag of kibble and poured some into the cat's bowl. Ninja stared at it and continued to yowl.

"What? You want Annie? Me too. But I got news for ya,

sister. She ain't coming home anytime soon. So, get the fuck used to it!"

Ninja stopped yowling and stared at her. Shea felt stupid for yelling at the cat. She opened the fridge, pulled out a carton of chicken broth, poured some into a small bowl, and set it on the floor. The cat sniffed it a few times and began lapping it up.

Shea pulled the vodka out of the freezer. The chill of the glass bottle made her shiver more. She returned it to the freezer and started a pot of coffee instead. It would keep her up half the night, but it was hot.

While the coffee brewed, she nuked a frozen dinner then settled on the sofa to watch the latest episode of *Pose*. Ninja curled up next to her.

She was still hoping to find Deirdre but had run out of ideas of where to look and had all but given up hope of finding her alive. During a commercial break, she texted Toni, asking if the BOLO on Deirdre had turned up anything. She fell asleep without a reply.

42

THE NEXT MORNING, Shea was heading to her bathroom to take a shower when her phone rang. "Yeah?"

"Happy Monday. It's Toni. Sorry I didn't reply sooner. Last night, I was with the Organized Crime Task Force trying to bust the Thunder and the Border Patriots for the stolen Wolf Ridge Arms weapons."

"You're back on the job?"

"I am."

"Are the Thundermen back in jail?" Shea asked, hoping for some good news.

"Unfortunately, no. The arms deal planned for last night at the laser tag place never happened. The Thunder and the Patriots were a no-show. A lot of wasted man-hours, and I looked like an idiot. Now I can't even get a warrant to search the Thunder's clubhouse."

"What about Deirdre? Any sign of her?"

"Detective Morris says no hits on the BOLO so far."

"Fuck."

"On a positive note, I understand trouble's brewing at Connelly's campaign headquarters. The *Chronicle* published a front-page article about his alleged affair and the covered-up abortion. Really shaking things up. Several major backers are already distancing themselves. You have anything to do with that?"

"Maybe. Does this mean you'll finally arrest Connelly?"

"Working on it. Morris confirmed that Connelly owns a dark-blue Mercedes-Benz SUV, which matches the description of the vehicle that ran Ms. West's Kia off the road. She's negotiating with his lawyer to bring him in for a talk."

"Negotiating? God forbid you pick him up and interrogate him like you'd do any other suspect."

"Shea, it's not that simple. There are two and a half million cars registered in Arizona. Roughly ten percent of them are dark blue, and a sizable portion of those are European imports. Fifteen thousand dark-blue European imports are registered in Cortes County alone. The odds that Connelly's Mercedes is the one that ran Ms. West's Kia off the road are remote. Even with the covered-up abortion as a potential motive to silence West, no judge will sign a search warrant based on that scant evidence."

The word evidence sparked a thought in Shea's mind. "Hey, do the initials LSC ring a bell?"

"LSC?" Rios asked. "No. Why?"

"No reason." Shea was sure the lapel pin held answers.

"On a completely different subject, that was a serious kiss the other morning. When are we going to have that dinner?"

"Look, Rios. That kiss was…I don't know what it was. It didn't mean what you thought it did. I've been dealing with a lot of stress lately. I ain't fit to go to dinner with no one. Maybe when all this shit is over. But no promises."

"I understand. Take care of yourself, Shea. Don't worry. We'll keep looking for Ms. West."

"Right." Shea hung up.

She no longer held out hope of finding Deirdre alive. Shea had failed her utterly. Even if Connelly lost the election, he'd never be arrested, much less go to prison. Meanwhile, three women and a pig were now dead.

After her shower, she dressed and headed to Iron Goddess. The road up Sycamore Mountain was closed because of the landslide. The ten-mile detour took her three times longer to get to the shop.

On the plus side, JuJu stopped by and picked up the broken remains of Shea's laptop. JuJu was a tall white woman with long, golden-brown hair secured with multiple hairbands to keep it from knotting while riding her bike.

"Can you fix it?" Shea asked her.

JuJu didn't look hopeful. "We'll see what I can do."

For the next two days, Shea threw herself into work to avoid obsessing over how much she missed Annie or had failed Deirdre. She and Lakota started working on the next show bike. Twice they got into a shouting match about the motorcycle's specs. Lakota had been right both times. She usually was. But Shea didn't want to hear it. She barked at her employees over the slightest provocation until most of the crew were avoiding her.

When Shea arrived home Monday night, an official-looking envelope had arrived with the mail. She opened it up, hoping for some good news. Instead, she learned that the paternity test had come back positive. Bryz was Annie's biological father. A custody hearing had been scheduled for July.

"Motherfucker!" She eyed the baseball bat and fantasized smashing Bryz's smirking face in. She'd have to call Dragon, but at the moment she was too angry to speak to anyone without erupting in rage.

The cherry on the shit sundae was when Rios sent a

text saying that Connelly had been at a campaign in Tucson the night that Deirdre disappeared. Dozens of witnesses and video footage of the event confirmed the alibi. So, it couldn't have been his SUV that ran her car off Cooper's Vista.

On Tuesday, JuJu dropped by the shop again. "Your laptop itself was beyond repair, but the solid-state drive was intact. I migrated the data onto a refurbished laptop, which actually came with a better motherboard and processor than what your old one had. So basically, you got a free upgrade."

"Thanks, JuJu."

Shea took a late-morning break next door at the Kokopelli Café. April, one of the cafe's servers, brought her a cup of coffee. "You want anything to eat?"

Shea shrugged but said nothing. Her appetite was gone. She felt numb.

"All righty, then." April shimmied away.

Shea picked up a copy of the *Cortes Chronicle* left on a nearby table. The front page bore the headline "Connelly's Numbers Plummet Over Abortion Scandal." Something close to a smile spread across her face. At least she wasn't the only one who was miserable this morning.

"Isn't that crazy?" said April, reading over her shoulder. "Can't believe a good God-fearing Christian like him had an affair with that tramp. And an abortion? Here I thought he was pro-life. Guess ya never know about some people."

Shea glared at her until she walked away and flipped to a story about the Phoenix Rising's latest victory against a rival soccer team. Her thoughts shifted to Annie and the upcoming custody hearing, which had her so worried for Annie that her body ached. She'd left messages for her niece but hadn't heard back. Not even a text. No doubt Julia's doing.

Enough was enough.

Shea tossed a few bucks on the table and waltzed back over to the shop's office. "I'm getting Annie back."

"Shea, you can't," Terrance replied. "They'll arrest you."

She threw on her mesh jacket. "I'm her goddamn legal guardian, T. I've done nothing wrong. Ain't no reason for her not to be with me."

Terrance tried to dissuade her, but Shea jammed in her earplugs and pulled on her helmet. "Sorry. Can't hear you."

She marched through the service bay into the parking lot and raced north to Bradshaw City.

A dark-blue Volvo S60 sedan sat in the shade under Julia Mueller's carport next to a Harley Davidson Screamin' Eagle Fat Boy. A quick inspection revealed a scrape of yellow paint on the car's right front quarter panel.

"Fuck me." Maybe the Thunder had Deirdre after all. Or at least had pushed her yellow Kia off the cliff.

Shea pounded on Julia's kitchen door with all her strength, fueled by anger and a need for violence.

Julia opened the door a moment later. "Shealene, what're you doing here?"

"Where's Annie?"

"In her room, but you ain't allowed to be here."

"Fuck you." Shea pushed past her. "Annie! Where are you?" She hurried down the hall and found Annie lying on the bed in the guest room with her laptop.

"Aunt Shea? What are you doing here?"

"Taking you home where you belong. Grab your things."

"Shea," Julia said, coming up behind her. "I understand why you want to take her, but it will only cause trouble."

"Don't tell me about trouble. Whose car is in the carport?"

"Hooch's. I borrowed it to run to Costco earlier this morning. Why?"

"He ran Deirdre West off the road. Probably killed her too." Shea started helping Annie pack her suitcase, gathering clothes from the dresser and stuffing them in Annie's suitcase.

"Baby, you're talking crazy."

Shea spotted a pair of Annie's French hook earrings on the floor and slipped them in her back pocket. "I saw the damage on the side. Yellow paint, just like Deirdre's car."

"That scrape is where I accidentally hit one of them damned posts at the Costco gas station. I'm not used to driving his car. Look, darling, I shouldn't tell you this, but it wasn't Hooch or the Thunder who went after that girl. It was a guy who works for Connelly."

"What guy?"

"Dunno his name. He's a fixer of sorts. When she got away from the motel, he chased her down and ran her off the road out in the woods somewhere."

Shea glared at her, wondering if Julia was lying or not.

"Shea, we got the DNA results from the paternity test. Bryz is Annie's biological father."

"I don't fucking care. I'm her legal guardian, and I say he ain't getting anywhere near her. They kidnapped and tortured a sheriff's detective. You know that?"

"Who did that?"

"Hooch, Bryz, and Mackey. Probably a few more. Had her tied up in a back room at the Church."

"That can't be true. Hooch would nev—"

"Bullshit, I rescued the detective. She told me all about it."

"Still, you can't take Annie. If DCS finds out…"

"They'll only find out if you tell them."

Julia held Shea's gaze until the doorbell rang.

"Just hold on a sec while I see who it is."

"Yeah, you do that." Shea continued to gather Annie's stuff. "How are you feeling?"

"Still sore, but better." Annie put her laptop in her computer bag. "I'm glad to be going home with you. Did my...did Bryz and Hooch really torture a cop?"

"Yeah. Detective Toni Rios."

Annie nodded. "Is she the woman they were talking about?"

"Yep. Thanks to you, she's safe. You're a hero."

"What about Deirdre?"

Before Shea could answer, a petite woman with a leather satchel walked into the room next to Julia.

"Excuse me, who are you?" the woman asked.

"Shea Stevens. Who the fuck are you?" But Shea had a feeling she knew.

"I'm Kelly Woods, a social worker with the Department of Child Safety."

43

She held up her name badge. "I'm here because I got a disturbing report that men with a known history of violence have been in this home and in close contact with the child."

Shea pointed a finger at Julia. "Talk to her. I'm the one that reported it."

Julia sputtered an explanation. "I-I haven't exactly allowed them in contact with Annie necessarily. They just..."

"Uh-huh," Annie corrected. "Bunch of them were here. Including Bryz, who raped my mama."

Woods narrowed her gaze. "A rapist? You let a rapist in here?"

"Far as I know, he ain't raped nobody in years."

"Ms. Mueller, we placed her here for her safety, not for you to put her further in harm's way!"

"That's why I'm taking her back home with me," Shea interjected. "Where she belongs and where she'll be safe."

"And how are you related to the child?" Woods asked Shea.

"I'm Annie's aunt and legal guardian. And her only blood relative aside from that fucking rapist Bryz. So, we're going home."

"DCS still has custodial authority over the child. I believe it would be best if we place the child in a foster home until the hearing."

Shea stepped into the woman's space. "Ain't gonna happen."

"If you try to take her, Ms. Stevens, I will call the police and have you arrested."

"You do that, lady. And then I'll let the cops know that you took custody from me to put her in a home with people who shot, kidnapped, and tortured one of their own. And of course, the child's rapist father. What do you think the cops will do then? And what will the media say?"

The social worker's eyes narrowed. "Someone who kidnapped and tortured a police officer was here?"

Julia blanched. "I...I'm just now hearing about this. I don't know."

"It's true," Annie said. "Hooch and his friends were bragging about it."

"You report me for taking Annie, and I'll call the detective who was tortured. We'll see who comes out on top. You'll be lucky to keep your job, lady."

The social worker stood there a moment. "This is disturbing news. I..."

"Look," continued Shea. "They only took custody from me after I refused to let the lab do a second DNA test. They ran the test anyway. You got the results. Why shouldn't she be in my custody until the hearing? In the four years I been taking care of her, we ain't had no problems."

"Young lady, where would you like to stay for the time being?" the social worker asked Annie.

Annie hugged Shea. "With her."

"Very well, Ms. Stevens, you may take her. But if you fail to appear with Annie at the hearing, we will intervene. Do you hear me?"

"Don't worry. We'll be there." Shea picked up Annie's suitcase. "Come on, Doodlebug. Let's go home. You ready to ride?"

Annie nodded. "Julia still has my phone."

"Get it," Shea ordered Julia.

Julia grabbed the phone from a kitchen drawer and followed them outside, where Shea secured the suitcase and computer bag to the back of her bike with a few strategically placed bungee cords.

"I had no idea about that cop, Shea-Shea."

"I don't care." Shea helped Annie get her jacket and helmet on. "I never wanna see you again."

"You can't mean that."

Shea climbed onto the bike then helped Annie onto the back. The two of them raced down the street without a word.

Traffic grew heavier while they approached Bradshaw's downtown area. While waiting at a stoplight, Annie tapped Shea on her shoulder. "Can we stop somewhere? I'm starving, and I haven't had lunch."

Shea's watch told her it was after two in the afternoon. It would take them at least forty-five minutes to get home with the detour. "I'll keep an eye out for a place."

Shortly before they turned onto the I-17 southbound, Shea pulled into a Culver's fast food restaurant.

Annie slid off the bike with a pained expression on her face.

"You okay?"

Annie put a hand on her abdomen. "Hurts a little. Could've done without all that bouncing around."

"Sorry. I should've brought the truck. Old habit grabbing Sweet Betsy. Maybe we should take you to the ER. Make sure you didn't—"

"No, please. I don't want to go back to the hospital. They'll just starve me more. It doesn't hurt that bad."

Shea studied her niece for a moment. "Okay, but if it gets to hurting worse or you start bleeding or feeling feverish or anything, you let me know. Deal?"

"Deal."

They went inside, ordered a couple of burgers, a truckload of onion rings, and a couple of shakes.

"I'm sorry I wasn't there for you when you had surgery."

"It's cool. You were trying to keep me away from Bryz."

"I didn't do a very good job." Shea remembered what Julia had told her about Annie being intersex. "There's something I gotta talk to you about."

Annie looked up with a mouthful of onion rings. "What?"

"Julia explained why you needed the surgery."

"It's 'cause I tore something in my belly. A hernia."

"Yeah, but there's more to it. You have what they call complete androgen insensitivity syndrome."

"What's that?" Concern clouded the girl's face.

"Nothing serious. At least, it shouldn't cause you any more health problems. You mentioned the other day you learned about DNA in Ms. Marquez's science class, right?"

"Yeah."

"You know most boys have an XY chromosome, and most girls have an XX chromosome."

Annie nodded.

"Except you have an XY chromosome."

Annie's jaw froze in mid-chew. "What? That's impossible. I'm a girl."

"Yes, you are. But sometimes people born with XY chromosomes have complete androgen insensitivity syndrome.

It means their bodies don't respond to testosterone. So instead of developing into boys, they develop into girls."

"You're saying I should've been a boy?"

"No, I'm not. You know about Uncle Terrance, right? He was born with a typically female body. But inside, he always knew he was a boy."

"Because he's transgender."

"Exactly. So, he changed his body to fit how he saw himself."

"Does that mean I'm transgender?"

"No. You're what they call intersex. It means you have characteristics of both. But whether you're a boy, a girl, or nonbinary is up to you to figure out."

"I always felt like I'm a girl."

"Then that's who you are."

Annie sat there processing it for a few minutes. "Why am I like this?"

"I don't know. I tried to read up on it. A lot of the stuff is technical medical jargon. Maybe if I'd finished high school, I'd understand it. But it's part of the reason why you ended up with a hernia. Some part of you down there didn't develop as it should. It caused the hernia, but it's been repaired."

"Will I ever...you know, fill out a little more?" Annie gestured at her small breasts.

"Far as I know, your body doesn't produce estrogen. That's what makes women grow breasts. Yours probably won't develop much more than they have." Shea glanced down at her flat chest. "Then again, I'm not exactly Dolly Parton here. You already got more up top than I do."

"Will I be able to have babies?"

"No. You have a vagina, but you don't have a uterus or eggs. No way to make a baby."

"That sucks. I always dreamed of having babies."

"You can always adopt. I adopted you."

"Not the same," Annie said with a sigh.

"No, it's not. Look, Terrance knows a doctor in Ironwood who works with transgender patients. She also sees intersex patients. We can make an appointment, possibly get you started on estrogen. If that's what you want. It's your body, your choice."

"Will estrogen allow me to have babies?"

"No, but your breasts might develop a little more. Look on the bright side: you don't have to worry about having a period every month."

"I wish I was a real girl."

"You're as real a girl as I am. Your body's just a little different."

"I don't want to be different."

"Annie, look at my face."

Their eyes met. "Yeah?"

"What do you see?"

"I see you."

"You see a butch lesbian with a scarred face and a flat chest. People stare at me all the time. People think I'm in the wrong restroom half the time. I've had kids run away screaming like I'm some kind of monster."

"You can be kinda scary." Annie chuckled.

"I suppose that's true. The fact is that I'm not normal. I'm different. You and me, we grew up around outlaw bikers. That's different too. Everybody's different in some way. Sometimes it's obvious, like my face. Sometimes it's not so obvious, like you being intersex. No one has to know, unless you tell them."

"Who all knows about me?"

"Only Julia, me, the doctor, and Uncle Terrance."

"Why'd you tell him?"

"Because I needed advice from someone who understands these things better than I do."

"I guess that's okay. He's family."

"Yes, he is. A big part of life is learning how to deal with the shit that comes our way. But you're not alone. We got each other, we got Uncle Terrance and Jake, and we got the Sisterhood."

"And Julia."

"We'll see about Julia. As long as she's with the Thunder, I don't want her around. You understand?"

Annie's eyes glistened. "I guess so. But I miss her. She was gone for three years. And after I get her back, all this happens."

"The Thundermen are dangerous. They hurt women. I don't want you to get hurt."

"So, what do we do now?"

"Let's head home instead. You and me got some catching up to do. Figured we deserve some girl time."

"Oh, you mean we'll braid each other's hair, paint our nails, and talk about boys?" Annie teased.

Shea ran a hand through her short spiky hair. "Well, I'll braid your hair and paint your nails, if you want. As for talking about boys, well, I'm all ears to whatever you have to say."

"I know, you're more into girls."

Shea felt a wave of warmth flow through her. She thought of Rios and felt bad with how she'd left things. "We can talk about whatever you want to talk about."

44

WHEN THEY GOT HOME, Annie stopped in the doorway and gasped. "What happened here?"

Shea pushed past her, afraid something else had happened, but it was the same as when she had left it that morning. "Oh, we had a bit of a break-in. It's okay. The insurance guy's coming out tomorrow to help us with the claim."

"Is it even safe to be here? What if they come back?"

"I don't think they'll be back. They got whatever they came for." Shea pointed to the small flat-screen on the TV stand. "Rah-Rah let us borrow one of her TVs until we can replace ours."

Annie still looked afraid.

"It's okay. Really. We're doing girls' night, remember? Put your stuff away. I'll nuke some popcorn, and we can watch that show about that Scottish woman solving murder mysteries. You've been looking forward to watching them. And in between episodes, I'll paint your nails."

"Yeah, okay."

Shea popped a large bowl of popcorn, and they settled

onto the sofa to binge-watch *The Dandy Gilver Mysteries* together. Annie was a diehard fan of the books by Catriona McPherson.

Between episodes, Shea got up to deal with a nagging thought.

"Where you going?" Annie asked. "Ain't we doing girls' night?" She wiggled her as-yet unpainted fingernails.

"I'll be right back. Gotta check something first."

In her bedroom, Shea picked up the lapel pin she'd found the previous day and reexamined it. She still couldn't think of anyone with the initials LSC, but maybe they weren't someone's initials.

She opened up the refurbished laptop and looked for LSC as an abbreviation. Several listings appeared in the search results. In astronomy, LSC referred to a local supercluster, whatever that was. In biology, it was short for lichen simplex chronicus. In applied sciences, it was a luminescent solar concentrator. Other meanings included Lake Superior College and London Symphony Chorus.

She kept scrolling through one explanation after another, but nothing seemed to fit until she came to the Loyal Sons of the Confederacy. She clicked on the link for the organization's website. Their logo matched the pin. And there was a chapter in Arizona. So, who dropped it at the crash site?

"Aunt Shea! Are you coming back?"

"Just a minute."

She searched for a directory of members but couldn't find one. Only post after post of racist nonsense dressed up as Southern heritage, whitewashed history, and imagined threats to "the white race."

Had she seen one of the Thundermen wearing the pin at the welcome-home celebration? It was possible. But a voice in the back of her mind told her she'd seen it elsewhere.

She pulled up Connelly's campaign website. In his portrait, he wore an American flag lapel pin. Nothing like the one she'd found.

Maybe it was someone who worked for Connelly. Hadn't Julia mentioned he had a guy who worked as a fixer? She clicked the link for his staff page and checked the photos of his top personnel. David Harriman, his campaign manager, was wearing a pin on his lapel. She enlarged the photo. It was the LSC pin.

"Motherfucker."

Harriman's bio on the senator's website didn't offer much information. A full web search led Shea to the guy's page on WorkConnect, a business networking site. David Harriman had grown up in Virginia, earned a bachelor's degree in political science, and served in the military. After getting out, he had worked for a military contractor then for a number of powerful security companies before becoming Connelly's campaign manager.

Further digging uncovered an article about a Henry David Harriman who had been involved with a scandal in which civilians in Iraq were murdered. There was no picture. Shea wondered if it was the same guy. And if it was, did Connelly know?

"Aunt Shea, can we watch the next episode already? Dandy and her partner are trying to solve the murder of a man found in a barrel of fish."

"Start without me. I gotta make a quick phone call."

"Whatever."

Pangs of guilt assaulted Shea. After the anguish she suffered when Annie was gone, Shea should spend time with her now that she was back.

But Deirdre was still missing. Maybe she was already

dead, and if that were true, Shea couldn't do shit about it. But on the slim chance she was alive, Shea had to find her. And this despicable lapel pin was her best lead.

Harriman had been at the crash site. Had he run her off the road? Did he have her? Or had he shown up afterwards looking for proof of his boss's indiscretions in the car? He'd probably ransacked Deirdre's condo and Shea's house.

She called Rios.

"Shea? What's going on?"

"I need to know if Connelly's campaign manager, David Harriman, owns a blue European vehicle."

"Why?"

"Would you answer my questions for once, Rios? Does Harriman own a vehicle that would match the one that ran Deirdre's Kia off the road?"

"Shea, even if he does, I can't provide you with that information. Whatever you know, tell Bello and Morris. They're working the case."

"I don't trust them. I trust you. Can you check this or not?"

Silence settled on the line.

"Let me make a phone call. I'll call you right back."

Shea returned to the living room, where Annie had resumed watching the show. "Dandy and her partner Alec are pretending to be linguists up in a fishing village in the Northern Isles, trying to find who killed the guy."

"What guy?"

"The guy in the fish barrel. These people in the village talk funny."

"Oh, okay."

Shea sat down and watched the show, checking the time periodically, wondering if Rios would call her back or if she'd blown her off.

Twenty minutes later, her phone rang.

"You were right," Rios said. "He owns a 2018 royal-blue Range Rover. How'd you know?"

"I found a lapel pin for the Loyal Sons of the Confederacy where Deirdre's car crashed off Cooper's Vista. Harriman is wearing a pin just like it in his staff photo on Connelly's website. It's him, I tell you. Where's he live?"

"I can't give you his information, Shea. But I'll let Bello and Morris know. If we can get a search warrant, we'll check out his place."

A surge of anger and frustration rippled through Shea. *Why can't she just tell me?* "Fine." She hung up and returned to the living room. Annie looked up from her iPad when she sat down next to her.

"About time."

"Sorry. I may have figured out who kidnapped Deirdre. Toni, I mean, Detective Rios confirmed he owns a blue Range Rover."

Annie tilted her head. "You like her, don't you?"

Warmth ran up Shea's neck and blossomed on her face. "Who?"

"Toni the cop." A teasing smile appeared on Annie's face. "You got a crush on her."

"Do not."

"Do too. I can tell by your expression every time you say her name. Not that there's anything wrong with that, I suppose. Just never thought Aunt Shea the outlaw biker would fall for a cop of all people."

"I'm not an outlaw."

"Maybe not like the Thunder. You break the law to help people."

"Fine example I'm setting for you."

"It's okay. Some of the best people in history have been that kind of outlaw. Like Harriet Tubman. She was a total badass."

"Harriet Tubman risked her life to rescue people from slavery. I just, hell, I don't know what I do."

"You rescued me from the kidnappers. You rescued Rios the cop from the Thunder. And you're trying to rescue Ms. Deirdre from whoever took her."

"I'm leaving the latter to the cops to deal with. So see, I'm not as badass as Harriet Tubman. Now let's just watch the show."

Annie pressed the play button on the remote.

An hour later, Shea's phone rang. "I gotta take this. It's...uh, Toni." She stood up to step into her bedroom.

"Shea and Toni sittin' in a tree K-I-S-S-I-N-G," Annie sang when Shea hurried into the other room.

"You find her?"

"Bello couldn't get a warrant. Not without more probable cause."

"Like what? Deirdre West's body lying out on his front lawn? You said his vehicle was a match. Did he have an alibi the night Deirdre disappeared? Did you check his staff photo for the pin I found?"

"His vehicle is a potential match. But so are a few thousand other cars in the county. And with this guy being Connelly's campaign manager, we have to tread lightly."

"Dammit, gimme the address. I'll check it out. By the time y'all get a warrant—*if* you get a warrant—it may be too late, if it isn't already."

"Shea, I can't condone vigilante justice."

"It was vigilante justice that saved your ass from the Thunder."

After a lengthy pause, Rios sighed and said, "I'm sorry, Shea. But giving you that information would cost me my badge and my pension. I simply can't."

"Fine. You go back to playing by the rules and protecting your precious pension. I'll do what I gotta do."

Shea hung up and texted Becca Alvarez, the skip tracer who had provided her the dirt on Connelly's shady financial deals. Five minutes later, Becca texted her back with Harriman's address.

Shea then called Indigo. "Hey, would y'all mind watching Annie for a bit? There's something I gotta look into."

"Sure. What's going on?"

"I got a lead on Deirdre West."

"You need some backup?"

Shea considered it. Shit was bound to get ugly, but after what happened at the Church, she didn't want to put anyone else in danger. "Nah, I'm good. I'll drop her by shortly. Thanks, Indigo."

Shea grabbed her Ruger from her gun safe and pulled on her biker jacket. "I gotta go out for a bit. I'm dropping you off at Indigo's."

"Now?"

"It won't take long. I promise."

"Where are you going?"

"To find Deirdre."

Concern bloomed in Annie's eyes. "Aunt Shea...I don't want you to go. Something could happen to you."

"Don't worry, Doodlebug. I'm a badass, remember? Now grab your jacket."

Shea locked the kitchen door behind them, helped Annie onto the back of her motorcycle, and drove out into the night.

45

SHEA HAD to stop a few times to double-check the route to Harriman's house in Ironwood's Shadow Hills District. Shea cruised past the swanky neighborhoods, some of which had signs announcing new homes available in the low 600s. She wondered how the campaign manager of a state senator could afford such digs.

State senators weren't paid much to begin with. But Connelly had a lot of family money, not to mention the funds from his illicit activities. Maybe Harriman had a piece of that pie as Connelly's fixer. Which would explain why he'd gone after Deirdre. Shea hoped she was still alive.

Harriman lived in the hilly Bedford Estates neighborhood. An orange-and-white-striped gate next to a small security guard shack barred the entrance. Shea pulled up, and a guard with lank hair below his cap approached. His uniform was wrinkled and smelled like a Philly cheesesteak sandwich.

"Can I help you?" he asked in a nasal voice.

"I...uh, I have a delivery for...uh...Dr. Mortimer Wiggins." The name just popped in her head, but it sounded ritzy enough to belong to a resident. "Very urgent."

"Dr. Wiggins? Not familiar with that name. Hold on." He stepped back inside the guard shack and tapped on a computer keyboard.

Shea noticed a two-foot gap between the orange-and-white gate arm and the adjacent fence. She ducked down and pinned the throttle, barely hearing the guard's shouts to stop while she whipped around the gate.

Large Victorian-inspired lampposts revealed two- and three-story mansions set on acre lots with an abundance of mature hardwood trees. No vehicles were parked on the streets or visible in driveways. No doubt all were tucked away in the three-car garages. Shea felt conspicuous on her motorcycle. She needed to get off the street before the security guards or the cops found her.

She zoomed past Harriman's residence, looking for a place to park that wouldn't alert anyone to her presence. The parking lot of the neighborhood golf course just a block away seemed to fit the bill. She pulled behind a small maintenance vehicle so that she was hidden from the street then killed the engine. She removed her biker jacket, popped on a black baseball cap, and backtracked on foot toward Harriman's, keeping to the shadows as much as possible. Twice she ducked behind a tree when a small security vehicle buzzed past with yellow lights flashing.

The first floor of Harriman's house was lit up inside. When she saw no sign of him from the front, she slipped around to the back of the house. The land sloped down enough to expose the basement windows but no doors. Far above, she caught the flickering blue glow of a TV reflected in the blinds of what must be one of the second-story bedrooms. Harriman was home. Possibly awake.

A quick examination of the basement windows

confirmed to Shea what she suspected. The house had a security system, which was probably armed with Harriman inside. Shea could pick locks but wasn't adept at bypassing the latest in security technology. Getting inside would require a little social engineering.

After a few minutes, an idea came to her. She sent a text to Connelly.

How's the campaign, Con Job? Perhaps voters should hear about your dirty business deals too. Payoffs to judges, federal regulators, and law enforcement. Secret accounts at Dubai Royal Bank. Arms deals with the Border Patriots. Meet me in 1 hour at your Ironwood office with $50K cash or this goes viral.

There was no immediate response. Maybe Connelly had turned in early. Or maybe he was calling her bluff.

She was about to try her luck with a basement window when a phone rang in the bedroom above her. A light flickered on, and Harriman began shouting. She couldn't make out many words, but she recognized Connelly's name and her own. The word "bitch" was mentioned more than a few times.

A moment later, Shea's phone vibrated from Connelly's reply.

Will meet you at parking garage with money. Alone. No tricks or else.

The light in the bedroom went out. Shea hurried around to the front of the house just as the garage door creaked open. As she suspected, Connelly was dispatching Harriman to deal with her.

The blue Range Rover backed out of the garage, Harriman clearly behind the wheel. Before the door closed completely, she slipped inside and disappeared into the shadows.

When the garage closed, she approached the door to the rest of the house. No dead bolt or anything. Just a common keyed lock. She checked the handle, and it opened. Instead of an ear-splitting alarm, she heard only the quiet hum of the air conditioning system.

A security keypad on the wall inside the door revealed the system was armed but not triggered. The door must not have been monitored. She breathed a sigh of relief. So far, so good.

She searched the main floor, looking for any place Harriman might keep a prisoner. She inspected the living room, the laundry/utility room, the Arizona room, the kitchen, the walk-in pantry, and both downstairs bathrooms. No sign of Deirdre.

She hustled upstairs, checking every bedroom, closet, and bathroom, as well as an office and a linen cupboard. But still there was no sign of Deirdre. In the office, he had a computer, but it was password protected. The desk drawers were locked, as was a three-drawer vertical filing cabinet.

Her watch showed Harriman had been gone for thirty minutes. He should be at Connelly's office, waiting to ambush Shea. How long would he wait before he realized she wasn't coming and returned home?

A thought occurred to her. Her search of the main floor hadn't revealed a door to the basement. Bizarre. She rushed back downstairs.

In the kitchen, she stopped at a tall bookcase. Dusty leather-bound titles and a collection of knickknacks filled the shelves. Odd thing to find in a kitchen. A narrow track ran along the baseboard next to bookcase. Could it be a hidden doorway?

She pushed on the bookcase, but it didn't budge. Of course not. Couldn't be that easy. She pulled on every book and knickknack, looking for a trigger, but nothing happened. When she felt along the back, her hand landed on a release switch. A latch clicked, and the bookcase shifted to the left. Shea pushed it further, revealing a solid door with a dead bolt.

"Well, well, well," Shea whispered and pulled out her lock picks. Twice she thought she had the tumblers aligned, but the cylinder refused to turn.

An idea came to her. Something she had seen on a video years ago. She rushed back up into the master bathroom, where she found Harriman's electric toothbrush. She removed the brush head and hustled back down to the kitchen, where she found a bag of baby carrots. She jammed a carrot onto the end of the toothbrush base, then stuck one of her picklocks into the other end of the carrot.

With the pick and the tensioner inserted in the lock, she activated the toothbrush. It buzzed, and the pick vibrated inside the cylinder. She jiggled it around, and in twenty seconds, the cylinder turned. The door opened, revealing a wooden staircase descending into the darkness.

She was about to flip on the light when a noise behind her caught her attention. Before she turned around, her head filled with blinding pain.

46

THUNDEROUS PAIN THROBBED in her skull when she came to. She was sitting on a concrete slab floor, her hands handcuffed behind her around a metal pole. Light streamed down from the top of a wooden staircase into the dim room. Harriman's basement. A naked female figure sat motionless in a chair ten feet from her, head slumped forward. This wasn't just bad. It was her worst nightmare.

"Deirdre? Is that you?" Speaking exacerbated the ache in her head. She ignored it. "Deirdre! You alive?"

There was no response.

She reached around the small of her back. Her gun holster was empty. She twisted her body to reach into her front pocket for a handcuff key she kept on her key ring. But her keys were gone as well.

"Dammit."

Tendrils of fear snaked through her mind. The dark walls closed in on her. She had often wondered how she would die. Getting wiped out by some distracted asshole in a truck making a left turn in front of her bike. Or maybe a bullet—from a Thunderman, maybe a cop.

Dying handcuffed in some creep's basement hadn't occurred to her. It was simply too humiliating. But here she was. And she was out of tricks. No weapons. No keys.

What would she have to endure before death took her? Rape? Torture? And what would happen to Annie? Would she end up some Thunderman's old lady? Would she be abused and die young like her mother?

She recalled her last argument with Julia. And then remembered one other detail. The French hook earrings she'd found on the floor. She'd never given them back to Annie.

She dug deep into her left rear pocket and found them.

With fingers going numb from cuffs pressing on her wrist, she pulled one earring free of the pocket. It slipped from her grip and fell to the floor. "Fuck."

She took a deep breath and relaxed the pressure on her wrists. The tingling in her fingertips faded and sensation returned. Male voices shouted upstairs. She couldn't make out who they were or what they were saying, but the tone was tense. She needed to free herself before they came down the stairs for her.

Her fingers wrapped around the earring. She bent the wire hook to form a ninety-degree angle at the tip. Doing so brought back a childhood memory of when her father had taught her to pick handcuffs. She'd been a natural. He'd pitted her against seasoned Thundermen to see who could pick cuffs fastest. She always won.

Shea inserted the wire into the handcuffs' keyhole, turning it first counterclockwise, then clockwise. The locking mechanism clicked, and the cuff released. She pulled her arms around, released the other cuff, and used the metal pole to pull herself to her feet.

She hobbled over to Deirdre. Her entire body was

swollen, bruised, and bloody. Shea pressed two fingers to Deirdre's neck. A weak pulse throbbed. She was alive.

A collection of tools rested on a nearby workbench. She grabbed a large survival knife and a ball-peen hammer. Time to finish this. She crept up the staircase, keeping to the edge of the wooden steps to avoid creaking and giving herself away. The door at the top was locked.

"When I asked you to take care of this, I never expected this." Connelly's muffled voice sounded appalled.

"You told me to make the situation go away. I did what needed to be done," Harriman replied.

"By murdering people? That's insane. That dead reporter's editor is now calling, asking me to comment on the story they're running about my history with Deirdre. You were supposed to keep Deirdre quiet and recover any evidence that De had. But instead you bring in biker thugs like this loser—"

"Hey!" It was Mackey. What the hell was he doing here?

"Don't 'hey' me, you pathetic bug. I got you sprung from prison so your little biker gang could help Harriman make my problems go away. Instead, you've made them ten times worse. Now, where is Deirdre?"

"Downstairs, along with that biker bitch," Harriman said.

"She still alive?"

"Deirdre? Last I checked."

"I want to talk to her. I...I want to tell her I'm sorry."

"Sir, I don't think that's wise."

"The damage is done. Give me the key."

"Fine. What do you want us to do with her?"

Shea pressed herself to the wall. The lock clicked, and the door opened with Shea behind it.

"I don't want you to do a gosh-darn thing. I'm through with you. I'm sick and tired of how this situation has played out. I'm going to call that editor back and tell him everything I learned tonight, and then I'm calling the cops. If I go to jail, so be it. But you two buffoons are going with me."

The crack of a gunshot made Shea's heart skip a beat. Connelly collapsed onto the landing in front of Shea. Their eyes met. He gasped and tried to stand, then another gunshot sent him tumbling down the stairs.

SHEA CAME around the door and stepped into the kitchen. Mackey stood ten feet away, gun in hand at his side. Before he aimed his weapon at her, she threw the hammer, hitting him in the forehead. He collapsed to the floor.

Harriman rushed toward the kitchen table between them where another pistol—her yellow Ruger LC9—sat next to her phone. Shea raced him for it, but he was faster. He fired twice, and a ceramic vase exploded on the bookcase behind her.

She slashed with the knife, driving him back against the double wall oven. With her free hand, she pushed the pistol away and drove her forehead into his nose. Scarlet blossomed down his face and onto his white shirt.

"Goddamn bitch." He snatched up a frying pan and delivered a series of blows that had Shea seeing stars. She lunged with the knife, but the pan knocked it out of her hand and sent it clattering across the tile floor. She cradled her throbbing hand.

With a surge of adrenaline fueling her survival instinct, she swung anything within reach. A canister of flour, a bottle of olive oil, a kettle. Harriman countered by wielding a fire extinguisher like a club.

Shea reached for the knife block only to find herself holding a ceramic honing rod instead. A blow from Harriman's fire extinguisher snapped it in half and nearly took her head with it.

Before she could grab another knife, a billowing yellow cloud filled the air. She choked on the bitter-tasting substance, struggling to see and breathe.

Harriman drove her to the floor, his hand crushing her throat. His bloodshot eyes blazed with hatred. "Fucking cunt!"

She drove her clasped hands up between his arms to break his grip, but he held on like a bulldog after a bone. Her vision grayed from lack of oxygen. A memory of an aikido technique she'd learned from an ex-girlfriend flashed in her mind. She'd always dismissed it as New Age nonsense, but she was seconds away from dying. What was there to lose?

She imagined herself forcefully throwing her life energy, her chi, down through the floor. Her body pivoted to the left, slipping Harriman's grip while he toppled as if following that imaginary chi through the kitchen tile.

Before he could recover, she lunged for the knife she'd brought up from the basement. He drove his foot into her jaw, but she barely registered the blow. Her fingers wrapped around the handle, and with the last of her strength, she threw herself at him and plunged the blade into his neck.

Warm blood sprayed across the floor. Harriman's eyes bulged. His mouth gaped open and closed like a dying fish in a silent cry of pain.

"You thought you could keep me locked up," she growled while the life ebbed from his eyes. "You were wrong."

Shivering and coughing, Shea pulled herself to her feet. The bitter taste of the fire retardant lingered in her mouth, combining with the metallic scent of blood. Every muscle in her body ached. Her head throbbed like the worst hangover she could remember.

She holstered her Ruger and tucked her phone and keys in her pockets. While she stood there trying to decide what to do next, a bullet struck the cabinet next to her. She ducked around the corner into a dining room, catching a glimpse of Mackey lining up another shot.

"Fucking cunt, I'm gonna kill you once and for all." A glass panel broke in a nearby china cabinet.

She fired a couple of blind shots then peeked out and hit Mackey's exposed boot with a third.

Mackey roared in agony and vanished into the living room on the other side of the kitchen. Shea followed, discovering a trail of blood on the living room carpet leading toward the front door.

Shea edged around behind a sofa, her eyes scanning the entryway for movement.

He popped out from behind a wall. They exchanged shots, then Shea ducked back down when her Ruger clicked empty. "Shit."

She hunkered down, trying to come up with another plan.

"I got you now, bitch."

She looked up to see Mackey leaning over the couch, holding the barrel of a nine-millimeter Glock inches from her face.

"Been waiting for this for a long-ass time."

The front door burst open. "Police! Drop your weapon. Get on the ground," multiple voices shouted.

When Mackey turned toward the door, Shea snatched the gun from his hand, flipped it around, and put two rounds through the side of his head. He dropped onto the couch, his head lolling over the back. Blood and brain matter dripped from the ceiling.

Shea dropped the gun and got to her feet with hands raised. Rios stood in the entryway alongside Morris, Bello, and Rios's partner, Detective Johnson. All had their guns pointed at her.

"You do have impeccable timing, Rios," Shea said. "Deirdre's in the basement. She needs medical attention. The entrance to the stairs is over in the kitchen."

Bello and Morris lowered their weapons and rushed downstairs. Rios lowered her weapon, but her partner kept hers trained on Shea.

"Where's Senator Connelly and Mr. Harriman?"

"Harriman's in the kitchen. Connelly's downstairs. Both dead."

"You killed them?" Rios asked with cuffs in hand.

"Just Harriman. In self-defense. After Mackey shot Connelly."

Rios stared at her for a moment then turned to her partner. "Put away your gun, Detective. And call dispatch."

47

Rios and her partner, Detective Johnson, escorted Shea to the dining room and peppered her with questions. They offered her medical attention but wouldn't let her wash her face or hands until crime scene techs had swabbed her for blood, gunshot residue, and the fire retardant. Shea refused to give them anything but her name and ID until Dragon arrived twenty minutes later.

After giving Dragon a rundown of recent events, Dragon told a deputy they were ready to answer questions. Detectives Rios and Johnson returned.

"Tell us what happened here," Rios said.

"I came looking for Deirdre West. Harriman opened the door and attacked me. Handcuffed me down in his basement next to where he'd been torturing Deirdre West."

"And what made you think Mr. Harriman was involved with Deirdre West's disappearance?" Johnson asked.

"I found a Loyal Sons of the Confederacy lapel pin where Deirdre's car crashed. Harriman is a member. Must've dropped it when he pulled her out of the car and dragged her back here."

Johnson's forehead creased. "You stole evidence from a crime scene?"

"I found what your crime scene people missed. I begged y'all to check him out, but you wouldn't. So, I came here to confront Harriman. He attacked me and handcuffed me down in the basement. When I managed to escape, Mackey killed Connelly, then he and Harriman tried to kill me. I'm lucky to be alive."

They continued to ask questions. Shea gave them a rundown of her escape and her fight with Harriman, as well as what Connelly had admitted about Harriman bringing in the Confederate Thunder.

"One thing confuses me," Johnson said. "Why did Mackey kill the senator?"

"I just caught the tail end of their last conversation, but it appears Mackey and other Thundermen were doing Harriman's dirty work to protect Connelly's so-called family values reputation. But Connelly was pissed that his affair with Deirdre still got out. Acted like he had no idea all the shit they were doing on his behalf. When he threatened to turn them in, Mackey shot him."

It was early morning by the time the detectives finished their interrogation. Toward the end, Shea was nodding off, despite Rios repeatedly offering her coffee.

"That's all we need for now," Rios said at last. "We may be in touch with more questions."

Every inch of Shea's stiff body ached when she trudged out of the house with Dragon at her side.

"Why'd you do this alone?" Dragon asked when they stepped out into the golden sunlight. "You could've been killed."

"Ever since I ran away from the Confederate Thunder as a kid, I had to rely on myself. I'd put y'all at enough risk already. Confronting Connelly on the highway.

Breaking into the Church. Didn't want to risk no one getting hurt."

"We're a sisterhood. You're smart and can kick ass, but you're just one woman. There's safety in numbers. Rely on your sisters."

"I called you, didn't I?" Shea elbowed Dragon playfully. "By the way, you mind giving me a lift back to my bike?"

They drove down to the golf course. Shea breathed a sigh of relief when she saw her motorcycle was where she'd parked it. Her phone pinged. "Shit."

"What's wrong?" Dragon asked after Shea checked her phone.

"Message from Indigo. She and Savage took Annie over to their place, but she's been up all night worried about me. I really suck as a parent."

"No more than any other parent. You've gone above and beyond to be there for her after her folks died. It's hard to raise a child that isn't your own."

"Bryz is still trying to get custody of her. The DNA results came back. He's her bio dad. I got her back from DCS, but I don't know for how long." Shea bristled with anger. "If he gets custody, even partial custody…"

"I've spoken with my associate, Kimberly Young. She specializes in custody cases. She'll keep that rapist away from Annie."

"And it will only take my entire life savings to do it."

"That's what I'm telling you, Havoc. The Sisterhood has your back. If you need help with money, we'll do what's needed to make it happen. Hell, you risked your home and your business to protect Indigo last year. Let us help you."

Shea locked eyes with her. "Thanks. Let me see how it goes. If I need help, I'll ask."

"Good. You okay driving home?"

"Yeah. Some wind therapy will do me good."

"Get some rest, girl."

"I will." She sent a reply to Indigo's text, asking her to bring Annie back home.

By noon, Shea and Annie were half dozing on the couch while the television played. Ninja sat curled up on Annie's lap.

"I was worried," Annie said sleepily.

"Sorry, kiddo."

"You saved that woman?"

"Yeah."

"You kill the person who took her?"

"I did. That bother you?" Shea looked over at her.

"No."

The doorbell rang.

"Shit," Shea muttered. "I hurt too much to move."

"I'll answer it."

"Hold up, kiddo. I got it."

She dragged her body across the living room and peeked through the peephole. Julia stood on the front porch. Shea opened the door.

"What the hell you doing here?"

"I'm leaving the Thunder." She held a large suitcase in her hand.

"Really?" Shea didn't bother to hide her skepticism. "And what does Hooch have to say about this?"

Julia straightened her back and raised her chin. "I don't give a damn what he thinks. I learned that he murdered that West woman's mother. Injected her with a load of insulin. There's a lot of things I can overlook, but killing innocent old women isn't one of them."

Julia wiped the sweat from her face. "Besides, I'm tired of being treated like someone else's property. For most of my life, that club's been my family. They were there for me for both my miscarriages and when Monster died. But only the club's old ladies. The men couldn't give two rat farts whether I lived or died."

"And this is news why?"

"I been watching you. A fierce young woman who ran away when she was a teenager, who had the guts to walk when I didn't. Who had the smarts to see the club for what it was. And who built a life for herself."

"You raised Wendy after Mom died."

"And look where it got her. Dead, just like your mother."

"You also helped raise Annie. She turned out all right."

"You helped. And now I want to make sure Bryz don't get nowhere near her."

"I appreciate that, but what can you do?"

Her face darkened. "You heard about the Wolf Ridge Arms truck that got hijacked? It was the Thunder. They're selling the guns they stole to the Border Patriots."

"I heard the cops tried to bust them, but the Thunder and the Patriots were a no-show."

"They changed the time and place. I know when the real deal's going down. Never thought I'd turn snitch, but if getting them locked up will protect my grandbaby, so be it."

Shea narrowed her gaze. Was Julia for real? "Wow."

"I'll need someplace to lie low for a while."

"You can sleep on my couch. Or you can stay with another member of the Sisterhood if you'd prefer your own room."

"I'd appreciate that." Julia reached out to hug Shea, but Shea held up her hand.

"But first, when's this deal between the Thunder and the Border Patriots going down?"

"Tonight at ten. Cortes County Fairgrounds."

"No bullshit?"

"No bullshit."

"I'll call my contact at the sheriff's office. You cool with that?"

"Anything to keep Annie safe. You find that girl you looking for? The one Connelly was after?"

"Aunt Shea rescued her last night," Annie said, appearing next to Shea.

"You done good, Shea-Shea. Your mama'd be proud of you."

While Annie and her grandmother talked, Shea called Rios. "I've got news on that arms deal." She gave Rios the new time and place.

"Thanks, I'll let you know how it pans out."

"How's Deirdre doing?"

"In the hospital under guard. Doctor says she should be released in a day or so."

"Good to hear."

"So. Friday night? Seven o'clock."

Shea let out a long sigh. "You never give up. Do you, Toni?"

"I owe you my life. But we can start with dinner. Cocina Maya. I'll text you the address."

"Friday night. See you there."

Before joining Julia and Annie in the living room, Shea pulled up the Border Patriots' website on her new laptop and left a note on their contact form. Just to stir the pot a little and make sure Bryz never got custody of Annie.

48

Two days later, Shea followed a hostess to a table at Cocina Maya. The decor had a Latin American style. One wall was painted with a blue-and-white Guatemalan flag.

She found Rios sitting at a table near the back. Rios stood and gestured toward the empty chair. She wore an off-the-shoulder, coral-pink dress that accented the warmth of her tan skin. Shea's pulse quickened.

The hostess handed her a menu, took her drink order, and disappeared back toward the front of the restaurant.

"Fancy place, Rios. What do you recommend?"

"The pepián de gallina was always my favorite growing up, although the chile rellenos are fantastic as well. And for the last time, it's Toni."

"Right."

"How's Deirdre West doing?" Toni asked.

"In the hospital with a bunch of broken bones and other injuries. On the plus side, she's been offered a job with Graciela Perez's campaign."

"I'm glad. Our narcotics division dropped the possession charges."

Shea shifted in her seat. They sure did keep it warm in this place. She pulled off her sport coat and set it on the back of her chair. "Thanks, uh, for saving my life. Again."

"You're welcome."

"I heard on the news that the task force's attempt to bust the Thunder and the Border Patriots on their arms deal didn't go as planned."

"That's an understatement. Seems the Patriots moved up the time for the deal again. When the task force got there, the Border Patriots and the Thundermen were already engaged in a full-on firefight with each other. Made the O.K. Corral look like a schoolyard brawl. Thirty-four men killed, most of them Thundermen. Turns out the Patriots were under the impression that the gun buy was a sting set up by the Thundermen and the feds."

"Is that right?"

A server named Marisol brought Shea a Dos Equis, took their dinner order, then hustled off to the kitchen.

"Who got killed?" Shea asked. "Anyone I know and despise?"

"I'm not at liberty to say."

"Come on, Toni. I'll find out eventually."

"Bryz, Hooch, Shank, and Basher, just to name a few."

"Well, I'm not losing sleep over any of them." Shea took a long pull on her beer. Bryz was dead. Mission accomplished. The rest were icing on the cake.

"You don't seem surprised by any of this."

"Like I said, I heard about it on the news."

"Shea..."

She looked up and met Toni's gaze. "You want me to be honest?"

"It's generally a good basis for a relationship."

"A relationship? Oh, so this is a date?"

"More an opportunity to get to know each other better.

And to do that, I would appreciate some honesty. Did you contact the Border Patriots?"

Every instinct in her told Shea to lie. *Never admit guilt to a cop.* Her father had drilled that into her. But where was he? Serving a life sentence for murdering Shea's mother.

"I sent them a message that someone involved with the Confederate Thunder was talking to the cops."

"As far as I know, we don't have a CI who's a member of the Thunder."

"Were you not there when that prospect Poptop told you about the hijacking and the gun buy? I told the truth."

A server brought a couple of bowls filled with ceviche. "Enjoy."

Neither Shea nor Toni reached for a spoon but sat staring at each other across the table.

It was Toni who broke the silence. "It could be argued that your message cost the lives of nearly three dozen people and put me and other law enforcement officers at risk."

"Guess this date ain't exactly going as planned neither, huh?" Shea held out her wrists, waiting to be cuffed. "Go ahead. Arrest me. Slap on them bracelets. You know you want to."

"Put your arms down, idiota. I'm not arresting you."

Shea lowered her arms. "Dare I ask why not?"

Rios put a spoonful of ceviche in her mouth. When she swallowed, she said, "I pulled the pin."

"Pulled what pin?" Shea started to eat her ceviche.

"I turned in my shield."

Shea nearly spit out the mouthful of fish and tomatoes. "You quit?"

"I'm taking my retirement and going private. I applied for a PI license."

"Wow. Just... holy fuck. What'd your boss say?"

"Lieutenant Goodman wasn't happy about it, but I'm sick of working for Sheriff Buzz Keeler. After the arms bust, Keeler did a press conference defending the Border Patriots, claiming they were protecting this country from rapists, murderers, and drug dealers."

Toni's eyes watered, and her voice grew strained. "I came to this country as a child refugee after government death squads in Guatemala murdered my parents. And this pinche pendejo is praising these racist vigilantes, calling people like me criminals? ¡Qué cabrón!"

"So, you pulled the pin."

"Sí."

Toni put down her spoon. "And now that I'm no longer a cop. I'd…" She took a deep breath and put her hand on Shea's. "I'd like to get to know you better."

A wave of heat started in Shea's face and moved down between her legs. "Really?"

"I've always admired you, ya know."

"A few years ago, you threatened to send me to prison when I refused to be your snitch."

"I did, and I'm sorry. I was trying to save lives. I respected your fearlessness, your resourcefulness, and your dedication to protect people you care about. That's why I wanted you as a CI. Granted, you didn't always obey the letter of the law, but you pursued justice as you saw it. I respect that."

"Wow, Toni, that's the nicest thing you've ever said to me."

"As a cop, I couldn't say it. But now that I'm a civilian, I felt you should know."

Shea wasn't sure what to make of this sudden burst of honesty and respect. The wall she'd kept up against Toni melted like ice cream on a summer's day. She let her gaze dissolve in Toni's honey-brown eyes.

"So, what do you say? Take a chance? See where this thing between us is going?"

Shea studied Toni's face, the warmth of her eyes. The way her dark hair fell about her bare shoulders. "Sure. Why the hell not."

"To new beginnings." Rios held up her glass.

Shea clinked it with her beer bottle. "New beginnings."

Ready for Another Adventure?

Download a free copy of "Kissing Asphalt", a Jinx Ballou short story, by subscribing to the Dharma Kelleher Readers Club newsletter at dharmakelleher.com.

This semi-monthly newsletter features release announcements, bonus content, giveaways, and more.

BOOKS BY DHARMA KELLEHER

Jinx Ballou Bounty Hunter series

Chaser

Extreme Prejudice

A Broken Woman

Shea Stevens Outlaw Biker series

Iron Goddess

Snitch

Blood Sisters

ABOUT THE AUTHOR

Dharma Kelleher writes gritty crime fiction with a feminist kick and is one of the only openly transgender voices in the genre.

She is the author of the Jinx Ballou Bounty Hunter series and the Shea Stevens Outlaw Biker. Her work has also appeared in anthologies and on Shotgun Honey.

She is a former journalist and a member of Sisters in Crime, the International Thriller Writers, and the Alliance of Independent Authors. She lives in Arizona with her wife and her feline overlords.

Learn more about Dharma and her work at https://dharmakelleher.com.

Lightning Source UK Ltd.
Milton Keynes UK
UKHW041859130920
369800UK00001B/69